THE DRAGON UNBOUND

THE TETHERING, BOOK THREE

MEGAN O'RUSSELL

Ink Worlds Press

Visit our website at www.MeganORussell.com

The Dragon Unbound

Copyright © 2017, Megan O'Russell

Cover Art by Sleepy Fox Studio (https://www.sleepyfoxstudio.net/)

Editing by Christopher Russell

Interior Design by Christopher Russell

Printed in the United States of America

To the readers who have waited so long for the next chapter in Jacob and Emilia's story. Thank you for believing in the Gray's type of magic.

May the person you love always be worth the wait.

THE DRAGON UNBOUND

DEXTER

*S*creams echoed in the distance.

"Kill on sight."

The words pounded into his head. Dexter's eyes fluttered open. He stared at the sparkling ceiling of the cavern above him. The stone swayed as he pushed himself up off the cold floor just in time to see the Pendragon tearing around the corner.

"Emilia," Dexter whispered, ignoring the pain slicing through the back of his head as he jerked around to see the chair behind him. She was gone. The stone bindings that had held her in place were shattered on the floor. The golden rope he had held in his hand lay on the ground, its color dull, the shimmer of magic gone.

He looked down at his hands. He had held the rope. There should be a mark on his palm. Emilia should he here.

A group of Dragons tore into the chamber, past the grand columns of ancient stone. The dragon tattoos that wrapped from their cheeks to their necks glistened with sweat. Something was wrong. Wrong enough to make the Dragon guards afraid.

"What's happening?" Dexter shouted at them, but they

ignored him as they ran through the exit on the far side of the cave.

Why would they run farther into the caverns? Someone had come from that direction.

Jacob.

Jacob had come from behind him while the Pendragon was performing the ceremony. Emilia must have gone with him.

Dexter scrambled to his feet, stumbling as the room swam in front of him.

"Emilia." Dexter ran after the Dragons, deeper into the tunnels. He glanced up and down the hall. There were shouts coming from both directions.

"Emilia!" Dexter screamed.

A *crack* echoed through the hall. For a moment, the ground shook before the sound of rock colliding with rock traveled toward him.

He had only an instant to shout, *"Primurgo!"* before the ceiling collapsed.

~

"It's been three weeks," Dexter said, fighting to keep his voice level with every word. "If the Pendragon is too afraid to go after Emilia himself, let me go."

"Do not ever think the Pendragon is afraid," Mr. Wayland said. "The Pendragon is no coward. But Emilia is broken. She is tethered to the Evans boy. We would have to kill him to bring her back and half the Gray Clan to get to either of them. Do you have any idea how well the Mansion House is guarded? Isadora Gray is no fool. It would take a huge effort to even attempt to break through their shield spells."

Dexter stared at his father. He was dismissing Emilia like she didn't even matter. "Emilia is the Pendragon's child. Surely it is worth some risk to rescue his daughter."

"When a child is broken, what good are they to their parent? If a child cannot obey, cannot fulfill the simplest request, why would you risk even one loyal Dragon to save them?" Mr. Wayland turned to leave the stone room Dexter had been kept in since Emilia's disappearance.

"She was taken, Father!" Dexter shouted, desperate to make his father stay and listen. "She didn't choose Jacob."

"I was not speaking of Emilia," Mr. Wayland said, the shrieking of stone on stone nearly drowning out his words as the door scraped shut behind him.

~

*D*exter sat alone amongst the tables of Dragons. It had been two months since he had been allowed out of his room. His mother's begging had finally worked, though being an outcast whose sole purpose was to help excavate the tunnels that had been damaged by the cave-in was not what she had had in mind.

Even with magic, moving the rocks was dangerous. The other workers treated him like filth. He was the one who had lost the Pendragon's daughter. At best, incompetent. At worst, a traitor.

The Dragons stood as one when the Pendragon entered. He had blood on his coat and wore it like a badge of honor, not bothering to clean himself before sitting down to eat at the table high on the platform at the end of the room. He looked like a king. But what kind of king would abandon a princess?

Dexter stood and crept quietly out the door and down to the excavating tunnels. He didn't need to be there yet, but it was better down in the dark alone than up here pretending to love the Pendragon.

It didn't take long for the rest of the men to arrive.

"The Pendragon's in a better mood. Maybe he finally got something out of her," John muttered.

"You wouldn't think a little blond thing could last that long." Jess shook his head.

John and Jess stared at Dexter, waiting for him to create the shield spell so they could begin digging through the rocks.

"*Saxurgo,*" Dexter said. A bubble blossomed from his hand, traveling through his companions. The bubble grew until it lay against the wall, creating a thin, glistening film that was their only protection from falling rocks.

"You'd think we might be able to get a few more people to work a proper shield down here," Jess grumbled.

All the strong wizards were guarding the compound, casting the shield that protected them from the outside, or away doing only the Pendragon knew what. The people working down in the tunnels barely had enough magic to be called wizards. That was the only reason they had been sent to do menial labor—they were as useless as humans. Except for Dexter. He had failed the Pendragon, and this was his punishment.

"I don't know what the Pendragon wants from blondie. *Elevare.*" A large rock in front of John shook as it rose in the air.

Dexter slammed himself into the wall just in time to avoid being hit by the boulder.

"Sorry about that," John said with a thinly veiled grin. "I just thought if the Pendragon wanted information on the Grays, he'd go out there and get it rather than making blondie Gray bleed every day."

Dexter's stomach turned. They had a blond Gray. Who?

"It'd be more fun. Going into that big estate and taking the information would be a lot better than sitting in the low tunnels every day," Jess agreed.

"Well, she won't make it much longer anyway," John said, no longer bothering to hide his smile.

∾

*"W*hat do you mean she disappeared?" The Pendragon's voice echoed through the hall.

Dexter edged closer to the door of the Pendragon's chambers, pressing himself against the wall so he could peer around the corner.

"You had Emilia in your sights, and she simply disappeared? *Tendicanis,*" the Pendragon said.

The Dragon who had run through the halls only an hour before, telling everyone he had finally caught a glimpse of Emilia, screamed.

"You are not fit to be called a Dragon. *Volucris calyculus somnerri—*"

The acrid stench of burning flesh reached Dexter's nostrils. The Pendragon was burning away the man's dragon tattoo.

"Bring me the little Gray bird!" the Pendragon shouted.

Dexter raced down the corridor to a crack in the rock barely wide enough for him to squeeze into.

"*Conformare,*" Dexter muttered as a guard dashed down the corridor to fulfill the Pendragon's order. All they would be able to see was broken stone.

Dexter had become adept at carefully hiding himself outside the Pendragon's chamber. He came here as often as he dared, desperate to find out who the Gray prisoner was. The tunnels where the prisoners were kept had been heavily guarded since Jacob escaped. He hadn't been able to get close enough to see anyone going in or out of the cells.

All he needed was for someone to say the name. Which Gray? Would they actually know anything that could help the Pendragon find Emilia?

Dexter held as still as he could, his arms beginning to shake from balancing awkwardly between the two slabs of stone.

Screams echoed through the tunnel as the Dragon dragged a

woman by her bound wrists to the Pendragon's chamber. The woman kicked, fighting to break free.

As she struggled with the man, the blood-caked hair fell away from her face. Dexter's gasp was covered by her shrieks. He knew this woman. She was battered and thin, covered in blood and filth. But it was Larkin Gardner. *She* was the Gray prisoner.

~

*T*here's magic in the wind. That's what Ms. Gray always said. As the wind whipped around him, Dexter hoped she was wrong. The only magic that could be in the wind tonight was the darkest kind. The freezing current bit his flesh, and he knew it would only get worse.

Her arms tightened around his waist. It was time. Dexter kicked off hard and felt the broom lifting them off the ground. He didn't look back as they flew away from Mount Graylock.

Larkin shook behind him. She was too weak to use any magic of her own.

"*Alavarus,*" Dexter murmured, and the air around them warmed. It wasn't much, but hopefully it would keep his hands from freezing to the broom—assuming the broom didn't fall apart and drop them out of the sky. Dexter had found the broom in the Pendragon's collection of relics. It was a Salem original. And nothing but sheer desperation could have convinced Dexter to ride it, or to risk Larkin's life flying high over the trees.

Dexter gazed up at the stars, following the constellations home. He had always hated learning astronomy. The only part he liked was keeping his arms wrapped around Emilia.

His throat tightened. The Grays might kill him on sight. He deserved it.

He aimed for the Mansion House. He didn't know where else to go. If the Dragons caught them...

Dexter pushed the broom faster. Falling off the broom was a better fate than being caught.

Hours passed. The broom swung suddenly to one side as Larkin slumped over, hanging dangerously in the air. He grabbed her wrist and tried to tighten her hold on him. He felt her jerk awake.

"Hold on, Larkin. We're almost there." The wind carried his words away, and she showed no sign of having heard.

Dexter flew over the lights of a town. In a few miles, they would reach the house. Dexter dipped the broom, flying as low as he dared over the tops of the trees. There were no lights coming from the Gray's house. They would be blocked from view by the *fortaceria*. Larkin should be able to get through Ms. Gray's spells, but not him. Not anymore.

Dexter landed the broom outside the gates. Larkin's legs buckled beneath her. He dropped the broom and caught her around the waist.

"Thanks, kid," she mumbled, trying to push the matted blond hair from her eyes with the back of her trembling hand.

"Go up to the house." Dexter helped Larkin to the gates. "Find Ms. Gray. Tell her to let me in."

Larkin placed her hand on the wrought iron gate. It shimmered and swung open. She stumbled down the dark drive without looking back. Dexter sank down in the snow next to the wall. All he could do now was wait.

REUNION

*J*acob woke with a start, his skin tingling as though tickled by a thousand frozen needles. He leaped out of bed, ripping the covers away from the mattress to search for whatever had been biting him, but the mattress was bare. Jacob looked around, itching his arms. The feeling was intense but not painful.

Jacob felt a twinge of fear in his chest the instant before Emilia's shout of "Jacob!" echoed up the stairs.

Jacob grabbed his wand and bounded from his room and down the steps to the second floor just in time to hear footsteps pounding down the stairs to the first floor.

"Emilia!" Jacob tore after her.

When he reached the front door, Emilia stood next to Aunt Iz, both of them staring out at the front gate.

"What is it?" Jacob asked.

"Someone came through the *fortaceria*. Stay here," Aunt Iz said before stalking carefully down the steps.

"Yeah, right," Jacob said, taking Emilia's hand as they followed Iz onto the lawn.

They crept silently down the drive, talismans ready to fight.

Something shimmered in the distance. A head of blond hair caught the moonlight. Before Jacob could see a face, Emilia gasped.

"Larkin!" Emilia ran past Iz.

Jacob took off after her, but before he had reached Emilia, she was holding Larkin in her arms.

"Larkin." Emilia steadied the frighteningly pale woman. "How did you get here?"

Larkin's voice crackled as she spoke. "He rescued me. He's at the gate. You have to get him...bring him in before they find us."

Jacob looked toward the gates. He could see a shadow just beyond.

Emilia's face spilt into a wide smile. "Stay here." She transferred Larkin into Jacob's arms and took off toward the gate.

"Emilia," Jacob called after her. He didn't want her to open the gates at night, not before Iz caught up.

"Go." Larkin lowered herself to the ground.

Emilia wrenched open the gates just as Jacob reached them.

"Samuel!" But the happy word faded on her lips as Dexter Wayland stood up out of the shadows.

"Em," Dexter said quietly.

Jacob stepped in front of Emilia. "You stay the hell away from her."

"Em, I'm sorry—" Dexter started.

But Emilia shoved Jacob out of her way. *"Perectus!"*

Dexter doubled over as though an invisible fist had punched him hard in the stomach.

Emilia's black hair whipped in the night wind. Jacob could feel the magic pulsating around her.

"You're sorry? *Subnicio!*" Dexter's legs flew out from under him, and he landed hard on the ground. "You betrayed me. *Alevitum!*" He crashed into a tree. "You destroyed my family." Dexter hovered three feet off the ground, clawing at his throat, gasping for breath. "You almost got Jacob killed." His face jerked to one side as though he had been slapped. "You horrible"—Dexter slammed into the ground hard on his left—"evil"—he flew back through the air to land on his right—"traitor!" Dexter flopped back and forth like a ragdoll, smacking hard into the ground with every swing. "You tried to tether yourself to me!"

"Emilia, drop him," Iz said in her quiet voice no one could ignore.

Dexter crumpled to the ground.

"We need to get back inside the gates." Iz strode over to Dexter and bent down. In one swift movement, she removed the cuffs that were Dexter's talisman. "Traitors will not be allowed magic in my house. *Maceragia secora brevis.*"

Dexter glowed silver for a moment, lighting the darkness with his frightened face before the light disappeared and he was cast into shadow.

"Now get back to the house." Iz pointed up the drive.

Emilia turned on her heel and strode away without a backwards glance. She wrapped her arm around Larkin, helped her to her feet, and led her up the driveway. Iz walked behind a limping Dexter, her wand trained on his back.

Jacob closed the gates behind him, smiling in the dark. Dexter and Emilia's reunion couldn't have gone better. Jacob caught up to the rest of the group as they reached the front steps.

"Where is everyone else?" Dexter asked, looking to the darkened windows of the house.

"Did you expect a welcoming committee?" Emilia snarled, helping Larkin through the front door. "One signal, and I'm pretty sure we could get a lot of people here who would *love* to see you."

Dexter's face blanched. "I meant is the rest of the family here? Are they safe?"

"The rest of the family is in a secure location," Iz said with a finality in her tone that made Dexter wince as though he had been slapped.

"Milluesco," Iz said. The lights flicked on as she entered the kitchen. *"Parese vaestus."* A pot flew out of the fridge and onto the table where it immediately began to steam. Emilia lowered Larkin carefully into a chair.

Larkin nodded feebly as Emilia handed her a spoon. The room went silent for a moment as they watched Larkin's hand move shakily from the pot to her mouth.

"But everyone's all right?" Dexter asked, his voice barely above a whisper as he stared desperately at Emilia.

Jacob kicked a chair, sending it flying halfway across the room. "No, they're not all right. Actually, none of us are all right. *All right* would be having all of us here, safe in this house, but you made sure that could never happen, didn't you?"

Emilia reached up and laced her fingers through Jacob's without taking her eyes off Larkin. He could feel the warmth of her touch calming him. Jacob took a shuddering breath. Yelling wouldn't help, not when they needed information. But he didn't miss the look on Dexter's face as Emilia pulled Jacob closer to her so his arm pressed into hers.

"Do you know anything about Samuel?" Iz asked.

"Why? Isn't he with the others?" Dexter moved as though to stand and look out the back door to the old carriage house where Samuel had lived.

Iz flicked her wrist, and Dexter slammed back down into his seat.

"You've already bound my magic. I'm no threat to any—"

"Samuel has been missing for months. The night Emilia was rescued, Samuel ran into the fire in the forest. We believe he may have been trying to rescue Larkin," Iz said in a calm, frightening tone.

"We were together in the woods," Larkin said, her voice a weak rasp, barely loud enough to be heard even in the silent kitchen. "He called me, asked me to come help when he found out Emilia was being held at Graylock. By the time I got there,

Jacob had disappeared from the shield Samuel had left him in. We waited in the woods. And then there was screaming, horrible screaming.

"I thought it was Emilia. I ran toward the sound, and I saw her being pinned to the ground by men. But when I tried to pull them off, Emilia's hair wasn't black anymore. It was a woman. A blond woman." Larkin's hands trembled so badly Emilia took the spoon from her and set it on the table. Huge tears left paths of white through the filth and blood that covered Larkin's pale cheeks.

"Domina," Jacob said. Pain surged into the burn scars that still marked his chest and cheek. "The blond woman was Domina." He knew he was right even before Larkin nodded.

"It was a trap," Larkin whispered. "The ground opened up, and I was locked in a stone room. That was the last time I saw Samuel."

Iz turned back to Dexter. "Did you ever hear anything about Samuel being captured?"

"No." Dexter's face was thin and drawn, nearly skeletal beneath his unkempt, black hair, but his eyes were wide and frightened.

"Did you hear about any other member of the Gray Clan being captured or killed?" Fire danced in Iz's eyes.

"No." Dexter rubbed the lines on his forehead that didn't seem to belong on an eighteen-year-old boy. "But after—after Emilia left, they didn't tell me anything anymore. I had to dig out the tunnels. I had to hide outside the Pendragon's chamber to hear anything."

"That must have been very difficult for you," Iz said, "but did you hear anything about a prisoner? Not only Samuel. Anyone. Was any area more guarded than before?"

"There were guards down the hall, farther down than Larkin's cell, but I don't know why. It could be anything."

"Or it could be Samuel."

"Ms. Gray," Dexter said, sounding suddenly as though he were explaining the logic he had used in solving a particularly complicated homework problem. "Even if there is a prisoner down there and even if it is Samuel, which there is no way of knowing if it is, there isn't a way to get him out." Dexter paused, but Iz remained silent.

"There are more guards down there. The tunnel gets narrow, and it's a dead end. There is no way out, and there are other things"—Dexter's eyes flicked toward Emilia—"more immediate things you need to know about."

"Such as?" Iz asked.

"The Pendragon is coming. I heard him last night. He said he knew where Emilia was and that he was going to come get her. He said he had been deceived and betrayed. That he would come to collect what was rightfully his from the Gray Clan."

"Did he say my name?" Emilia asked, turning to look at Dexter for the first time since they had entered the gate. "Did he say my name?" Emilia shouted when Dexter didn't answer her.

"No," Dexter said, "he said he was coming to take back his family. That the years of separation were over. He was going to bring her home. That's you, Em. He's coming for you."

Emilia gripped Jacob's hand. Fear flooded her grey eyes. The Pendragon wasn't coming for Emilia. He was coming for her mother. For Rosalie.

"How soon is he coming?" Iz asked, her tone cold and crisp.

"I don't know," Dexter said. "He was rounding Dragons up. He wanted to make sure the compound was guarded when he came to get Emilia. He isn't coming by himself. He's bringing an army."

"Do you have anything else to add?" Iz asked, staring hard into Dexter's eyes.

"I'm sorry, for everything. I'm so sorry—"

"Any information," Iz cut across his apology.

"You need to leave here. Soon. Tonight. The Pendragon is coming, and he will kill anyone who gets in his way."

"Your concern has been noted." Iz stood. "I will escort you to Samuel's home. You will not be staying under this roof."

Iz took Dexter by the arm and led him out the backdoor of the kitchen, Emilia close behind. Jacob followed, unwilling to allow Dexter to be alone with them.

The door to Samuel's little house swung open before they reached it.

Iz steered Dexter into the darkness of the carriage house. The air smelled damp and musky. The months it had been empty had taken their toll.

"Sit," Iz commanded, pointing to a wooden chair in the far corner.

Samuel had sat in that chair outside. It seemed hollow now without him.

Dexter walked into the dark corner and sat without argument.

"*Silva alescere,*" Iz said. The wood of the floor and the wood of the chair began to meld, growing together to form long tendrils that wrapped themselves around Dexter's ankles and wrists, binding him to the chair.

Emilia slid her trembling hand into Jacob's. That was the spell the Pendragon had used to tie her down when he had tried to tether her to Dexter.

"Come on, Emi," Jacob whispered, leading Emilia through the yard back into the light of the kitchen.

Emilia leaned into Jacob's arms, staring at the door. Iz appeared a moment later.

"*Foretio,*" Iz said. The walls of the carriage house shimmered.

"He's coming for Rosalie," Emilia said, stepping toward Iz.

Even that foot of distance made Jacob panic. It didn't matter if the Pendragon wasn't coming for Emilia. He would kill all of them to get to Rosalie.

"I know," Iz said. "Emilia, go and get Molly. She's guarding Rosalie's room."

"Aunt Iz, I'm sorry. I didn't know she was tethered to him. I didn't know he could track her when I brought her back. I just wanted..."

"To meet your mother," Iz said, tucking Emilia's long black hair behind her ears. "Get Molly."

Emilia ran into the hall.

"What do we do?" Jacob's heart raced as though the Dragons had already arrived. The floor creaked over his head. He knew it was the sound of Emilia running to get Molly, but his pulse told him it was the Pendragon, come to kill them all.

Iz paced the kitchen. "First, we find a safe place."

"The Pendragon will be able to find her," Jacob said. "Wherever we put Rosalie, he'll be able to feel it."

Jacob wanted to tell Iz being tethered felt like a cord had been tied around your heart, and the Pendragon would be able to follow that cord to Rosalie wherever she went. He wanted to say it felt like you couldn't breathe right when you were apart from your *coniunx*. That Rosalie was the other half of the Pendragon's soul. That the Pendragon must not have been able to breathe or relax for years. Not with a hole where his heart should have been.

That if he, Jacob, had been apart from Emilia for years, he would be here in the next five minutes just to feel whole again. Apart from loving Emilia, apart from losing her being the worst thing he could ever imagine, the feeling of being broken in two for years on end would make him run to someone, even if he hated them, just to make it stop.

But how could he explain that to Iz? How could he explain it to anyone?

"We can't go to the Elis tribe," Jacob said. "We can't lead the Pendragon to Connor, Claire, or the professor."

"The professor isn't with the centaurs." Iz's head snapped toward Jacob. "Why would you think he was there?"

"You said the rest of the family was safe," Jacob said, trying to sort through everything Iz had told him in the twelve hours since he and Emilia had been back at the Mansion House. Had it really only been half a day? "I assumed you meant they were together. Emilia and I ran away from the Elis. I thought you sent him there as extra protection for Connor and Claire. To teach them."

"The professor is ill. He was sent to stay someplace safe and away from stress until all this is over," Iz said, her hands trembling. "He is not as young as he used to be."

"What happened?" Jacob asked. The professor was old. But he was magical. He was happy. "How did he get sick?"

"Two of his children ran away," Iz said, looking past Jacob as Molly and Emilia ran into the kitchen.

Jacob's heart twisted. The professor was sick because of him and Emilia. He knew the professor was old, but not that much older than Iz. And he had always seemed so lively and happy. Jacob shook his head, clearing his mind of the kind man's smiling face and trying to catch up with the hurried conversation between Aunt Iz and Molly.

"We can't keep her safe. Not here." Molly ran a hand over her wrinkled forehead. "Not if the Pendragon is coming to get her himself."

"Can we call for help?" Emilia asked. "Make a stand here?"

Iz turned toward Emilia.

Emilia clutched the counter so tightly her knuckles were white. "He's already sent someone to kill Jacob and me. I'm sure he wants all the Grays dead at this point. If he's coming to get Rosalie, this might be our chance. Make a stand on our ground. Isn't that better than running away and hoping he doesn't pick us off one by one?"

Molly looked at Emilia with a sad smile. "You think like Samuel. And if we had anyone to call for help, perhaps it would work."

"The wizards who live on the preserves are fighting to defend their homes," Iz said. "The centaurs are struggling to protect Claire and Connor. Dragons have been appearing on preserves, picking off wizards who are alone and weak. If we take any protection away from those in the forest, it will only mean the Dragons will be able to kill them more efficiently."

"But if everyone came here," Jacob said, his heart leaping at the thought of having a real and final plan, "the Dragons would have to come at us head on."

"The wizards from the preserves won't come here." Emilia shook her head. "They don't live like we do. The idea of making them all come to the Mansion House, all live together in this one small place—it would be like a prison to them. They would never agree to it."

"Even to save their lives?" Jacob asked.

"Asking them to abandon their homes would make us as much the enemy as the Dragons," Larkin said, her head hanging low over the pot of soup.

"Then we take Rosalie back to her Clan," Molly said. "Ask for their help in protecting her."

"Which Clan is she?" Iz asked, turning to Emilia.

"The Virginia Clan," Emilia said. "But Rosalie won't have seen any of them since before she had me. They might not want to help her. I don't even know if her family is still there."

Iz sighed, closing her eyes and resting her head in her hands. "We can try to ask for Edna's help. See if she is still fond of whomever Rosalie's family was last associated with. We'll leave at daybreak."

"What do we do about him?" Jacob pointed out the back door at Samuel's house.

"Take him with us," Iz said, standing. "If we leave him here alone, the Pendragon will murder him. And I don't want blood spilled in my home."

SOMEPLACE SAFE

*T*he large, black SUV waited in the drive as the sun began to peer over the tops of the trees. Emilia helped Larkin down the front steps, her arm wrapped tightly around Larkin's waist. She knew they shouldn't be moving Larkin so soon. Larkin needed to rest. But the sight of Dexter walking toward the car with Molly's wand pointed at his back quickly shook all thoughts of sleep from her mind.

Molly opened the hatch. "Lie down." She pointed to the trunk of the SUV.

Dexter looked shocked only for a moment before lying down on the floor.

"*Cordus,*" Molly said coldly. Ropes appeared, wrapping around Dexter from shoulder to ankle. "And keep quiet." Molly slammed the trunk closed. "I will not have traitor filth sitting on the upholstery." She stalked back to the house.

"Come on," Emilia said, helping Larkin to the car. Larkin climbed into the backseat, and within seconds her eyes drifted closed.

Rosalie's voice carried from the front door. "I just want to know where we're going."

"We're going someplace we can be safe," Jacob said, leading Rosalie to the car.

Rosalie stumbled, squinting at the early morning light. "You keep saying we're going someplace safe. I really don't think you understand what that means. Safe for you is away from me." She turned her gaze toward Emilia. Rosalie's eyes looked clearer now than they had the night before.

"We're trying to find a place that's safe for all of us," Emilia said, gesturing for Rosalie to sit next to Larkin.

"I suppose you are naïve enough to believe in a place like that." Rosalie brushed a long strand of black hair from Emilia's face before climbing in next to Larkin.

It was strange to see the black hair next to the blond. All Emilia had wanted was to save Larkin and Samuel and find her mother, and now she had two of them in the same place. But Samuel was still gone, and they were all running again.

The gates swung open as the car crunched down the drive. Emilia glanced out the back window, trying to appreciate the beauty of the morning light bathing the house in its gentle glow. But her mind couldn't move beyond wondering who would be with them when they got to come home.

~

*A*unt Iz sped south, weaving through the cars on the highway, driving on the road's shoulder when rush hour traffic had brought all the other cars to a halt.

"Won't we get a ticket?" Jacob whispered in Emilia's ear.

"No," Emilia whispered back as the SUV dove through two lanes to swerve onto an exit ramp. "This car has a *tellumor* on it. Like a magical fire siren. We dart around, nobody notices."

Aunt Iz slammed on the brakes as a yellow sports car swerved in front of them.

"Unless you hit them." Emilia dug her fingers into Jacob's leg.

"They're banned except for emergencies, and really tricky to do. But…"

At this rate, they would be in the Virginia territory before noon. Emilia slipped her hand into Jacob's. Every car that came near was a threat.

One of the tires hit a pothole, and a stifled grunt came from the trunk.

Rosalie turned, looking into the trunk. "Did you know there's a boy back here? Is he supposed to be tied up like that?"

"Yes, Rosalie," Emilia said. "Just ignore him."

Rosalie kept staring at Dexter. "What did he do to make everyone so mad?"

Emilia tightened her grip on Jacob's hand. She could feel his heart racing in her own chest.

"If I get to ride in a seat, and he has to ride in the trunk, he must have done something awful," Rosalie muttered, her gaze shifting to land on Emilia's shimmering hand. She twisted in her seatbelt to whisper into Emilia's ear. "He's the one, isn't he? The one your daddy tried to tether you to. And now you have him tied up in the trunk." Rosalie laughed. "I leave you for a quick seventeen years, and this is the trouble you get yourself into? I think I might have to admit I gave birth to you after all."

"Just stop it," Emilia said.

"And who's the blond one?" Rosalie asked, looking at Larkin as though noticing her for the first time.

"She's a friend," Jacob said. "She was captured by the Pendragon. Now she's back, and we need to keep her safe, too."

"Good God," Rosalie laughed, her voice filling the car. "At this rate, the next time you try to take me *someplace safe*, we'll need a school bus."

"Rosalie, please be quiet," Iz said in her quiet tone that anyone with a self-preservation instinct knew to obey. "Larkin needs to rest."

"Don't worry. I'm sure they make some rich people version of a school bus." Rosalie smiled, sitting back in her seat. "Or maybe you'd feel more comfortable in a stretch limo?"

As Rosalie drifted back into silence, Jacob leaned close to Emilia's ear.

"She's right," Jacob whispered so softly only Emilia could hear. "If we keep hauling everyone around like this, the Pendragon will catch up."

"What else can we do?" Emilia whispered back. "We can't very well trust Rosalie with a broom, or *him* for that matter." She raised an eyebrow in the direction of the trunk.

"We could use the spell from Newport. The one *she* gave us."

Emilia knew who *she* was without asking. The Hag. The Hag had sent them a spell in Newport. A spell that had somehow, impossibly, transported them instantly hundreds of miles away, saving both their lives. But magic like that didn't exist.

"Disappearing and reappearing is impossible." Emilia shook her head.

"But I saw Iz do it," Jacob said. "In her office, the first day I was at the Mansion House."

"That's different," Emilia said. "She was just projecting herself across the room. Not moving her body across the country."

"We did it," Jacob said.

"I know." Emilia bit her bottom lip. "But you can't just move yourself from one place to another. Disappearing is fine. It's the reappearing part that doesn't work. The second you disappear, your magic doesn't exist anymore. There's no way to bring yourself back."

"But we've already done it once," Jacob said.

"Unless you want to explain to Iz how we got the spell and see if she thinks we could pull it off again without getting ourselves killed, I say we wait and hope something better comes up." Emilia turned back to the window just in time to see a red car dive out of the way as Aunt Iz sped past.

"Flying carpet then?" Jacob said.

She chuckled and leaned into Jacob's shoulder. Her heart slowed as his arm wrapped around her. She was asleep before the next mile marker.

~

The rumbling of the car as it sped down an uneven road of dirt and rock jerked Emilia awake. She blinked at the bright light. The sun was high in the sky, but her watch said it wasn't quite noon.

"Where are we?" Emilia asked, sitting up and running her fingers through her hair.

Jacob was asleep next to her. His head drifted to one side, but his arm was still wrapped around Emilia as though he were protecting her even in his sleep.

"We should be there soon," Molly said, twisting in her seat to shake Jacob's knee. "Wake up, Jacob. You don't want sleep in your eyes when you meet the Virginia Clan." Molly gave Emilia and Jacob a hard look before turning back to the windshield.

"Why do you say it like that?" Jacob asked. "The *Virginia* Clan."

"Not all wizards live like the Gray Clan," Aunt Iz said. "The leadership of the Gray Clan is passed down generation to generation. We groom our heirs to take on the responsibility. We spend our lives amassing the resources necessary to care for our Clan and the creatures we guard. But the Virginia Clan is different. They haven't kept the same family in charge. There are skirmishes and coups. Whoever wins the latest battle ends up in charge, even if they don't have the knowledge or wisdom to rule with any sense of order."

"Or the money," Rosalie muttered behind them.

"Edna is in charge at the moment," Iz said without any sign she had heard Rosalie. "She is a very wise woman who has done everything within her power to look after the good of her Clan. I knew Edna long before the Sable family took control of the

Virginia territories, and I can only hope she will be as reasonable as I have always known her to be."

Iz turned onto a small drive that had a painted iron fence hanging open in front of it. The peeling white paint of the fence matched the house behind it. The car shuddered and stopped as soon as the back bumper was within the gate. Starting from a point in the very center of the windshield, a faint light began to flicker. The light grew into a shimmering bubble the size of Emilia's head. Within seconds, the bubble had grown to be twice the size of the car.

The glittering, transparent sphere moved toward them, engulfing the car, leaving only a few feet on either side, blocking them from the outside world.

"Good," Iz said, opening her car door, "she knows we're here."

4

THE VIRGINIA CLAN

*T*he front steps were slanted with deep grooves worn into them from years of footsteps. An old swing and wind chimes hung in the shade on the porch. The faint tinkling of the chimes made the hair on Jacob's neck stand up.

Aunt Iz stepped out of the car, her gaze fixed on the porch. Emilia shrugged and opened her door to follow. Jacob slid across the seat and climbed out Emilia's door. Even the distance the SUV would have put between them felt too far trapped inside of the shimmering bubble, staring at the peeling front door. Jacob wrapped his arm around Emilia's waist and shut the door before Rosalie had a chance to follow.

"*Compingere,*" Emilia murmured, and the door sealed itself shut.

Rosalie smacked the window and scowled at them before climbing through the car to sit in the driver's seat.

"Do you think she'll be okay in there with Larkin?" Jacob whispered to Emilia.

"Larkin can take care of herself, and if Rosalie kills Dexter..." Emilia shrugged.

The loud squeaking as the front door swung open pulled Jacob's mind away from the occupants of the car.

A woman walked onto the porch, her wand held aloft. Her hair was dyed shoe-polish black, which matched the overly arched eyebrows she had painted on. Even through the faint shimmer of the bubble, Jacob recognized the woman. He had seen her before. She was one of the wizards who had judged him when he had been called in front of the Council of Elders for destroying his school and murdering humans by breaking apart a dam. The dam, at least, had not been his fault.

The sallow color of the woman's wrinkled skin gave Jacob the impression of someone who had not seen sunlight in a long time and had tried to give herself features she could see in dim light. Now, standing in the bright sunlight, the effect was almost comical.

"Isadora," the woman said, still not lowering her wand.

"Edna." Aunt Iz gave a polite bow of her head.

"These aren't good times for dropping in on someone unannounced," Edna said, her voice rasping. "You never know who might be trying to get in through the gate."

"Nor is it a good time for lingering too near gates," Iz said. "I was hoping we might be able to talk. I have a problem, and I was hoping for your assistance."

"What sort of problem?" Edna walked up to the edge of the bubble and stared at Emilia.

Jacob stepped in front of Emilia, blocking her from Edna's gaze.

"So, she did manage to get herself tethered." Edna shook her head. "I thought that was just another rumor."

"Please, Edna," Aunt Iz said, "I am coming to a Clan head in search of aid."

Edna paused for a moment before flicking the tip of her wand. There was a loud *pop*, and the bubble around them disappeared.

"Come inside," Edna said, walking up to the house without looking back.

"*Compuere,*" Emilia said. The car door unsealed, and Rosalie climbed out.

"You know she won't help you," Rosalie said, her gaze darting from the house to Emilia's face. "Not in the way you want."

"We have no one else," Emilia said.

Rosalie followed Aunt Iz, dragging her feet in the dirt like an angry child.

Molly had moved around to the trunk and reappeared holding her wand out in front of her, Dexter's still bound body bobbing ahead of her like a dog on a leash.

"Larkin," Emilia whispered, touching Larkin's knee.

Larkin jerked awake with a shriek, fighting to get free from her seat while the seatbelt held her pinned.

"Shh," Emilia cooed. "You're fine. We're here, and it's time to go inside."

Larkin looked up at the house, her breathing still ragged. "Sorry. I'm sorry."

"Do you want to go inside with us?" Emilia asked.

Larkin nodded.

Emilia reached in to help Larkin from the car, but Larkin pulled her hand away. "I'm fine. I can do it alone."

Jacob felt Emilia's heart drop. Larkin had been left with the Dragons for months. Tortured. Alone. Could damage like that ever be undone?

"Emi." Jacob touched her shoulder.

But Emilia shook him off, wiping the tears from her cheeks and following the rest of the group into the house.

The house smelled of age and disrepair. Emilia had been right. Not all wizards lived like the Grays.

Edna had settled herself on a faded flower print armchair facing the front door, leaving the rest of them to stand with their backs to the wall.

As soon as Jacob had shut the door, Edna flicked her wand. The lock gave a dull *thunk* behind him.

"No offense, but these are terrible times." Edna pulled a cigarette from her pocket.

"I take no offense at all." Iz gave another small bow. "I appreciate your caution."

Edna pointed at Dexter who lay on his back, hovering a few inches above the floor. "How did you get the Wayland boy?"

"He rescued me." Larkin's eyes darted to Dexter, then she squeezed them tightly shut, taking a breath before continuing. "I was held by the Pendragon for months."

"But you're still keeping him tied up?" Edna asked.

"As you said, these are terrible times," Iz said.

"I do still have access to one of the dungeons. One of the few perks of being from the Virginia Clan. There is always someone trying to kill you with a spell to your back. But if they miss and you catch them, at least we have a nice dark hole for them to rot in."

Dexter shook his head, mumbling through his gag.

"That will not be necessary," Aunt Iz said, speaking over Dexter's muffled grunts, "yet. He spent a good deal of time with the Dragons and may still have information that could be useful to us."

Edna nodded. She put the cigarette to her lips and touched it with the tip of her wand. A tiny burst of fire appeared where the two met, and Edna sighed, sinking back into her chair. She made a noise somewhere between a growl and a purr as smoke blossomed from her mouth. "If you don't want me to throw the traitor down a hole, what *do* you want, Isadora?"

"This is Rosalie Wilde," Iz said, pointing to Rosalie, who gave a halfhearted curtsy while glaring at Emilia.

"A Wilde, huh?" Edna leaned forward, studying Rosalie's face. "She sure is, but that family is gone. They tried to take power from the Walker family when they were the Clan heads about fifteen years ago. The Walkers killed every Wilde they could. I'm surprised this one survived."

"They killed everyone?" Rosalie's voice was tight and small, and what looked like a tear glistened in the corner of her eye.

"Everyone. It was that massacre that led to the Sable family taking power and my becoming the head of this Clan. But surely someone from the Virginia Clan would know that. And what has she got to do with you?" Edna scanned all of them, her gaze stopping on Emilia. "Emilia Gray, the orphan. I'm guessing you finally found Emilia's mother. Doesn't surprise me that a Wilde would leave a baby alone on a doorstep, and with a different Clan no less. Did you go crawling back to the Grays? Did you want them to pay you for giving Isadora an heir?"

"I found her." Emilia stepped forward.

The air in the room seemed to shift as all eyes turned toward Emilia. Jacob could feel her nerves shaking.

"*We* found her." He stepped up to stand next to Emilia. The backs of their hands brushed, and a tingle flew up his arm. If Emilia was going to have to explain how she found Rosalie, Jacob wouldn't let her do it alone.

"How did you find her?" Edna's eyes narrowed, her painted black brows scrunching together.

"My father is the Pendragon. He kidnapped me. Once I knew who he was, I managed to find out my mother's name and track her down." Emilia stopped. That was really as much of the story as could be told without admitting to breaking the laws of Magickind.

"And what rock was she hiding under for so many years?" Edna asked. When Emilia didn't answer, she turned her glare toward Rosalie.

"Nowhere that will make this any better for anyone." Rosalie spun to face Iz. "Did you really think this was going to keep Emile from finding me? Did you really think the Virginia Clan was going to save the day? They can't even keep from murdering my whole family!"

"Rosalie, please try to stay calm," Molly said, putting a hand on Rosalie's shoulder.

"Stay calm?" Rosalie screamed, her black hair flying as she rounded on Edna, holding out her left palm, the one that glistened with a streak of gold. "We're here because eighteen years ago, I tethered myself to Emile LeFay, and now he's coming to kill me and anyone who stands in his way."

Silence overtook the room.

"We won't let him kill you," Jacob said softly. He jumped as muffled shouting came from the corner. He had forgotten Dexter was still there.

"Stop it," Emilia whispered at him, but Dexter shouted louder, his eyes bulging from the effort.

"Just shut up."

Dexter kicked backward, banging his feet against the floor, sweat streaming down his face from the effort.

"*Evocio.*" Iz waved her wand, and the gag flew out of Dexter's mouth. "What?"

"He didn't mean Emilia?" Dexter asked, struggling to keep his head up. "He's coming for Rosalie instead?"

"Yes," Jacob said.

"Then why don't we let her go back to him?" Dexter asked. "He won't hurt his *coniunx*. She'd be safer with him than running with you."

"Because death is better than sharing a bed with a monster." Rosalie tore the sleeve from her shirt and stomped over to Dexter, shoving the fabric into his mouth.

"Do you mean to tell me you brought the Pendragon's *coniunx* to my house?" Edna said.

"Yes," Aunt Iz said. "He is coming for her. The Gray Clan is stretched to its limits. We are being attacked from every side. The

Pendragon will come for her, and if our Clans stand united when he does—"

"There is no Virginia Clan to stand with anyone." Edna took a long draw on her cigarette. "As soon as the Council fell apart, we lost most of the travelers. Why should they listen to me if there is no Council to stand behind me? The Grimes family tried to take power. I caught a few of them and put them into the dungeon for rebellion. The rest ran to the Pendragon. I have a few members of my own family left. But all they can do is try to keep their own children alive."

"I am so sorry, Edna," Molly said.

"The Pendragon is evil." Edna dropped her cigarette, which disappeared before it hit the carpet. "I have spent my entire life fighting for a strong Virginia Clan. Fighting to make this territory something to be proud of. We were so close. So close to having a Clan my grandchildren would be proud to lead. Then darkness came out of the Gray woods and destroyed it all."

Edna stood and walked to Rosalie, taking her chin in her hand. Rosalie shuddered but did not back away.

"This one is a Wilde. She is of my Clan, and I will take care of her. That one"—Edna pointed to Dexter—"is a Wayland and a captive of the Grays. Unless you want him in a dungeon, he has nothing to do with me. The rest of you are welcome to stay for lunch. But if the Pendragon is coming for the Wilde girl, I suggest you leave. I won't be responsible for what he does to you."

"We can't just leave her here," Emilia said, turning to Aunt Iz.

"We didn't come to leave her on your doorstep," Iz said, "though I do appreciate the offer. We came to seek your help in finding a solution."

"How did you hide from the Pendragon for the last seventeen years?" Edna asked.

"I fell off the earth." Rosalie's hands trembled as she picked at her curls. Her eyes seemed to grey and her frame to shrink. She looked more like the Rosalie Jacob had carried through the Siren's Realm than the one whom he had ridden with in the car.

Edna waited, drawn-on eyebrow raised.

"I went to the Siren," Rosalie whispered. "I couldn't feel him there. It was quiet. I was safe."

"Then why did you bother coming back?" Edna asked.

Jacob remembered Edna from his trial. She had voted to let him go. She had seemed so nice and reasonable. But now her voice dripped with venom.

"I brought her back," Emilia said. "I thought she could help us"—Emilia paused for a moment, and Jacob could hear the word *kill* hovering in the air—"defeat the Pendragon. I didn't know they were tethered."

"And you didn't think to warn her?" Edna asked, her sharp eyes flaring at Rosalie.

"Thinking wasn't something I did there," Rosalie muttered. "I said I didn't want to come back."

"She is of the Virginia Clan." Edna's voice rose, echoing through the empty house. "She will be punished according to our laws."

"Punished?" Jacob asked, taking a step in front of Rosalie, blocking her from the tip of Edna's wand.

"She wanted to leave the world of Magickind. Then she will leave it," Edna continued.

Jacob glanced at Aunt Iz. Her face was calm, but Emilia's was white with panic.

"Rosalie Wilde, you will have your powers bound tonight at sunset."

Emilia gasped and took a step toward Edna. "You can't!"

Jacob grabbed Emilia and pulled her to stand behind him, shielding her from Edna's cold glare. Edna continued to speak, unfazed by Emilia fighting to push past Jacob.

"As your life is threatened, the Clan will continue to protect you until the threat has past. After you are no longer in danger, you will be sent to live in the world as a human." Edna stopped and looked at the group. "Now, would any of you like lunch?"

"You can't just bind her powers," Emilia said, finally managing to shove past Jacob. "The Pendragon is coming for her, and she needs to be able to defend herself."

"And does she still have use of her powers? Can she control them? Should someone who bound herself to the Pendragon be trusted with a talisman?" Edna took a longer stride than seemed possible with her tiny frame to glare right up into Emilia's face. "You wanted my help. I'm giving it. But on my terms. I won't have a crackpot who doesn't know which way a wand should be pointed running around my territory. I may not have much of a Clan left, but I sure as hell plan to protect what I've got."

"We understand, Edna," Aunt Iz said. "And I must say I agree."

"Aunt Iz, you can't!" Emilia shouted. "We rescued her. We should be protecting her, helping her! Not stealing her magic!"

Emilia turned to Jacob, and his heart sank. She wanted him to be on her side, to say Rosalie should be allowed to remain a witch.

"Maybe you could bind her powers temporarily?" Jacob said. "Until she's more herself. Then once this is over, we could undo the spell and give Rosalie her magic back."

Emilia turned away from him. He wanted to hold her, to tell her he was on her side, but they needed help. There was no one else to ask.

"What happens once the Pendragon is destroyed will be up to those who are still alive," Edna said, turning and marching through a door at the far end of the room. "And considering what you've dragged into my house, I doubt any of us will qualify."

5

THE BINDING

*E*milia sat on the porch, ignoring the cold wind that seeped through her coat. The sun was starting to fade. Soon they would bring Rosalie out to bind her powers. A sunset ceremony. It felt like an execution. The door creaked open behind her. She knew it was Jacob before he'd draped the blanket around her.

"Some day, huh?" Jacob sat down beside her.

"Some day." Emilia took Jacob's hand. Her heart began to hum the moment their skin touched. She pulled him closer, moving the blanket to cover them both.

Emilia took a deep breath. His scent of grass and life filled her lungs as she relaxed into his shoulder. But her stomach was still tight. "You really think binding her powers is the right thing to do?"

"No." He lifted Emilia's chin and looked into her eyes. "But I think it's the only way to get the Virginia Clan to help us. And without Edna, we might not make it through the night."

"The Grays have never needed help before," Emilia said. "We can fight without outside help." But even as she said it, she knew it wasn't true. Without Edna, they could be dead before morning. Even with her, they still might be.

"Emi," Jacob whispered, "you are the most important thing in the world to me. I would do anything to keep you safe, and right now *safe* means we need Edna's help. We'll find a way to get Rosalie her powers back. We dragged her back from another world. We can find a spell to help her. Iz bound Dexter's magic, and it didn't hurt him."

"This won't be like that. " Emilia shook her head, trying to find the words to explain. "Iz just blocked Dexter's magic. It's still inside of him. It just can't get out. It's what they do to kids who can't control their magic. Iz had to bind Claire a few times, but it's temporary. That sort of binding is easy to undo, and it won't hold forever. What they're going to do to Rosalie...they want to take the magic out of her completely. That isn't something we can fix by looking in a book and picking out a spell."

Emilia rubbed a hand over her eyes. How long had it been since they had had a full night's sleep? More than a month, now? Since before the Siren's Realm. "The binding spell was protected by the Council of Elders. Not many know the incantation. What if none of them will give us the reversal spell?"

Jacob lifted her hand from her face. The golden streak on her palm began to glow. Jacob trailed his finger along the mark, and heat flooded up Emilia's arm.

"Jacob," Emilia whispered. She leaned in, her heart beginning to race, but footsteps came toward the front door.

Jacob smiled, and Emilia's breath caught in her chest as his lips gently grazed the gold mark on her palm.

"It's time," Aunt Iz said as she stepped onto the porch, Rosalie close behind.

Someone had given Rosalie a bath. Or perhaps she had managed it on her own. Her hair flowed behind her in long, black curls, tumbling down the back of her deep purple coat.

Rosalie turned to Emilia. "I suppose you wouldn't want to

miss this. After all, you did risk your life to get me here." Rosalie turned and walked down the steps. She stood under a barren tree and stared up at the sky.

Emilia glanced at Jacob before following Rosalie. "We didn't save you for this." Emilia spoke softly, not wanting Aunt Iz to hear. "And this won't last forever."

"He'll still find me. And he'll take me away. He'll kill anyone who tries to stop him. He wants me back. It feels like hunger, but a thousand times worse. He'll take me back to his caves." Rosalie's voice trembled. "But this time, I won't be able to escape." Rosalie pointed a shaking finger at Edna. "You're making sure of it."

"I am being asked to protect two traitors who have fraternized with the Pendragon," Edna said as she strode over to Rosalie, knocking her accusing finger away. "You made a mistake. You joined yourself to a killer. You will pay the price. I have a Clan to protect, and I don't trust you not to kill me in my sleep. So unless you want to be locked in the closet and chained up like the Wayland boy, I suggest you stand still. The sun is setting."

Edna was right. The sky was shifting from orange and red to a dusky blue.

"Hold still," Molly said. "Take a deep breath, Rosalie, and it'll be over soon."

"Thanks." Rosalie turned to gaze into the west at the last bit of color left behind by the sun.

Molly, Aunt Iz, and Edna all stepped in to form a circle around Rosalie.

Rosalie's hands started to shake. Emilia wanted to comfort her mother, to hold her and protect her, but Jacob wrapped an arm around her waist, holding her back.

Jacob had become a part of a spell that was not meant for him. Emilia laced her fingers through Jacob's. Her place was with him. Not getting her powers bound with Rosalie. Rosalie would need Emilia's magic whole.

"*Laxo sua calyxis*," Molly, Aunt Iz, and Edna began to chant, all three tipping their heads back with their eyes shut.

Tears slid down Emilia's cheeks as Rosalie began to glow with a strangely cold light. A gleaming, silver thread flowed from Rosalie's palms. Rosalie balled her hands into tight fists, as though trying to keep her magic from drifting away.

"*Venefecto modo magus—*"

Bright, golden light pulled away from Rosalie as though someone were separating her from a mold of herself.

"No!" Rosalie screamed, clawing at her chest. "Stop! Please!"

"Rosalie!" Emilia tried to pull away from Jacob. The spell was going wrong. They were going to kill her. "Aunt Iz, stop!"

Rosalie fell to the ground, screaming as she clutched her chest.

"You're killing her!" Emilia shouted. "*Rasus!*" Jacob jumped away from her as though stung, and Emilia ran toward the circle.

"*Sevoco vita exsaura.*"

She was too late. The three women dropped hands, and the light around Rosalie faded into darkness.

"Rosalie," Emilia said, kneeling next to her, "can you hear me?"

Rosalie lifted her head, blinking at Emilia, her eyes unfocused.

"You're alive," Emilia whispered, relief flooding through her.

Rosalie pushed herself to her feet, shaking.

"Careful," Emilia said, reaching to steady her, but Rosalie took a step toward Iz, swaying as she moved.

"Rosalie." Jacob dove forward, catching her as she tripped and toppled over. He lowered her gently to the ground.

Rosalie stared up at the night sky.

"It's all right, Rosalie." Emilia said. The cold of the frozen ground bit her knees. "You're going to be fine."

"It's gone," Rosalie murmured. "It's gone. How could they do it?"

"I know it's hard," Jacob said. "But this was the best way to keep you safe."

"Safe?" Rosalie pulled away from Jacob, struggling to stand. "How did you do it? Tell me how!"

"Binding is an extremely old spell—" Molly started.

Rosalie spun to face Emilia. "It's gone," she whispered, holding out her left hand. A hand without a trace of gold.

6

BROKEN

*E*milia held Rosalie's palm, twisting it in the fading light, trying to catch a glimpse of gold. But there was no shimmer of the golden mark left on Rosalie's trembling hand.

"It's gone," Rosalie whispered, her voice shaking as much as her hand. "Everything's gone." Tears shone in her eyes. "He's gone. Emile is gone."

"What happened?" Aunt Iz said, taking Rosalie's hand from Emilia.

"It's quiet. So quiet and empty." Rosalie clutched her chest as though trying to staunch a wound. "You did this." Rosalie rounded on Edna.

"*Elutio,*" Edna said, waving a hand at Rosalie.

This time Emilia leaped forward to catch her mother before she fell to the ground.

"Why did you do that?" Jacob asked, glaring at Edna. He reached down and scooped Rosalie into his arms.

"She was getting hysterical," Edna said.

Emilia brushed the hair away from Rosalie's face. "That was nowhere near hysterical for her." Rosalie was breathing deeply, though her eyes twitched behind their lids. "What happened to her mark? Nothing can make a tethering mark disappear. It's not possible."

"I have no idea," Aunt Iz said.

"Does it matter?" Edna asked. "We bound her powers. If it broke her tethering, is it such a bad thing? We can hide her somewhere, and the Pendragon will never be able to find her."

Edna turned and walked into the house.

She didn't understand. If the binding had broken the tethering, it had broken Rosalie.

"We should take her inside," Jacob said, starting toward the house.

Emilia followed, not taking her eyes from Jacob. He kicked the front door open and headed up the stairs to the small bedroom they had locked Rosalie in to wait for her binding.

The room was tiny and dusty with a faint stench of cat. As soon as Jacob had lain Rosalie down on the faded, moth-eaten comforter, Emilia took his arm and turned him around.

She buried her face on his chest, struggling to keep her breath even. His fear pounded through her, and Emilia knew he could feel her panic as well.

Rosalie had been torn in half. The constant pull in her chest would be gone. The hum of every breath her *coniunx* took. The jolt when he was afraid. The tingle when they touched.

"Maybe it's better," Jacob said softly, as though he were afraid Rosalie might hear, "if their tethering really is broken."

"Jacob—"

"He's a monster, Emi," Jacob said, pulling Emilia even closer. "She hated him. If he can't find her…if she doesn't have to feel him…"

Emilia shuddered. What would be worse? Losing half of your soul, or having that half of your soul be a murderer?

"Don't leave me," Emilia whispered, looking up into Jacob's bright blue eyes. "Promise me, Jacob. No matter what, we stay together." Hot tears streamed down Emilia's cheeks. She had never wanted to be tethered. Not to anyone. But now, she couldn't even bear to think of the spell being broken. "I can't lose you."

Emilia leaned up and kissed Jacob. The moment their lips met, every thought of their ever being apart slipped away. She pulled herself closer, slipping her fingers through Jacob's hair. Her chest thrummed, not just with her heartbeat, but with his as well. And as she deepened their kiss, her heart raced faster. This was where she was meant to be. This was home. This was life.

Jacob pulled away with a gasp, taking his arms from Emilia's waist as though burned. He turned to pace the room.

Emilia tucked her hair behind her ears, trying to hide a grin. "You all right?"

"Yep," Jacob said, his voice sounding unusually tight. "That was"—he paused and quickened his step—"interesting."

He glanced to Emilia, then at Rosalie sleeping on the bed. "I'm going to go and check on"—he looked back to Emilia, his face turning bright pink—"uh, see what Iz thinks we should do."

Jacob strode out of the room and closed the door sharply behind him.

Emilia let herself smile for a moment, remembering the warmth of his touch before turning to Rosalie.

"*Resipisco,*" Emilia said, placing her hand on Rosalie's forehead.

Rosalie began to stir, rubbing her eyes like a small child before sitting up. Her gaze drifted around the room, finally focusing on Emilia and then moving down to her hand.

"How do you feel?" Emilia asked, knowing it must sound like a horrible question, but she didn't know what else to say.

"Hollow," Rosalie mumbled. "*Inluesco.*" No ball of light appeared. She turned to the window. "*Aperestra ab externum.*" The window stayed shut tight. "My magic is gone."

"I know." Emilia sat down next to Rosalie.

"I can't feel him." Rosalie rubbed a hand on her chest, as

though searching for a hole. "It's so empty. Like that ugly little woman stole my heart or a lung or..."

"Soul."

Rosalie took Emilia's hand, clutching it so tight it hurt, staring silently into Emilia's grey eyes—eyes Emilia knew matched the Pendragon's.

"Did you know?" Emilia asked, when she couldn't stand the silence anymore. "Did you know binding your powers would break your tethering?"

"I thought it could only be broken by death. That's why I went to the Hag. I was too afraid to die. So I left. I thought the Siren's Realm was the only safe place. I could have been living as a human in Cleveland this whole time."

"Cleveland?"

"Doesn't it sound like such a normal place?" Rosalie laughed. It sounded cold and hollow.

"Does it hurt?" Emilia whispered.

"I don't know." Rosalie wrapped her arms around her chest as though trying to hold the broken pieces of her heart together. "It hurt when I could feel him. It tore my soul in two knowing I was bound to a monster. Now I've been ripped in half." Rosalie's brow wrinkled. "I don't know which hurts worse." Rosalie's chin trembled. Her eyes looked like a frightened child's.

Emilia studied her mother's face. Now, away from the Siren, Rosalie seemed younger. Yesterday she had looked like a wasted version of the picture Claire had shown Emilia months ago. Her face had been creased and drawn, but now, even through Rosalie's puffy eyed tears, she looked no older than twenty-five or twenty-six. Definitely not old enough to be Emilia's mother.

"How much time passed for you?" Emilia asked. "With the Siren."

Rosalie tensed and began twisting her curls around her fingers. "I don't know." She chewed on her bottom lip, tugging even harder on her curls.

"You never wondered?" Emilia gently moved Rosalie's hands away from her hair, worried she might start to pull it out.

"It didn't seem important. I didn't think I would ever come back."

"But if the Pendragon can't feel you, you could start a life here," Emilia said.

"It's too late. He's too angry. Emile will find me. Whether he can feel me or not, he'll find a way."

"We can hide you. We can find a safe place."

"I thought I *had* found a safe place," Rosalie said, touching Emilia's hair. "But it didn't last. Safe never does."

7

LOST BIRD

"*I* was starting to think you all forgot I needed to eat," Dexter said, struggling to twist the heavy chain around his wrists in such a way that he could manage his spoon.

"We didn't forget," Jacob said. "We just didn't care."

Dexter finally managed to get the spoon into the soup and began to eat greedily. The soup had been boiling. The bowl nearly burned Jacob's hands as he carried it to the closet. It must have been scalding Dexter's mouth, but he ate it without pause.

"What happened at the binding?" Dexter asked between giant mouthfuls.

Jacob clenched his fists. It was none of Dexter's business what had happened to Rosalie. He stood to leave, and Dexter clutched the bowl to his chest as though afraid Jacob would take it from him.

"You can keep eating," Jacob said, making his voice as even as he could. "We won't starve you to death. We aren't monsters here."

Jacob turned to leave.

"The Pendragon is a monster," Dexter said quietly.

Jacob punched the door. The pain that shot from his knuckles to his elbow didn't stop him from wanting to punch Dexter. Jacob took a deep breath, shaking his fingers to make sure nothing was broken before turning back to Dexter.

"Finally figured that out, did you?" Jacob spat. "It wasn't breaking a dam and murdering people. It wasn't trying to kill Emilia, Iz, and me on a plane. It wasn't kidnapping Emilia. So what was it then? They made you work?" Jacob knocked the bowl from Dexter's hands and watched it clatter to the floor with grim satisfaction. "Did they take away your food? Or was it just that the tethering didn't work out the way you planned? If she had been bound to you, you would still be living in those caves. You would have everything you want, and she would be the prisoner. Chained to you."

"I never asked to be tethered to her." Dexter stared at the wooden floor.

"I saw the book you had," Jacob said, remembering a day before the world had fallen apart. Before Emilia had been kidnapped and taken to the Graylock Preserve. "I saw you lock a book in your desk. A book about how tethering works."

Dexter looked up, his eyes wide and confused.

"You were trying to figure out how to bind Emilia to you," Jacob said.

"I wanted us to be tethered," Dexter said. "But I wanted it to be her choice."

"Bullshit."

"You may not believe me, but I would never do anything to hurt Emilia. I love her."

"Kidnapping is a sign of love?" Jacob laughed coldly at the absurdity of Dexter understanding love at all.

"I had nothing to do with that." Dexter pulled against his chains, struggling to his feet. "I love Emilia. All I ever wanted was for her to want me. For her to choose me."

Jacob kicked Dexter's feet out from under him, sending him sprawling to the ground, hitting his head on the wall.

"It's too late. She's already chosen me." Jacob spun and swung the door open.

"She didn't choose either of us," Dexter called after him. "And now she never will."

Jacob didn't look back as he slammed the door behind him.

He couldn't breathe. Everything had been settled. Emilia had said she wanted him just...was it really yesterday? She said she had chosen him. She wanted him without spells or magic.

Jacob walked past the living room and out the front door onto the lawn, ignoring Molly's call of, "Jacob, aren't you hungry?"

The cold air hit his lungs, chilling him from the inside out.

"Jacob," Emilia called softly from the porch.

He didn't turn around. All he wanted was to hold Emilia, to protect her and love her. But Dexter was right. The tethering had cheated him of the chance to win her fairly. Even if she did want him, evil had gotten them here. And that would never go away.

The porch steps squeaked, and Emilia wrapped her arms around his waist, her head resting between his shoulder blades.

Jacob took her hands. They were small and freezing. He rubbed them between his own. Their palms began to glow like embers, illuminating the night around them.

Emilia moved around him to place her head on his chest. "How did we get here? How did we end up in Virginia with my mother a human, Dexter chained up in the closet, Larkin practically a ghost, Molly and Iz in negotiations about where we're all supposed to hide, and the rest of the family God knows where? Maybe it would have been better for you if you hadn't been a wizard."

"It wouldn't have been better. I never would have known about magic, I wouldn't have had a family, and I wouldn't have you."

"And if he finds us?" Emilia asked. "If he kills all of us?"

Jacob could hear the tears in her voice. He searched for something brave to say, something to make her feel better, but all he could think of were words Samuel had spoken when the Dragons still seemed like a far away threat. "It would still be worth it. None of us are willing to let the Pendragon win. The more we fight him, the more we lose, but it's worth it. Because letting him take over, letting him kill humans and tell them about all of us, we can't let that happen. And protecting you, protecting this family, it's worth risking everything."

$\sim$

*L*arkin stood behind the house, staring at the stick in her hand. Emilia watched from the kitchen window. Molly had convinced Edna to let her do the cooking. No one but Edna could argue with the change. With Molly in charge, everything they ate no longer tasted like cigarette ash.

"Do you think Rosalie might join us for dinner?" Molly asked from her spot at the stove.

"I can try," Emilia answered, guilt curdling in her stomach. She hadn't really spoken to Rosalie, not since the binding two days earlier. She wanted to ask Rosalie about herself. About Emilia's grandparents. But it all came back to the same thing— Emile LeFay was Emilia's father. If she asked her mother about her past, it would end with him.

Instead, Emilia watched Rosalie. Every time Rosalie left her room, Emilia studied her. And every time Rosalie caught her staring, Rosalie would shrug and walk away.

And now Emilia watched Larkin, standing out in the cold garden, holding a stick.

"You should talk to her," Molly said, making Emilia jump as she placed her hand on her shoulder.

"And say what?" Emilia sank into Molly's side, feeling like a little girl again. But now Molly couldn't fix all her problems with cookies and a warm hug. "Say I'm sorry you came after me? I'm sorry I left you in Graylock? I'm sorry my father tortured you for months?"

"Or you could tell her you love her and you're glad she's home," Molly said, tilting Emilia's chin to look into her eyes. "She's been through a lot. And we are far from the other side of this mess. The only thing we can do is cling to the people we love the most and make the best of each moment."

"You're right." Emilia stood and took Jacob's coat from the hook by the door. "Thanks, Molly."

The sun was bright enough to make Emilia squint as it peered through the winter-bare trees.

Larkin still stood, holding the stick in her hand, just staring at it.

"How's it going?" Emilia said, instantly wishing she had thought of something better to say.

Larkin spun on the spot, pointing the stick at Emilia. She froze for a moment, glaring at Emilia before shaking her head and lowering her hand.

"Sorry," Larkin muttered. "I didn't hear you."

"It's fine." Emilia took a slow step forward. "Did you decide to go with a wand for your talisman?"

"I need something." Larkin broke the stick in two and tossed it to the ground. "I need to be able to fight. But I've never really been a wand person I guess."

"I have your ring," Emilia said.

Larkin's head snapped toward her, her pale eyes dark with confusion.

"Jacob has it, technically." Emilia resisted the urge to back away.

"That's impossible. The woman in the caves, she took it."

"Her name was Domina," Emilia said. "She hurt Jacob. He killed her and took a ring from her. He gave it to me when we were escaping." Tears stung Emilia's eyes as she remembered the woods and the fire. "I didn't look at it then. And when we got home, I threw it in the back of a drawer without looking at it.

"If I had seen the bird on it when he gave it to me, I would have known it was yours. We could have stayed, gotten you out. Samuel went back in after you, but he didn't tell us why." A sob caught in Emilia's throat. Her words came out in strange gasps. "He made us leave. Leave both of you in that place."

Emilia heard the back door *squeak* open. She didn't need to turn to know Jacob was on the porch. Watching, protecting.

"You had to go," Larkin said quietly. "Do you know what the Pendragon asked me about when he was torturing me? Not MAGI. Not Iz. He asked me about you. You're what he wanted from me. If he had had you, I'd be dead."

"Th-that's ridiculous," Emilia stammered. "He wants me dead. You're a MAGI. You're more valuable than I am. Why would he hurt you to find out about me? You were in the caves. You had no way to know where I was. You had nothing else to tell him."

"*Manuvis.*" A shimmering red ball appeared in Larkin's hand.

"Be careful," Emilia said, taking a quick step forward, fighting the urge to grab the sphere from Larkin. "You don't have your talisman."

"Probably for the best," Larkin said. "Never practice with a talisman, right?" Larkin tossed the ball high into the air where it exploded with a *bang*, shaking the window panes.

The door squeaked open again.

"He didn't want to know where you were," Larkin said. "*Manuvis.*" Another larger, brighter ball formed in her hand. "He wanted to know about you. About what you like—food, books, clothes. What it was like to live with you, watch you grow up." She tossed the ball into the air, and it curved in a long arc, exploding right above the roof of the house.

"Larkin, be careful," Emilia said. They couldn't afford to make Edna mad enough to throw them out of the house.

"He wanted to know if you were careful, too," Larkin said. "If you were one to run wild through the woods or stay where Iz told you. *Manuvis.*" The new sphere was large enough Larkin had to hold it with both hands.

"I've never seen that spell." Emilia took a few steps forward, trying to close the distance between her and Larkin. "Is it a MAGI spell?"

"There is no more MAGI," Larkin grunted as she tossed the sphere into the air. But it had been too heavy. It wasn't going to fly high enough.

"*Primurgo!*" Emilia shouted, forming a shield over them as the ball began to career back toward the ground. The explosion shook Emilia's lungs.

"Nice one, Em," Larkin said.

"Don't call me that," Emilia said, looking toward the house, wishing Jacob were standing with her.

"Because that's what Dexter calls you?" Larkin asked, raising a blond eyebrow.

"You look like Claire when you do that," Emilia said.

"Actually, she got it from you, who got it from me, who got it from Iz." Larkin laughed. But the laugh was hollow and dry, not what it should have sounded like at all. "And Dexter picked up *Em* from me. But the Pendragon, he calls you plain old Emilia. I think he likes that you were named after him. That you're his."

"I'm not his."

"You're his blood." Larkin knelt, trailing her hands lazily over the dead grass, scorching a pattern into the earth. "You're the most important thing there is."

"I'm not."

"You are," Larkin said, her voice low and her words coming at a frighteningly even rhythm, "because he thinks you are. We have what he wants. As long as we have that, we can fight him. As long as we have you, we have a hand left to play. The minute we lose the thing he wants, he will take everything and kill everyone who stands in his way. His castle will be complete with Emilia LeFay."

"Don't call me that!"

Larkin turned to look at Emilia, but Emilia didn't meet Larkin's eyes. She couldn't stop staring at the scorched grass. A perfectly drawn Dragon. Identical to the tattoo the Dragon warriors wore, wrapping from their cheek to their neck.

"*Manuvis.*" A manic anger gleamed in Larkin's eyes.

"Larkin, you shouldn't—" Emilia began a moment too late.

The shining, crimson sphere was already blossoming into being in Larkin's hands. But this time the spell crackled with fire, sending sparks raining down onto the scorched dragon.

Larkin gasped and fell to her knees, her eyes still bound to the sphere in her hands that grew with every second.

"No!" Emilia screamed, but there was nothing she could do. Larkin was pushing too much magic through her body. She had no talisman.

Larkin screamed.

Emilia reached for the blazing sphere in Larkin's hands. The heat of the spell scorched her palms.

"*Elutio!*" The shout came from the door.

Larkin's eyes grew wide with panic for an instant before she crumpled to the ground.

Emilia stared in horror as the sphere continued to grow before a flash of light knocked her off her feet.

"Larkin!" Molly shouted, running down the back steps, but Jacob was already halfway across the lawn.

Emilia didn't know how, but she was lying on the scorched earth. She crawled over to Larkin, her hands bursting with pain every time they touched the grass.

Larkin lay on the ground, her blond hair framing her face like an angel.

"Larkin," Emilia whispered, reaching for her face.

"Back away Emilia." Molly knelt next to Larkin.

"Emi." Jacob lifted her into his arms, holding her close to his chest.

"No. Larkin." Emilia tried to push away, but Jacob held her tighter.

"*Medamo facilinox requietas—*" Molly muttered, laying her hand over Larkin's heart.

"Is she okay?" Emilia asked, terrified to hear the answer.

Seconds ticked past as Molly continued to chant.

"She'll be fine." Molly sat back on her heels.

"I should have stopped her," Emilia whispered. "I should have—"

"She's in pain," Molly said. "She's been hurt. Sometimes there's nothing you can do. She'll heal on her own time."

"Will she?" Tears slid down Emilia's cheeks.

"We can hope." Molly stood, dusting the ashes off her knees.

"Should we give her her ring?" Jacob asked, still keeping Emilia cradled to his chest.

"It's either that or bind her powers," Molly said, reaching a hand out to Jacob.

He lowered Emilia gently to her feet before reaching into his pocket and pulling out a silver ring with a tiny bird etched on the front.

Emilia took it from him and knelt next to Larkin, slipping the silver band onto her finger.

"We'll need to wrap your hands," Molly said.

"Jacob can do it." Emilia looked down at her hands. Her palms were burned and blistered.

"Go," Molly said, trailing her fingers over the scorched grass. As her palms passed, the grass began to sway with an unseen wind, growing and changing until it was bright green and healthy.

Emilia watched over her shoulder as Jacob guided her to the house. Before he could close the door behind them, a bright green dragon had appeared in the grass.

Banging shook the closet door by the stairs.

"Hey!" Dexter screamed. "Hey!"

Jacob led Emilia past the door that vibrated with Dexter's kicks.

"Is she hurt?" The noise stopped as Emilia paused in front of the door. "Is Emilia hurt?"

Emilia walked up the stairs.

"She's fine." Jacob's words followed her.

Emilia walked into her room and sat down on the bed, resisting the urge to start throwing things. Jacob was there a moment later, a roll of gauze and some ointment in his hands.

"Let me see," Jacob said, gently lifting Emilia's hands onto this lap.

As their hands met, the golden glow began to shimmer from the streaks on their left palms.

"Ouch," Emilia gasped, pulling away. Her left palm had stung at Jacob's touch, but when she looked down, the skin around the golden mark had healed perfectly. Her fingers were still burned, but her palm was perfect, marked only by the line of gold.

"How did you do that?" Jacob asked, looking at Emilia's hand and carefully avoiding touching it.

"I didn't."

"*Pelluere*," Jacob said, touching the tip of his wand to Emilia's right hand.

She bit her lips as the sting of healing spread across her skin. When the pain faded, her right hand was still pink and raw. Jacob carefully wound the gauze around it.

"You'd think they would have made spells to heal spell damage," Jacob said, his brow furrowed in concentration.

"They exist." Emilia traced her thumb along her healed left palm. "But every time someone creates one, someone else makes a spell that does more damage than the healing can mend."

"We should ask Iz to take a look when she gets back." Jacob leaned against the wall at the head of Emilia's bed.

He looked exhausted. Shadows of purple lay under his bright blue eyes.

"Where is Aunt Iz?"

"In the barn with Edna," Jacob said. "At least that's where I saw them go after breakfast."

"I would have thought all that exploding might have made her come see what was happening." Emilia rested her head on Jacob's shoulder, letting her eyes drift shut.

"She must have thought we could handle it." Jacob kissed Emilia's forehead.

"Larkin says the Pendragon wanted to know about me. That's why he was hurting her, to know more about me. She said I'm important because he wants me. That we have to keep me away from him because he wants his daughter." Emilia hated saying the words, but Jacob was a part of her fate. He needed to know. "I always wanted to know who my parents were. I just never pictured all the death and destruction that would come with it. The Pendragon knows I hate him. Why does he want me? Why do I have to be important?"

"You're important for a lot of reasons, and the Pendragon sharing a bit of your DNA is barely on the list. And it doesn't matter why he wants you. I will never let him take you. I will do whatever it takes to keep you safe."

Emilia held Jacob tight, feeling him relax with every breath. "I'll keep you safe, too. We're in this together."

"And together we'll find a way to make this right. We'll find a way to get everyone home."

"Do you think Larkin will be all right?"

"She'll be fine," Jacob said, his voice fading as he yawned. "She needs time to heal."

Emilia let the steady rhythm of Jacob's breathing carry her into sleep.

8

THE HIDDEN CONSEQUENCE

Bang, bang, bang.

"Wake up!" Rosalie's voice pounded through the door.

"What's wrong?" Emilia called, clambering off the bed and to the door.

Jacob dug through the sheets, feeling for his wand. It had been with him when he was trying to fix Emilia's hands. He dove to search the ground as Emilia opened the door.

"What's happening? Is Larkin all right?" Emilia asked.

"Are you trying to hide your boyfriend under the bed?" Rosalie asked as Jacob scrambled beneath the frame after the shadow of his wand.

Jacob froze.

"No," Emilia said, "I'm not hiding *Jacob* from anyone. Now what's wrong?"

"Apparently one of the joys of being the human is getting sent to run errands," Rosalie said in a disinterested voice. "The angry ginger—"

"Molly," Emilia corrected.

"—wants you both to come down to dinner," Rosalie said. "Thanks for saving me the trouble of having to go to his room."

Rosalie pushed past Emilia into the room as Jacob sat up, banging his head on the bottom of the dresser.

"And a word to you, lover boy," Rosalie growled. "I may be human now, but I can still skin you alive."

Rosalie turned on her heel and strode out of the room without a backwards glance.

"I don't know why she thinks you're, we're—" Emilia spluttered. "I don't think she's earned herself the right to care." Emilia blushed bright red before following Rosalie down the creaking stairs.

Jacob glanced into Emilia's mirror, brushing the dust from under the bed out of his unruly blond hair.

If Molly thought they'd been, not that they had—Jacob's reflection blushed more than Emilia had—Molly would peel him like a carrot.

Jacob ran down the stairs and made it to the dining room right behind Emilia. Not that it could really be called a dining room.

Larkin and Rosalie were already seated at the wooden card table in the far corner of the living room where they had eaten all their meals. The kitchen was too tiny for all of them to gather there, and even the card table wouldn't have been large enough to hold all of them if Aunt Iz or Edna showed up or if someone let Dexter out of his closet.

Jacob shared one of the longer sides of the rectangular table with Emilia opposite Rosalie who glared at him. Larkin sat at one end. Molly came bustling from the kitchen preceded by a parade of dishes that all floated down onto the table with perfect synchronization.

Smelling the wonderful food through the faint haze of smoke made Jacob miss the Mansion House more than anything else had. They should be there right now, all of them together, talking about the day's lessons, eating together. As a family. Jacob's family.

Emilia laced her fingers through Jacob's under the table.

Rosalie smacked her palm on the table, making the whole flimsy thing shake. "No holding hands at the table."

Emilia glared silently at her mother, holding Jacob's hand even tighter.

"I can see the glow," Rosalie snapped.

Emilia and Rosalie glared at each other, looking more alike than ever in their anger.

"I've made your favorite, Larkin," Molly said after a tense moment. "Beef and dumpling stew."

"Thanks, Molly," Larkin said in an awkwardly cheerful voice.

But Emilia and Rosalie still glared at each other.

"Any chance you could pass the potatoes, Emilia?" Larkin asked.

"Fine," Emilia said, dropping Jacob's hand and turning to Larkin with a smile. "I'm glad you're hungry." She passed the giant tureen of perfectly fluffy, whipped potatoes to Larkin.

"Maybe I should have stayed around," Rosalie said, ignoring the plate Molly was trying to give her. "I think I could have been good at this angry mother thing."

Emilia dropped the fork that had been halfway to her mouth back onto her plate with a *clatter*. "I think it's a little too late to find out."

"You know, I think you're more angry at me for interrupting your time with him than you are for me leaving you." Rosalie took a bite of the stew.

"What?" Molly said.

"I'd like to apologize," Larkin said loudly, pulling Molly's angry gaze from Jacob's face.

"For what?" Emilia asked.

"For losing control earlier." Larkin took a deep breath. "I'm MAGI trained. I should know my limits. I shouldn't have been using the *manuvis* if I wasn't in control of my magic, and not without a talisman. I'm sorry, Emilia."

"It's fine," Emilia said, reaching across the table and taking Larkin's hand. "We've all lost it before."

"I blew up my school." Jacob shrugged. "Well, just broke all the glass really."

"But you didn't know you were a wizard," Larkin said.

"I trashed a room at the Mansion House when I got out of Graylock," Emilia said, not mentioning the fact that it had been Dexter's room she had smashed to pieces.

"I jumped off a cliff and into the Siren's Realm." Rosalie stabbed a dumpling with her fork. "Not that I had lost control of my magic, but I know *some people* here don't agree with that decision."

"Thank you, Rosalie," Larkin said, her tone still somber.

"And what about you?" Rosalie turned to Molly. "Tell us about how you've lost control and destroyed an entire roast goose."

"Rosalie," Emilia warned.

"There are some things best left alone." Molly paused. "But I will say that we've all lost control. We've all done something we're not proud of. And no one was hurt. That's the best you can hope for."

"But I'm a MAGI agent," Larkin said, her pale face desperate. "Or I was when there was an agency. I'm not supposed to crack. I'm not allowed to lose control."

Emilia stood and walked to Larkin, wrapping her arms around Larkin's boney shoulders. "It doesn't matter how well trained you are. You've been through Hell. You're allowed to not be okay. We'll get through this together."

"Thanks, Em," Larkin said, leaning her head on Emilia's arm. Tears glistened in her eyes as she twisted the silver ring on her finger.

～

*R*osalie spent the next morning following Emilia and Jacob around the house, never speaking to them but constantly staring at Emilia and glaring at Jacob. She stood in doorways, her arms still wrapped tightly around her chest as though afraid she might shatter if she let go. But even through the angry glares she shot at Jacob, Rosalie's face had begun to change. The longer Rosalie was away from the Siren, the more like Emilia she looked. It was hard to believe she was the same woman. The dark rings under her eyes had disappeared. And every passing hour seemed to take away the sunken look of her cheeks.

Larkin, too, was looking healthier. Jacob had come down to lunch to find her standing in the corner with Aunt Iz and Molly, the three of them talking in hushed tones over cups of tea.

"I'll make room," Molly said, noticing Jacob and walking over to the table. "*Prolares.*" The table began to grow like a telescope, expanding a few feet before stopping just short enough to allow people to squeeze between it and the wall. "Grab a few chairs please, Jacob."

By the time Jacob had managed to squeeze seven chairs around the table, Rosalie and Edna had taken their seats.

"Good. Everyone's here," Aunt Iz said as Emilia arrived a few minutes later. "Please sit." Aunt Iz waited while Emilia and Jacob squeezed in next to the wall.

"We've made a decision," Iz said, taking a seat at the head of the table. "While I am sure we can all agree Edna's hospitality has been gracious, it is time for us to leave. Larkin and Rosalie are both well enough to travel again. The Pendragon knows Rosalie is from the Virginia Clan. It's only a matter of time before he comes here looking for her. For the sake of the Virginia Clan, it is best if we are not here when he does."

"Who does *we* include?" Emilia asked, looking from Aunt Iz to Molly.

"Molly, Larkin, and I will be taking you and Jacob to stay with Professor Eames," Aunt Iz said. "I have already discussed it with him, and he is thrilled to have you."

"And what about Rosalie?" Emilia asked.

"I'm going to live with the humans." Rosalie reached across the table, touching Emilia's hand for a moment before leaning back in her chair. "It really is for the best. It'll be safest if I simply disappear." Her voice was softer and gentler than Jacob had ever heard it.

"But you said he could find you," Emilia said, her voice becoming shrill as she gripped the edge of the table, turning her knuckles white. "You said he'd track you down even if you weren't bound to him."

"Arrangements have been made," Aunt Iz said. "Rosalie will be living as a human, but she will be very well protected."

"Protected how?" Emilia asked.

"In ways that will be much more effective if fewer people know about them." Molly inclined her head toward the door to the closet where Dexter was still being held.

"We are doing everything we can to make sure she's safe," Larkin said, leaning forward and taking Emilia's hand. "I've made the arrangements myself. I just need you to trust me."

Emilia nodded, chewing on her lower lip.

"We'll leave in twenty minutes." Iz stood up.

"What about him?" Jacob pointed to the door that hid Dexter.

"He'll be staying with the Virginia Clan," Edna said, following Iz out of the room. "Indefinitely."

Jacob left his plate and headed up to his room. They were throwing Dexter into the dungeon. They had talked about sending Jacob there when they thought he was helping the Dragons. A place so horrible they give you a choice—a life trapped deep in the darkness or suicide.

Dexter was a traitor. He had hurt Emilia. But did he really deserve that? Why couldn't wizards have a normal prison? Jacob lifted his bag onto the bed, tossing in the two pairs of pants he had put in a drawer. Maybe he should just keep everything in a bag all the time from now on.

"Tell me it'll be okay." Emilia spoke from the doorway. She was pale, and her eyes were bright. "That somehow we can figure out a way to get all of us back together. That we can get Samuel out, give Rosalie back her powers, and..." Emilia's voice faded as tears began to stream down her face.

Jacob brushed her tears away and kissed her softly. "Emi..."

There was no way to promise they would all be together again. He had always thought that with Emilia he could do anything. But what if he was wrong?

"I promise you we will fight, together, until we can be safe and with our family."

Emilia nodded and pressed her lips to the burn that still marked Jacob's cheek. "We'll fight."

Jacob picked up his bag and led Emilia to her room. Her bag lay open on the floor, still full. "You didn't unpack either?"

"We've spent so much time running." Emilia laughed feebly. "I didn't want to lose any more socks."

Emilia zipped her bag, and Jacob flung it over his shoulder.

Gravel crunched as Molly pulled the car up close to the house.

Emilia squeezed Jacob's hand. "They won't send us different places?" She turned to Jacob, fear filling her eyes. "They won't split us up to keep us safe?"

"I won't let that happen," Jacob said, pulling Emilia close to him with his free arm. "We'll stay together, I promise."

Together, they walked down the stairs and out onto the lawn.

Rosalie leaned on the hood of the car, her head in her hands. Molly took the bags Larkin had been lifting into the trunk, insisting on doing the work herself. Edna stood just off the front steps, shaking hands with Aunt Iz.

"Thank you for everything," Emilia said, taking Edna's hand. "Your hospitality has been very kind."

Jacob listened to the polite replies, looking up at the sky. Where would they be when they slept tonight? If they even got to sleep at all.

In the bright sunlight, dazzling purple flashes appeared against the sky. Jacob blinked and rubbed his eyes. Squinting up into the blue sky, he could still see the bright bursts of color above the house.

"What's that?" Jacob asked, pointing to the flashes.

But Emilia was nodding at something Edna was telling her in her crackling voice.

"Emilia." Jacob took her shoulders and turned her away from Edna's speech. "What are those lights?"

Emilia squinted, looking up into the sky. "Aunt Iz," Emilia said, her voice loud enough to cut through the rest of the noise, "there's something wrong with the shield spell."

"Nonsense," Edna said, "I have those sweet boys in the barn chanting all the time. There's no way for anyone I don't..." Edna's voice trailed away as her eyes focused on the dancing purple lights. "I suggest you go out the back way." Edna ground the butt of her cigarette into the dirt.

"We will not leave you under attack," Aunt Iz said, her stance wide and her wand trained on the gate. "Larkin, get the children and Rosalie into the car."

Rosalie looked up, her eyes focusing on the flashes in the sky, before nodding and obediently moving to her car door.

"We are not children." Emilia raised her hand, her silver ring glinting in the light.

"Now is not the time to argue semantics, Emilia," Aunt Iz said as she stalked slowly toward the front gate.

"We can fight," Jacob said. "We've done it before."

"No, you don't." Rosalie leaped forward and seized Emilia's arm, trying to drag her toward the car.

There was a *crunch*. Jacob spun toward the gate, raising his wand, expecting to see it buckling under attack. But the gate was solid and still.

"There!" Larkin pointed at the ground.

The dirt around the gate pulsed and squirmed. Jacob's skin crawled at the clicking and rustling barely muffled by the earth.

"Get out, Isadora," Edna growled.

"I think it's a bit late for that."

9

BLACK AND BLOOD

*T*he ground pulsed higher and higher until a seething mass of shining black exploded from the dirt.

The creatures stood, stretching their horrible limbs. They looked like men. Or what had been men. Now their arms hung past their knees, and their fingers disappeared into sharp talons. Black glistening armor had taken the place of their skin.

One of the men-made-monsters turned to Jacob. He felt a scream tear from his throat, but the noise of his cry was lost in the bellows of the attack. The monster raised its horrible face, scenting the air. Its eyes were white, but its voice was human.

"In the name of the Pendragon!" The creature let out an almighty roar and ran straight toward Rosalie.

"Emilia, get back to the house, now!" Jacob pointed his wand at the creature closest to Rosalie and Larkin. "*Alevitum!*"

The monster in the lead soared backward, knocking over the beast behind him and breaking the formation of the rest. Jacob spun around, searching for Emilia. She was racing toward Rosalie.

"Emilia, take Rosalie and—"

"Jacob, look out!" Emilia cried.

Jacob whipped around to see a great shining blackness bearing down on him. He raised his wand a moment too late. Pain shot up Jacob's arm as one of the creature's sharp talons sliced his right hand, sending his wand flying across the yard. The cut burned, searing his flesh as the skin around the wound bubbled and frothed.

"*Perectus!*" The spell sent the creature stumbling back.

"There's something on their claws!" Jacob shouted the warning to Molly as she leaped away from one of the beasts. Jacob gagged as the monster's talons missed Molly's throat by mere inches.

"Death to the thief!" the creature cried.

Jacob dove for his wand. Black talons clicked together as the beast charged.

"*Primionis!*" Emilia screamed. Black claws tore at Emilia's shield inches from Jacob's face. The creature swiped again, roaring in frustration.

"*Regnitio!*" came Edna's voice.

The creature froze for a moment, its right arm raised above its head before the beast began to move in slow motion, its face twisting in a silent scream as though tortured by an unseen force. The creature shook for a moment before lowering its arm. The monster's white eyes darkened to a deep, stormy grey, and it turned on its fellows.

"*Tentutio impevis,*" Edna commanded, and the possessed creature ran at another, tearing at its armored chest, sending shreds of shining black flying through the air.

Jacob needed his wand. He needed to fight. But he couldn't look away from the beast's attack. Inside the terrible hard black skin lay ribs, lungs, and horribly red blood.

They were wizards. These awful things used to be wizards.

"No!" Emilia's voice jolted Jacob back to the fight. She was screaming, running toward Rosalie, but Larkin got there first.

Larkin raised a shaking hand and stammered, "*P-profindo.*"

The creature stumbled back. It looked at Larkin, letting out a laugh that sounded like a roar, before charging again with its talons high in the air.

"*Profindo!*" Larkin screamed, and this time, her spell resounded with a loud *crunch* as the creature's chest caved in.

The creature gasped, suffocating as it writhed on the ground.

A shout of victory made Jacob turn back to Aunt Iz. She was still fighting two of the beasts, but one had broken away, running toward Jacob, pointing a talon dripping with blood at Jacob's chest.

"*Recora,*" the monster hissed.

Jacob threw himself to the ground on his right, rolling over something hard in the grass. "My wand," Jacob gasped, lurching forward to grasp it, but the creature was closer. Jacob looked around. Everyone else was fighting their own battle. No one could help him.

The creature let out a low, rasping laugh that raised the hairs on Jacob's arms.

The creature's talons closed around Jacob's wand.

"*Evocio!*" Jacob shouted. The wand flew from the beast's grasp and into Jacob's outstretched hand. "*Scorepio!*"

The creature's black shell turned muddy brown, starting at its feet and moving to its chest. The beast let out a high-pitched, terrified scream as its armor began to *crackle*. Its feet crumbled, and the monster fell, hitting the ground as a pile of dust.

Panting, Jacob pushed himself to his feet, searching the lawn for the others. Emilia and Larkin had one of the creatures pinned to the ground. Molly leaned against a tree, her wand pointing at her own arm as she chanted a healing spell, but Edna and Iz were each fighting three at once.

As Jacob ran toward Iz, something big and black passed him on his right. The beast that Edna had been controlling leaped in front of her, like a puppet defending its master. One of the creatures clawed at the puppet's chest, sending a flood of deep red blood pouring onto the dirt. As though its strings had been cut, the creature under Edna's control fell lifelessly to the ground.

"*Fulguricio!*" Edna shouted, and bright blue lightning flew from her wand, piercing two of her attackers through the heart.

The last creature jumped backward and hissed.

"*Calvinis!*" the monster shouted. Flames licked the clapboard sides of the house, creeping up toward the roof.

"You sorry little bastard. *Immospatha!*" Edna ran forward, slashing her wand through the air.

The creature screamed as blood gushed from a fresh wound on its leg.

"Help!" A scream came from inside the house. "Help me!"

Dexter was still inside.

"Take Rosalie to the car!" Jacob shouted to Emilia. He saw the look of horror in her eyes for only a moment before he leaped into the flames.

The skin on his legs screamed as he raced through the fire. "Dexter!" He shouted, coughing through the smoke. "Dexter!"

"In here." The muffled cry came from the closet by the stairs where Dexter had been locked for days.

The door burst open before Jacob had reached it.

Dexter was crouched on the ground, straining uselessly against his chains.

"*Prolaxio.*" Jacob touched the tip of his wand to the thick chains.

"That won't work," Dexter coughed.

"Should I go then?" Jacob asked through gritted teeth.

"Try *torfacio*," Dexter said.

"*Torfacio.*" The manacles glowed white hot.

Dexter screamed. The stench of burning flesh joined the thick smoke as the metal crumpled and fell away.

"Let's go." Jacob grabbed Dexter by the front of his shirt and yanked him to his feet.

The smoke billowing through the house was black and unnaturally thick.

"Where's the door?" Jacob shouted.

Screams filtered through the smoke. He turned to move toward them and slammed face first into a wall.

"*Inluesco,*" Jacob said, but the pale blue glow from the ball of light in his palm barely reached his eyes.

"This way." A hand closed around Jacob's shoulder, steering him.

Jacob hacked and gagged. His lungs burned, heavy with smoke as he gasped for breath. His head spun. Dots of brilliant white light danced before his eyes. The spots were joined by bright orange flames and blue skies. Jacob tripped and fell to his knees, landing hard on the grass outside the back door. Dexter heaved on the ground next to him.

"How did you know the way out?" Jacob coughed, pointing his wand at Dexter's face. "There was no way to see in that smoke."

Dexter spit a clump of horrible blackness onto the ground.

"I was plotting an escape. I knew where the doors were."

"Why did you bring me?" Jacob stood up. His knees tried to buckle beneath him.

"I didn't do it for you," Dexter said, but the sneer Jacob had expected wasn't there.

The sounds from the fight on the other side of the lawn carried past the *roar* and *crackle* of the burning house.

"Where is she?" Dexter asked.

"With Rosalie." Jacob turned to run to the front of the house.

"Is she—"

"She's fine," Jacob said as Dexter stumbled after him. "I can feel it."

As they rounded the corner to the front of the house, Jacob thought he had entered another world.

Molly and Emilia stood in front of the big black car, each

fighting one of the creatures. A blur of curly black hair covered Rosalie's face as she pounded on the windows, screaming to get out of the car.

In the middle of the lawn, Aunt Iz, Larkin, and Edna had surrounded a knot of the black beasts.

"Get to the far side of the car," Jacob shouted to Dexter, running to join Emilia's fight, all thoughts of fatigue and smoke forgotten.

"No," Dexter said, "I can fight."

"With what?" Jacob didn't have time to hear the answer. *"Perectus!"* he cried, shooting a spell at the back of the creature Emilia was fighting. The beast turned, focusing its white eyes on Jacob.

The creature moved forward, and Jacob lifted his wand. Before he could think of a spell, a rock came flying from the right, striking the creature's head. Jacob and the beast turned together and saw Dexter, stooping to pick up more stones from the ground.

The beast turned and ran for Dexter, its arms trailing behind, talons reflecting the flames still licking the house.

"Dexter, move!" Jacob shouted, but Dexter stood his ground, throwing rock after rock at the creature. *"Talahm delasc!"* The red of Jacob's whip shot out of the tip of his wand and wound itself around one of the creature's arms. Jacob wrenched his hand to the side, forcing the creature to turn on the spot.

The creature bellowed. Something stuck out of its chest at a grotesque angle. Blood dripped from the wound and onto the grass. Dexter circled the beast and pulled a broken fence post from its chest. The thing swayed and, with a shuddering *gurgle*, collapsed to the ground.

The lawn had gone quiet. The *crackle* of the house burning was the only noise left. Jacob turned, looking for Emilia. She ran across the lawn toward him.

"Are you all right?" Jacob asked, taking Emilia's face in his hands and searching her for any sign of pain or injury.

"I'm fine," she breathed. "Where did you go?"

"Dexter was in the house," Jacob said, turning back to Aunt Iz's fight.

She and Larkin had cornered the last of the creatures. Edna was watching, her hands on her hips, her chest rising and falling with each labored breath. Molly was still leaning against a tree, her face pale. Rosalie was pounding on the car window. When she caught Jacob's eye, she pointed to the lock.

"I had to lock her in there," Emilia said. "She wouldn't stay put."

"*Immospatha!*" Larkin shouted. The beast she was fighting roared.

Jacob took a step toward Larkin.

"Watch out," Emilia said, grabbing Jacob's elbow as he tripped over an arm lying in the grass.

"What were those things?" Jacob asked, swallowing the bile in his throat.

Iz stood in front of Larkin now, her wand raised high.

"*Recora,*" Aunt Iz said calmly. Without a sound, the creature crumpled to the ground, still and lifeless.

"*Somnerri,*" Dexter said, walking up behind them, carrying the bloody, broken piece of fence in his hands. "I had heard rumors about the Pendragon wanting to use them. But I never thought he would do it."

"Because he's such an upstanding guy?" Jacob asked.

"No, because—" Dexter's face turned white, and he sprinted across the lawn toward Aunt Iz.

"Jacob!" Emilia shouted, pointing to the far side of the house. Two dozen more shining black creatures ran toward Aunt Iz and Larkin.

"*Gelethra!*" Jacob shouted, but his spell did nothing to slow the attack.

"Aunt Iz!" Emilia screamed, bolting toward Iz. Her back was still turned. She hadn't seen the new group coming to join the fight.

"*Primionis!*" Emilia shouted, but the creatures with their sharp, black talons would reach Iz first.

Dexter was ahead of them, but he had no magic.

"Ahh!" Dexter screamed as he launched himself at the monster at the head of the pack, sinking his piece of broken fence deep into the creature's neck.

Bellows issued from the pack as the monster fell to the ground, gurgling as blood spouted from his neck.

"Run," Edna said, her voice low as she turned toward the beasts. Her gaze was fixed on the barn. The front wall had been ripped off. Torn bodies littered the ground.

Molly ran forward and stood next to Edna, wand raised, ready to fight.

"Take the children and go, Isadora!" Molly shouted. "*Lancanus!*" Something like a silver harpoon erupted from the tip of her wand, striking the nearest beast in the heart.

"Molly, get out," Edna said. "I'll hold them off. *Radictus.*" Two giant trees collapsed in front of Edna, forming a barricade.

"I'll fight with you," Molly said.

"You'll go. I don't want house guests' blood on my hands."

"Thank you," Aunt Iz said, glancing at Edna before grabbing Molly's arm and dragging her away.

Emilia's hand wrapped around Jacob's, and they ran back to the car.

"We have to help her," Jacob said as Emilia wrenched the car door open.

"We have to go!" Emilia shoved Jacob into the car and scrambled in behind him.

"We can't just leave her. She can't fight all those things. She'll die." Jacob twisted to the window, trying to see Edna.

"She knows." Dexter leaped into the car and slammed the door shut behind him.

Larkin was behind the wheel. As she sped out through the shattered front gate, Jacob caught only a glimpse of the fight in the rearview mirror. But that moment was enough to see one of the creatures' black talons sink deep into Edna's chest.

10

PIKES

"*W*hat were those things?" Larkin wiped the blood from her forehead with her sleeve as she drove.

"*Somnerri*," Dexter said.

"What?" Emilia asked.

"They were Dragon guards before. It's a spell, an awful spell. I heard rumors in the tunnels about the Pendragon wanting to make *somnerri*. But I didn't think it was true." Dexter shook his head. "The spell isn't reversible. Those people will be stuck like that for the rest of their lives."

"Well, if we kill them all, they won't have to worry about it for too long, now will they?" Larkin said.

White eyes and taloned hands swam through Emilia's mind. "Who would choose that?"

"Who said Emile gave them a choice?" Rosalie said from the far back of the car where she was crammed in next to Molly.

"How could the Pendragon even know about the *somnerri* spell?" Aunt Iz said, her gaze scanning the road and her wand still poised, waiting for another attack. "That magic was sealed by the Council."

"There was a book," Dexter said.

"What book?" Iz asked.

"*The Taboo Magic*," Dexter said, his voice crackling and low. "My father had me read it. I gave it back to him. He must have given it to the Pendragon."

"You should have burned the book," Larkin said.

"You should have burned yourself with the book," Rosalie said. "What else was in that book? How many other people have been hurt by those spells?"

"Only two I think," Dexter said. "But he already knew how to do that spell."

The car fell into silence. Blood pounded in Emilia's ears, thundering with each beat of her still racing heart.

Her right leg felt hot. It was probably another cut or bruise. But at least they had all survived.

She pressed her knuckles into her eyes, trying to erase of the images of Edna's last moments. They had gone to her for help, and now she was dead. The people from the barn were dead. The rest of the Virginia Clan, gone.

A hand touched her shoulder, and she knew it was Jacob's before she opened her eyes.

His brow was furrowed beneath the layers of blood and ash. Soot stained his face and arms. Each breath he drew rattled in his chest. But still, he was worried about her. He had almost burned to death rescuing her ex-boyfriend who was now stashed in the backseat with Molly and Rosalie, both of whom looked like they might strangle Dexter at any moment merely for existing.

Well, Molly would kill him with magic. Rosalie would strangle. It just depended on who got there first. And still, Jacob was worried about her.

She tried to smile for him, but she couldn't make herself do it.

"Ouch," Emilia said. Her right leg was burning again. She rubbed the spot and felt something hot in her pocket. She pulled out the tiny mirror she always carried. The face of the mirror glowed bright blue. "*Sutrevalov.*"

"What's going on?" Iz asked, twisting to see Emilia from the front seat.

But a voice was already coming from the mirror.

"Finally," Claire said, "I've been trying for an hour to get a hold of someone who is supposed to love and care for the two kids ditched in the woods."

Dirt, and something else that looked horribly like blood, was streaked across Claire's face.

"Claire, are you and Connor all right?" Emilia asked, trying to see past Claire to the scene behind.

"Oh we're fine, no thanks to the Dragons that attacked us this morning," Claire said casually.

Molly leaned over the seat to speak into the mirror. "How did they find you? How did they get in? Is anyone hurt?"

"Oh, there was lots of blood and things exploding. Swords slashing, arrows flying. It was very exciting. Then the centaurs killed them all, except the one they're torturing for information. Judging by the screams, he's still alive," Claire said. "But that can wait. We're coming home."

"Claire, you can't come home. We're not at home," Jacob said over Emilia's shoulder.

"Doesn't matter!" Connor shouted from the background.

"The centaurs killed the Dragons and put their heads on pikes," Claire said. "We're coming home."

Emilia shuddered at the mere thought of centaurs decapitating people. "Claire, if the centaurs won, you're safer where you are."

"You're not listening to me." Claire spun the mirror to show a line of dripping, bloody heads on spikes twelve feet tall. Crows had gathered, nipping at the unseeing eyes of the dead.

"There are heads on pikes." Claire turned the mirror to show her face again. "We're coming home."

"Tell them to stay where they are," Aunt Iz said. "We'll be there in a few hours."

In Emilia's entire life, she had never seen Aunt Iz like this. It wasn't even that her hair was a mess, or that there was blood all over her shirt. There was an air of quiet fury about her as she gave Larkin directions to the Green Mountain Preserve. Larkin drove more than twice the speed limit. Iz had done all sorts of spells on the car to make it faster. Now she was shooing cars off the road.

Emilia gripped Jacob's hand as a semi pulled off the road an instant before Larkin would have rear-ended it.

"She did the same thing in Manhattan," Jacob whispered to Emilia, "when you were taken."

Night had only just begun to fall when the car turned to bounce down the dirt road that led to the meeting point between the Elis Tribe and the outside world.

Before the car had stopped, a dozen centaurs came out of the trees with swords and bows raised.

"Are we going to be killed by centaurs?" Rosalie asked from the backseat with only the faintest hint of interest in her voice.

"Wait for a moment." Aunt Iz climbed slowly from the car with the tip of her wand pointed toward the ground. "I am Isadora Gray, come to assist the Elis Tribe and recover the Gray wards the Elis Tribe has been caring for."

A jet-black centaur stepped out in front of the rest and bowed deeply. "Welcome, Isadora Gray." Raven turned to the car. "And welcome, Jacob Gray."

"Thank you, Raven," Jacob said, climbing out of the car and bowing. A young, white centaur came forward to stand at Raven's shoulder.

"Hello, Loblolly." Emilia took a step forward. "Was anyone hurt?"

"Some were wounded," Raven said, his voice growling and low. "The Dragon scum attacked our old and our children. They didn't want to fight the strong."

"Sabbe," Emilia said, a fist clenching around her heart. "Did they hurt Sabbe?"

The white centaur was ancient. If they had attacked the weak, Sabbe would have been first.

"They attacked Sabbe," Loblolly said, his normally bright voice cold with anger. "And we slaughtered them."

"She wasn't hurt?" Jacob asked.

"We would never allow our elder to be harmed," Raven said. "Three were wounded defending her. And then we killed the Dragons. Please come to the camp." Raven looked to Aunt Iz. "Or rather what is left of it. Proteus has requested your presence."

"We would be honored to meet with him." Aunt Iz bowed.

"Was Proteus hurt?" Molly asked as they wove through the trees.

"He was slashed through the flank," Loblolly answered from his place next to Emilia.

She wanted to lay her cheek against his soft white fur. He had carried Claire once when the centaurs were mourning their dead. There had been too much death today. Even though they had escaped, Edna had died. And the centaurs had won, but their home had been ruined. As they approached the camp, the stench of death hung heavy in the air.

Would Loblolly hate her for wanting to curl up against his warm side and hide? Just pretend to be a little girl again who wondered at the magic of centaurs?

"There were no deaths?" Dexter asked.

The entire party stopped to look at him.

"Not yet." Raven turned his back on Dexter. "But night has not yet fallen." He led them into the clearing.

The camp was in ruins. Scorched piles of still smoking ash lay where the centaurs' tents had been. Bright red, blue, green, and purple tents had stood side by side, filling the clearing with color and life. But now the ground was brown with winter, black with fire, and red with blood. A few very new tents stood in the center of the clearing, all twelve feet tall, high enough to allow even the tallest centaur to stand comfortably.

Beyond the tents, at the tree line on the far side of the clearing, stood four pikes, tall enough to be seen over the tents. On top of the pikes were four severed heads, still gently dripping blood as the crows fought for ownership of the flesh.

Emilia felt herself sway, and two hands moved toward her waist. Dexter had reached to help her.

"Don't touch me," Emilia said, moving to stand next to Jacob. She took his arm and wrapped it around her waist, just in case her head started to spin again.

"Your wounds should be tended." Raven pointed to a white tent at the far side of the clearing.

"We're fine." Emilia scanned the clearing for signs of Connor and Claire.

"As you wish. The prisoner is waiting for you, Ms. Gray." Raven gestured toward the red tent in the center of the clearing. "And I will take the human someplace quiet to wait." Raven nodded to Rosalie.

"Great, now I'm being called *the human*." She sneered at the word. "Can *the human* take a nap?"

"Of course." Raven pointed to the one wizard-sized, green tent barely visible behind the tall, white one.

"Are Claire and Connor in there?" Jacob asked as Larkin, Molly, and Iz strode toward the red tent.

"No," Connor answered, so close behind Emilia's ear she almost knocked Jacob over spinning to see him.

There was a cloud of muddy blond hair, and Claire's arms were around her neck.

"I'm glad us almost getting killed made you finally talk to us again," Claire said, switching to hanging from Jacob's neck.

"It wasn't like we didn't want to talk to you," Jacob said.

"Really? 'Cause the whole running away in the middle of the

night thing—" Claire began, but Connor stepped in front of her, cutting her off.

"What is he doing here?" Connor asked, aiming his wand at Dexter.

"He rescued Larkin," Jacob said.

"And we haven't tossed him in a pit yet why?" Claire asked.

"They were going to, but we were attacked," Dexter said.

"How convenient," Connor said.

"Well here's a down payment on your suffering." Claire took a running start and kicked Dexter in the shin.

Dexter hopped on one foot, breathing through his teeth.

"Well, that was satisfying." Claire smiled. "Now, is anyone who hasn't betrayed us all hungry?"

Emilia's stomach growled at the mention of food. She had forgotten they hadn't eaten since breakfast. "I'm starving."

"You"—Connor pointed to Dexter—"can wait there." He pointed to a soggy patch of dirt in front of the tent where the Dragon was being questioned.

A scream issued from the red tent, and Proteus's voice carried across the clearing. "Do not turn to Isadora for mercy. You attacked a centaur tribe. You will be dealt centaur justice. *Talahm delasc.*"

Emilia pictured the red whip forming in Proteus's hand.

A *crack* and a wail came from the tent.

"Maybe once Proteus is done with that guy he'll have a few questions for you, too," Claire said cheerfully, taking Emilia's hand and leading her away from the still screaming Dragon.

Emilia looked back to see Dexter's face pale as he sat outside the tent between the two centaur guards.

Connor and Claire led them past the dripping heads to the tent the four of them had shared before Jacob and Emilia had run away. The tent was collapsed, trampled, and muddy, but the fire in front of it was lit. Food was laid out on the tree stump beside it.

Emilia sat down next to the fire and relished the heat on her face. She closed her eyes and pictured herself in front of the fire in the living room at the Mansion House, warm and safe with Molly's homemade hot chocolate.

"The food here has changed a bit since you abandoned us."

"Claire," Connor warned.

"Sorry," Claire said, throwing her hands up. "Left us here without any warning to assume you were dead for a really stinkin' long time."

She looked to Connor who shrugged.

"We've moved up from weird leafy green plants and small woodland creatures to oddly shaped tubers and small woodland creatures." Claire handed Emilia a chunk of roasted squirrel.

"Bon appetite." Connor took a bite of a strange looking root.

Emilia contemplated how best to eat the squirrel for a moment while the others ate their food. Connor and Claire had dispensed with silverware altogether, picking up everything and eating with their hands. They really had been living with the centaurs for months.

"How did it happen?" Jacob asked after a minute.

"We heard the attack when we were in the field for morning lessons," Connor said. "There was screaming and shouting. Raven told us to wait in the training ring. We had been doing combat archery, but…"

"We didn't wait." Claire picked up for him. "We ran back to the camp. There weren't many centaurs here when they attacked. Everyone was gone for the day."

"Two of the Dragons were already on the ground when we got here," Connor said. "The other three were still fighting. As soon as they saw us, one of them ran at us. None of the centaurs noticed since they didn't know we were there."

"But I don't think the Dragon thought we were going to fight back," Claire continued. "It was bad for a minute, but then we had him on the ground. He's the one Proteus is talking to."

"Centaurs aren't really into letting enemies surrender or trying to keep the people they're fighting alive, so ours was the only non-dead Dragon when the spells stopped flying," Connor said as a blood curdling scream came from across the clearing. "He might not wish he were alive, but I don't think that's our problem."

"He was trying to kill us, so…" Claire shrugged.

Emilia opened her mouth to argue with Claire. But Claire was right. Emilia couldn't feel sorry for the people who were trying to kill her family. Not anymore. Too much had happened.

"There were only five Dragons?" Jacob picked up another portion of squirrel.

"Five was a lot. We almost lost a few centaurs," Connor said.

"But none of the Elis were killed?" Jacob pushed further.

"Nope." Claire shook her head. "The Elis are badass fighters."

"Exactly." Jacob pointed to the heads on the spikes. "None of those men had the Dragon tattoo."

"This doesn't feel right." Emilia chewed on her bottom lip.

"How?" Claire said.

"The Pendragon sent five men," Emilia said, looking around to be sure no one was listening, "and they weren't even fighters. The Dragon fighters all have a dragon tattoo that wraps from their cheek to their neck."

"Really?" Claire asked. "I didn't take the time to look when they were trying to kill us all, and once they'd been decapitated, it seemed rude to stare."

Emilia shook her head, ignoring Claire's sarcasm. "Why would he send five men who weren't even the best fighters against an entire centaur tribe?"

"Maybe he thought they could get in, grab us, and get out before the centaurs noticed," Connor said. "They did almost kill us, remember?"

"No, they didn't," Claire said, smacking Connor on the arm.

"You were great. It would have taken twice that many to kill either of us."

Connor nodded. "Fair enough."

"I think the point is," Jacob said, "it doesn't seem like the Pendragon."

"Two failed attacks on hidden Gray Clan members in one day? It doesn't seem like the Pendragon at all. It feels like I'm missing something." Emilia studied the scorch marks on the grass and the slashes in the trees. "Something deeper or darker. Something more." Emilia dragged her hands through her hair, giving a frustrated growl. "I know it's there—"

"But you just can't see it."

11

DAUGHTER OF ROSALIE

The screams from the red tent didn't stop for hours. Loblolly, the bright white centaur they had spent so much time with during the fall, came to make sure they had enough to eat. He was limping and looked exhausted. With a few words, a new tent appeared for them, covering the torn one.

"Sleep well, Grays," Loblolly said before disappearing into the night.

The inside of the tent was bare—no beds or blankets—like the ones the centaurs slept in.

"Better than nothing," Connor said, moving to curl up on the ground.

"Wait." Emilia pressed her palm to the tattered tent beneath them. "*Alavarus.*" The canvas warmed under her hand.

"That's a new one." Claire stretched out like a snow angel on the ground. "How come you never used that when you were here before?"

"It's for warming people, but if the earth is alive, it should work the same." Emilia curled up on the ground. It was as warm as if the summer sun had just been shining on it.

"How daring of you," Claire yawned.

"Not daring," Jacob said. "Necessary."

"I've decided I really hate being cold," Emilia said, pulling Jacob's arm to cover her shoulder. She felt his heartbeat slow and his worry ebb as they drifted to sleep.

∾

*E*milia could see the white light dancing even before she opened her eyes. It was a tiny sphere, no bigger than a firefly.

"What are you?" Emilia wanted to reach out and touch the light, but what if it was dangerous? Or just didn't want to be touched?

"Jacob." Emilia shook his shoulder, but he only grumbled and rolled over.

The light moved slowly toward the tent flap.

"What do you want?" Emilia asked.

But the light kept moving away.

Emilia knew the settlement had been attacked. Knew she shouldn't go wandering out of the tent alone at night. But something in the light felt familiar, old, and inexplicably good.

Emilia touched the sapphire pendant around her neck, making sure she had her talisman before standing up and stepping out into the night. The light waited for her outside, drifting gently in the breeze.

As soon as she was once again close enough to touch it, the light began to move through the center of the clearing, right past the centaurs standing guard. Emilia crept forward, wondering if they would be able to see the light as she did.

As the light floated past the centaurs, they nodded to it. One even muttered something to the sphere in the centaurs' language, which Emilia could not understand.

"You will tell us where the prisoner is held," Aunt Iz's voice carried out of the red tent, followed by a *buzz* and a scream. "You tried to murder children of the Gray Clan today. Do not wager your life on the misguided assumption that I will hesitate for a moment to kill you. Talk, and the pain stops. Keep silent, and you die. Painfully.

"Or perhaps death is too kind an end for a murdering Dragon scum. Perhaps I should let you stay with Proteus for the rest of your days. The centaurs' hospitality is legendary." A whimper came from inside the tent. "You will tell us where the prisoner Samuel Ireson is being held." Another crackling *buzz* and scream.

Emilia walked faster, wanting to get away from the voices. They needed to find Samuel, to save him, but this…it didn't feel like Aunt Iz at all.

The lights from the clearing vanished as she reached the trees, leaving only Emilia and the dancing white light in the woods. The screams faded in the distance until the only sound was Emilia's feet on the frozen ground.

"I know you're leading me somewhere," Emilia said, more to break the eerie silence than hoping for an answer. "Why wouldn't you let me bring Jacob with me?"

"Because it is not him I wish to see." An ancient, low, and musical voice came from the shadows.

"Sabbe," Emilia said, even before the bright white centaur stepped into the light.

The white orb made her coat glisten so brightly she shone blue. Sabbe's clouded eye turned to Emilia for a moment before she twisted her head, looking at Emilia with her good, blue eye.

"It is not he who has pulled his blood from another world," Sabbe said.

"You told me to go find my mother," Emilia said, unsure if her shivering was from the cold or from Sabbe's one-eyed glare. "You told me she would have the answer."

Sabbe nodded.

"But she doesn't have any answers," Emilia continued, her

words tumbling out. "She doesn't want to be here. She doesn't want to help us stop the Pendragon."

"Your father."

"Fine. *My father*," Emilia spat. "My mother doesn't even want to help me kill my father. Is that what you want me to say?"

"It is what you must understand."

"That she doesn't want to fight?" Emilia asked, her voice halfway to a shout. "Well, now she can't since her powers have been bound. What was the point? What was the point in any of this?"

"You need her."

"It doesn't matter what I need." Tears burned in the corners of Emilia's eyes. "Rosalie Wilde will never be any part of it."

"She can make you the fighter you need to be." Sabbe turned to leave the clearing.

"How can she make me a fighter when she can't even use a talisman? They're sending her away. I won't even be with her." Emilia chased Sabbe through the trees. Even though Sabbe was old and withered, her long centaur's legs carried her fast enough that Emilia had to run to keep pace. "She's just disappearing all over again."

"She gave birth to the girl you were. She can make you the warrior you must become."

"How?" Emilia reached out, seizing Sabbe's wrist. Her skin felt like wrinkled paper under Emilia's touch.

"It will be her choice." Sabbe stepped away from Emilia. "And she alone can make it."

Emilia didn't follow as Sabbe disappeared into the shadows.

Emilia's feet carried her back toward the camp without thought. Her mind was too busy trying to figure out what Sabbe had said. There had been a reason Emilia needed to bring Rosalie back, even though she couldn't see it right now. Rosalie was important. She could help Emilia stop the Pendragon.

But it would be Rosalie's choice. And if Rosalie got to choose, she would run to Cleveland and never look back.

Emilia reached the clearing. The guards nodded but didn't stop her as she passed the red tent. Voices still came from inside.

"I just don't see another way," Larkin said. "If they had kept that one alive—"

"He had given us all he could," Proteus cut in. "His mind had split open. There was nothing else to pull out."

"I think they might be right." Molly's voice sounded muffled, like her head was in her hands. "I don't like it. I hate it, but I think it might be our only chance."

There was a pause. Emilia held her breath, not wanting to miss a word.

"Larkin," Aunt Iz said. Her voice sounded weary and afraid. "Skry Stone. Tell him you're back. Tell him we need him. I'll contact Eames."

"Thank you," Dexter's voice came softly through the canvas.

Emilia dug her fingers into her palms, willing herself not to wake Jacob with her rage. They were meeting in the middle of the night, and Dexter was with them. Helping them.

Part of her wanted to run into the tent, screaming that Dexter had betrayed them. That his head belonged on a pike with the other Dragon scum.

But he had saved Larkin. He had brought her home.

She slipped into her tent, stepping over Claire's outstretched arm. Jacob's breath was steady as she curled up next to him, letting his warmth calm her.

Never trust a traitor, even one without magic.

DEAD

*J*acob stared at the roasted squirrel in his hand. He was hungry. He needed to eat. But the idea of eating another squirrel made him nauseous. The pale, grey light of dawn made the meat look more decaying than tasty.

"Stone will be here soon," Larkin said, her voice strong even though her face was still drawn.

Of course she would be happy to see her old MAGI partner. Jacob would be glad to see him, too.

Tall, muscular, bald, and terrifying, Stone had the sort of presence that made you feel sure no one would be foolish enough to attack you.

He had been in the MAGI headquarters when it was destroyed. He had been wounded, and Larkin had barely managed to save him. That was probably the last time they had seen each other.

Jacob shuddered at the thought, taking a bite of squirrel to hide his shaking hands. It was easy to forget that other people had lost the ones who had mattered most to them.

"Iz has decided you four will be safest with Professor Eames,"

Larkin continued. "Stone will be taking you to him while I take care of Rosalie."

"What do you mean *take care of?*" Emilia asked.

Jacob could feel how tense she was, like an open trap waited in his chest, ready to spring.

"Iz has arranged a safe place for her," Larkin said, taking Emilia's hands in hers. "She has a place to stay."

"Hidden inside and alone?" Tears glistened in Emilia's eyes.

"Better than outside and dead," Larkin said. "She'll be provided for."

"And what about you and Molly?" Emilia asked. "Where are you going?"

"To find a way to get Samuel back—"

"I'm sorry." Molly's trembling voice came from behind Jacob.

Jacob turned to find Molly, her face ashen and tear-streaked, wringing her hands.

"Aunt Molly." Connor ran over and took her arm. "What's wrong?"

"I'm afraid I have some bad news. We just spoke to—" Molly paused, working her lips as though trying to force words from her mouth. "Professor Eames is dead."

Jacob shook his head, trying to make the buzzing in his mind stop. Trying to reason through which of Molly's words he had misheard.

"What do you mean *dead?*" Claire asked.

"We spoke to him last night to tell him you would be coming," Molly said, reaching out for Claire who backed away, tripping over a root and tumbling into Emilia. "Iz just tried to contact him again, make sure everything was safe, but his guards—" Molly paused again. "They found the professor dead in his room."

"He was attacked?" Emilia said, standing Claire back up. "Why weren't there shield spells? Why didn't his guards protect him?"

"He wasn't attacked," Molly said. "He passed quietly in his sleep. They found him in his bed."

"No!" Claire shouted. "The Dragons got to him. They poisoned him or used some other kind of weird magic. Like those bug men." Claire turned to Emilia. "One of the bug men killed him. We have to go find them. Make them pay for hurting the professor."

"There is no one to make pay," Larkin said, pulling Claire into her arms. "There is nothing we can do. He's gone."

"You can't know that," Connor said. "We have to go. We have to investigate. He could have been kidnapped. Maybe the guards are lying. Maybe Professor Eames is fine."

"He's gone, Connor," Molly whispered. "I'm so sorry."

"We have to go to him." Jacob dragged his hands through his hair. "We have to go."

"He has already gone, Jacob," Proteus said, walking up behind Molly.

"But he deserves a funeral," Jacob said. "He deserves to have his family say goodbye."

"Isadora has decided it's too dangerous," Molly said.

"But we have to." Emilia took Jacob's hand.

"It's like the Shadowing you do for your dead," Jacob explained, willing Proteus to understand. "We have to say goodbye." Jacob choked on the last word. He hadn't spoken to the professor since they had been sent to the Elis. And now he never would again.

"Isadora has gone," Proteus said. "MAGI Stone—"

"She's gone?" Emilia shrieked, tears streaming down her face. "She couldn't even come tell us herself, and now she's just shunting us away again?"

"We're taking you someplace safe," Molly said.

"Rosalie is right," Emilia spat. "There is no such thing as safe." She turned and stalked away into the trees.

"Emilia!" Jacob shouted, running after her, ignoring Molly's calls that they needed to leave. "Emi, stop!"

"Why?" Emilia rounded on him. "So we can run away again?

So we can hide some other place while people get hurt. So we can watch our family crumble. Are we just supposed to forget someone in our family died today?"

"No, but Iz is gone. Molly and Larkin need to go with her. To help her find Samuel. But they can't until Rosalie is safe."

Emilia snarled at the word.

"Stone is coming for us," Jacob said. "And the longer we stand out here hating Iz for leaving, the more time it will take before they can get Samuel out."

"We could go with them." Emilia took Jacob's face in her hands. "We've been to Graylock. We can fight."

Jacob's pulse raced.

Back to Graylock. Back underground.

"No." Jacob took both of Emilia's hands in his. "We can't."

"Why not?"

"Because, Samuel made me promise I wouldn't go in after him if he tried to rescue you."

"But now he's trapped. Doesn't that change things?"

"If Iz, Molly, and Larkin go in and something goes wrong, we need to be out here," Jacob said, remembering hating Samuel for saying the same thing to him. "Because if something goes wrong, they'll need people on the outside trying to save them. That's us, Emi. We're the backup plan."

Emilia took a deep breath and pressed her forehead to Jacob's chest. "You want us to wait and see if they die, so we can go in and save them if they've only been captured to be tortured instead of killed?"

"I want to stop the Pendragon." Jacob held Emilia tight. "That's what all of us want."

"Promise we'll go after them?" Emilia looked up at Jacob with desperation in her eyes.

"Promise." Jacob slipped his hand into Emilia's, leading her back through the trees.

Claire sat next to the dampened fire, her dirt-streaked, pink duffle in her lap. Her face was blotchy and stony. She didn't look up as Jacob and Emilia came out of the trees.

"Stone is here," Molly said, looking up from the cleaning spell she had been doing on Connor's bag.

"Most of our stuff got trampled," Connor said, shrugging at Jacob's confused look.

"Let me see your bag," Molly said, moving toward Claire.

Claire still didn't look up.

"You have to go soon." Molly reached for the pink duffle.

"Don't touch it," Claire said, her voice dull. "Please don't pretend you care that my bag got ruined. Go to Isadora and tell her thanks for not even checking in on us before she left. Thanks for ditching us in the woods and not even coming to see us once, not even to tell us herself that the professor was dead. Give her my gratitude for handing us over to strangers again, to be sent some other mysterious place to be kept out of her way." Claire stood up and strode through the trees in the direction of the road. "Oh, and Merry Christmas!"

"I'm sorry, Aunt Molly," Connor said, giving her a hug around the middle. "I'll talk to her. She's just sad."

"I know. Be careful." Molly ruffled Connor's bright red hair before he ran off into the trees.

"So you're going to meet Aunt Iz now?" Emilia asked.

"She's taking me to her," Dexter said, appearing through the trees, walking next to Proteus.

"Why?" Jacob asked, resisting the urge to step in front of Emilia.

"We're going after Samuel," Molly said, raising her hands as Emilia began to protest. "Dexter knows the caves."

"Dexter," Emilia spat, "is also a filthy traitor."

Dexter flinched at her words.

"Who is willing to risk his life for the Gray Clan," Proteus said, his deep calming voice seeming to rile Emilia even more.

"Or lead them into a trap!" Emilia shouted.

"I would never do that." Dexter took a step forward.

"Don't give me that bullshit about what you would never do. I think we've learned you're best at stabbing people in the back." Emilia rounded on Molly. "You're going to take him with you to try and get Samuel, and you're leaving me and Jacob behind?"

"Emilia, it's time to go." Larkin strode out of the trees, head held high, every bit the MAGI agent she had been the first time Jacob saw her.

"Are you coming with us?" Jacob asked Larkin.

"I'll be riding with you until we've secured Rosalie in her new location," Larkin said, taking Emilia's hand when she tried to cut in. "I'll be joining Molly, Iz, and Dexter later today."

"While the rest of us hide." Emilia lifted her hand from Larkin's grasp.

"If there is anything I have learned from Isadora Gray, it is to trust," Proteus said. "She would never cause pain without need, even if the pain is only that of being left behind."

"Thank you, old friend," Molly whispered to Proteus.

"Let's go," Jacob said, taking Emilia's hand and leading her away.

He managed to get her to follow for a few steps before she turned and ran back to Molly. Emilia threw her arms around Molly's neck. "Bring him home. And take care of Larkin and Iz."

"I will." Molly tucked Emilia's hair behind her ear.

"And take care of yourself, too," Emilia whispered, tears in her eyes.

"And you take of the others," Molly said. "We will come for you as soon as we can."

"I love you, Molly," Emilia said, gripping her in a hug for one more second before rounding on Dexter. "If anything happens to any of them, if you betray them, if you let a hair on any of their heads get hurt, I will track you down, and so help me, I will make you wish the Pendragon had found you instead."

With that, Emilia turned and took Jacob's hand, dragging him through the trees toward the road.

Branches cracked as Larkin ran to catch up. "I had forgotten how much of Iz's temper you had in you."

"Don't trust him, Larkin," Emilia growled, not slowing her pace. "Use him if it'll help Samuel, but don't ever trust him."

Jacob wanted to say something about the fire in Edna's house. Dexter could have left him in there to burn, but he didn't. He had saved Jacob. But the anger he could feel pulsing from Emilia made him bite his tongue.

They emerged from the woods to find Raven and Stone standing next to the car. Stone's arms were crossed as he glared at the trees. It wasn't until he saw Larkin that he smiled. It was the first time Jacob had ever seen Stone have an emotion.

"Hey there, little bird," Stone said, pulling Larkin into a hug. She was so tiny against his large frame she almost disappeared. "Don't go scaring me like that again."

"I won't, Jeremy," Larkin said. "Thanks for taking care of this lot for me."

"Anytime," Stone said, stepping back and opening the passenger door for Larkin.

Claire and Connor spoke to Raven on the other side of the car.

"When it is time," Raven said, "come back to the Elis. You might be great warriors yet."

"If we survive long enough, I'll definitely take you up on that." Claire stood on her tiptoes and gave Raven a somewhat awkward hug around the middle before climbing into the car.

"Tell everyone goodbye for us," Connor said. "And thank you."

Connor took the seat in the far back, squeezing awkwardly in between Claire and Rosalie.

"Time to go," Stone said.

"Goodbye." Emilia turned toward Raven. "And sorry for all the trouble."

"Bye, Raven," Jacob said lamely.

He squeezed into the car. It smelled strangely new and sterile. The scent made Jacob's head spin after the fresh crisp air of the woods.

Emilia lifted Jacob's arm, draping it around her shoulder as the car trundled down the dirt road.

Jacob wanted to say something about the professor. About how he hadn't known him as well as the others had but that he had been a wonderful man and teacher. That it wasn't fair for him to be gone. But the car had fallen silent. Jacob squeezed his eyes shut so tight, spots danced in front of them.

They would talk about it later. If they managed to survive the day.

13

GOODBYE

*"W*e're here."

Emilia woke as Jacob whispered in her ear. She blinked at the noon sun pouring in through the car window. She hadn't meant to fall asleep. She had wanted to look at Rosalie. Even if Rosalie had refused to talk to Emilia, she wanted to study every black curl, and the face that looked so very much like her own. Even to hear her breathe or talk to Claire would be something. Anything to memorize just one more detail of her mother.

But instead, she had slept, and now they were going to leave Rosalie behind. Emilia looked out the window, hiding her face as she wiped her tears on her shirtsleeve. The town could have been Fairfield. Quiet, pretty, perfect. But Aunt Iz couldn't leave Rosalie there or anywhere else the Grays had ties to. So instead, they were going to dump Rosalie in the middle of some strange town and wish her luck.

"Good God, I'm being hidden at the North Pole," Rosalie said as they drove past a giant Christmas tree in the town center. There was a bright red sleigh in front of the tree, complete with a jolly Santa Claus. Children fidgeted in a line that wound around the glistening tree, waiting for Santa to pull a special present just for them from his big red sack.

Emilia wished for a moment that she could jump out of the car and go tell Santa her Christmas wish. But a man in a red suit couldn't make sure her family survived until New Year's Eve, let alone until they actually stopped the Pendragon. Santa couldn't bring the professor back.

"Let them out here," Rosalie said.

"We aren't there yet," Stone said, pulling over despite his words.

"That's the point." Rosalie squeezed forward, opened the car door and climbed out, beckoning Emilia to follow her.

Emilia took Jacob's hand and pulled him out of the car with her. She didn't want to say goodbye. And she couldn't do it alone.

"Why can't I come with you to the safe house?" Emilia asked.

"The fewer who know exactly where I am, the better," Rosalie said.

"So you don't trust me." Angry tears stung the corners of Emilia's eyes.

"I trust you," Rosalie said, taking Emilia's hands. "But I know Emile, and when he can't find me, he'll look for you. Even knowing the Grays left me somewhere might be too much. Besides, I've never been good with goodbyes."

"We'll come back for you. As soon as it's safe, we'll come get you."

"As soon as Emile is dead," Rosalie said. Her voice was cold and filled with an awful knowing. The only real way out for her was for the Pendragon to die.

"I'll come back for you." Emilia stepped forward, pulling Rosalie into a hug before she could argue.

Rosalie nodded but didn't say anything before climbing back into the car. Larkin, Connor, and Claire stood on the sidewalk.

The five of them watched the car pull away without speaking. Emilia didn't bother to wave. Rosalie wasn't looking anyway.

"It's safer this way," Larkin said as the car turned out of sight.

"It's not about safe," Emilia murmured. Her throat felt tight. She wasn't sure she could speak anymore.

"Let's go see Santa," Claire said with a false brightness in her voice.

"Now is not the time," Larkin said.

"Now is the perfect time. It's Christmas! It doesn't get much better than that," Claire said, grabbing Connor's and Larkin's hands and dragging them away. "All those with their souls bound to one another aren't invited."

"I am supposed to be guarding you all," Larkin said, planting her feet and letting Claire tug uselessly on her arm.

"In case you haven't noticed, we've had a really crappy morning with a sincere lack of jingle bells. So unless you are trying to make it worse, I think we should go see Santa," Claire spoke through gritted teeth, tipping her chin up and raising a blond eyebrow significantly at Larkin. "Do you really think the Pendragon would just drive quietly up and try and snatch any of us?"

"He did it before," Connor said.

"Exactly," Claire growled. "He'll try something new with lots of bangs and noise. Let's give Emilia a minute without us all staring at her."

"Don't leave the square," Larkin called back to Jacob and Emilia as Claire and Connor dragged her away.

"Emi," Jacob said.

Emilia buried her face on his chest.

"I'm sorry," Jacob whispered.

"For what?" Emilia asked, keeping her face pressed to the warmth of his coat.

"For all of it." Jacob kissed her lightly on the top of her head.

Emilia could feel the pain trapped inside him. Hopeless grief and guilt that echoed her own. She held Jacob tighter.

"You have nothing to be sorry for. No one does. Except the

Pendragon. I just"—Emilia took a breath, willing herself not to cry—"thought it would be better. I thought—"

"You'd get your mom back," Jacob finished for her.

"We keep losing people. Samuel, the professor—" Emilia's voice caught in her throat. "And we can't even go to him. And now Rosalie." Emilia turned away from Jacob toward the Christmas lights and laughing families. "How does this end?"

These happy people were all spending Christmas together, but not the Grays.

Emilia felt like someone had punched a hole straight through her stomach. She was hollow. The world, the fighting, had taken too much of her. And now she was empty.

Children were lining up by the tree, getting ready to sing carols. Emilia's head began to pound at the thought.

"There is no way out," Emilia said. "I keep trying to think through it, to find a way for us to make it to the other side, but all I can see is more fighting, more people dying, and…" A sob swallowed her words. She wrapped her arms over her head like a child hiding from a monster.

Jacob held her close, whispering in her ear, "There is a way out. And there's fighting, and we might not all make it. But we have to try, Emi."

"What's the point? So we can all suffer more?"

"The Pendragon is just a wizard. He's powerful and evil. And it might take all of us to do it. But we can beat him, Emilia. We *have* to beat him."

The hole in Emilia's stomach filled with anger and fear. "Because no one else will."

She wiped her face with the palms of her hands. Jacob was right. The Grays were the only ones left fighting. The Elis would help them, but the Grays would have to lead.

"We should get the others," Emilia said, taking Jacob's hand and feeling warmth flood through her.

The black SUV pulled back up to the curb. Stone climbed out and circled around to Emilia.

"Is it done?" Emilia asked.

"She's hidden," Stone said.

"Good." Emilia nodded, gripping Jacob's hand and willing herself not to run down the road where Stone had taken Rosalie, screaming for her to come back.

"Em," Larkin said, nodding for Stone to go to Connor and Claire, who were waiting in line by the Christmas tree. "I have to go." She reached out to Emilia. "I have to meet Iz."

"Don't you need the car?" Jacob asked.

"I've made arrangements." Larkin shrugged.

"Aren't you going to say goodbye? What about Claire and Connor?" Emilia asked, trying to push away the panic squeezing her lungs. Larkin had just been saved. Now she was leaving them, too.

"They know I'm going, and I'll be back in a few days. Take care of her, Jacob." Larkin tucked Emilia's hair behind her ear. "She's important."

"I know." Jacob nodded.

Larkin smiled, waved over Emilia's shoulder at the Christmas tree, and turned to walk away.

Emilia didn't turn to see Connor, Claire, and Stone waving back. She wanted to watch Larkin.

Larkin crossed the street and walked up the steps into a white clapboard church, closing the door behind her.

"How did it go with Santa?" Jacob asked as Claire ran over to them empty handed.

"Not well. He didn't appreciate my sarcasm," Claire said, waving to the closed door of the church.

"Where are we going?" Claire asked for the twelfth time that hour.

"We're almost there," Stone said. His voice was calm, but Jacob could see his eyes flicking toward the rearview mirror, checking for cars driving behind them every few seconds.

But the night was dark, and no headlights chased them. Of course, the Pendragon didn't need headlights or a car. Not if he wanted to attack. It wasn't as though he minded the humans noticing magic.

"Does it bother you that every time Aunt Iz needs to drop us off some new *safe* place, she makes you do it?" Claire asked.

"We are very lucky to have Stone protecting us," Emilia said.

"There is no one else to bring you. Not who can be trusted." Stone turned onto a road running alongside a lake. In the darkness, it was impossible to see to the other side. It might have been as big as an ocean. "When we get out of the car, I want you all to be quiet."

"Does that mean we're getting out of the car?" Claire leaned as far toward the front seat as her seatbelt would allow.

"Yes. Do not use magic unless we're attacked."

Jacob felt Emilia tense beside him. "Do you think we were followed?"

"Each of you will take your bag and walk directly to the boat. Understood?" Stone stopped the car and turned around in his seat, staring at them all.

"Yes, sir," Claire whispered loudly, giving an exaggerated salute and knocking the heels of her sneakers together.

Connor elbowed her in the ribs.

"Get your bags, and get to the boat. Let's go." Stone opened his door and stepped out into the night.

Jacob's breath rose in cold clouds before him. He was the first to the trunk and started grabbing everyone's bags and passing them out. Pink duffle for Claire, rucksack for Connor, a black camping pack for Emilia, and an overstuffed school backpack for him. Stone stood at the top of a path that led to the lake, pointing for them to follow the thin trail to the dark shore.

They walked down to the boat, Jacob cringing with every *crackle* and *crunch* of the rocky path that led them to the sand. The lake only seemed to make the night colder. The frozen sand sent a chill through the soles of his sneakers.

A rowboat bobbed at the end of a long wooden dock.

Stone stopped in the middle of the beach, his gaze sweeping the horizon.

Claire tapped him on the arm and pointed to the rowboat, her blond eyebrows climbing up her forehead. Stone nodded, and Claire led the way to the dock.

Claire was the first to climb into the boat. Connor helped her down while Jacob held the tie line taut, wondering how the little boat could carry them all. Connor climbed down next. Jacob reached out to help Emilia, but she shook her head, pointing for Jacob to go first. She stood on the dock, her hand held out in front of her as though waiting for an attack.

Jacob climbed down ungracefully, holding his breath when the boat began to sway. Emilia was a step behind him. She settled into the seat next to Jacob as Stone climbed into the boat and uncoiled the rope.

Stars danced on the surface of the lake. The boat moved without oars or engine, their movement leaving only the smallest trace of a wake.

Connor took off his hat and handed it silently to Claire, who hit him in the face with it before tugging it onto her head.

Emilia twisted in every direction, her gaze scanning the darkness. She shivered, and Jacob moved closer, wrapping an arm around her waist. Emilia sank into his side but didn't stop searching the night.

Nearly twenty minutes passed before the dark in the middle of the lake became even darker. Standing out against the stars was a line of trees surrounding a small island.

Stone began to murmur a chant.

Jacob tried to recognize the words. It was something about water and ice, protection and fire, but he had never heard the spell before.

The boat slowed, as though the air around it was being compressed. Jacob rounded his shoulders as the spell squeezed him so tightly he could barely breathe. He wanted to spread his arms and stop the magic, but it was no use. The spell that surrounded him was too big.

What if the spell never ended? What if they were crushed to death? But Emilia wasn't panicking. Jacob could feel her. Alert, tense, but not afraid. The spell pulled at Jacob's skin and hair, working its way from his nose to his back.

With a lurch, the boat leaped forward.

"Welcome to Elder's Keep," Stone said.

From the inside of the barrier, Jacob could see lights flickering in the windows of a small log cabin.

The boat scraped the beach with a *crunch* and ground to a halt.

Jacob stood in the wobbly boat and climbed over the side.

Freezing water seeped into his sneakers as the waves lapped at his feet.

"Come on," Jacob said, reaching to help Emilia out of the boat.

"Thanks," she murmured, not taking her eyes off the cabin.

Jacob reached back to help Claire, but Connor had already scrambled over the side and was steadying the boat as she climbed out.

"Let's get inside," Stone said, his gaze sweeping through the shadows of the trees.

"Can we be seen through the shield?" Emilia asked, taking Jacob's hand before walking to the cabin.

"No," Stone said. "But that doesn't mean anything."

The cabin was built of logs so wide Jacob couldn't have wrapped his arms around them. Even in the dark, he could tell the wood was weathered and grey. Vines grew up the corners of the cabin, clinging to the edges of the windowsills. Storm shutters with peeling paint flanked every window.

Claire was the first to reach the cabin. She pulled the door open. "Is this really Elder's Keep?"

"Do you have a problem with it?" Stone walked into the living room.

"Well, I was expecting a computer and a few giant monitors. Or swords and armor. Really, either way would have been much better than abandoned cabin chic." Claire picked up one of the threadbare paisley pillows that decorated the couch.

"Sorry, but this is what you get," Stone said, ushering Jacob in before shutting the door.

"Is there a bathroom?" Claire asked as Stone slid a shining golden bolt into place across the door.

"Yes."

"Well, then I guess it's a step up from the Green Mountain Preserve." Claire ducked as Connor tossed a pillow at her head.

"Enough," Stone said. "Stay here while I check the cabin."

"What is there to check?" Claire whispered as Stone left the room.

Five doors led out of the living room, and Stone went through each of them in turn, starting with the one next to the tiny kitchen in the corner.

"No wonder Molly didn't want to bring us here," Connor said as Stone slipped into the third room. "Can you imagine her in a place that calls that corner a kitchen?"

"The cabin is clear," Stone said after exiting the last room.

"Clear from what?" Jacob asked. "I thought this was a safe house. Can the Dragons get in here?"

"No. But that doesn't mean they won't do it anyway," Stone said. "None of you are to leave this island under any circumstances. There is enough food here to last months. You have everything you need. You will stay here until Ms. Gray comes to get you or sends one of us to do it for her. Do you understand?"

It took Jacob a moment to murmur, "Yes," with the others. He had never heard Stone speak that much at once.

"If there were to be an emergency, a life threatening attack, there is another way out of the cabin without crossing the water," Stone continued.

Jacob pictured each of them climbing into the stove and being magically transported.

Stone walked to the corner of the living room and stomped his foot on the floor a few times. Layers of dust and dirt sifted through the cracks in the planks as a section of the floor barely three feet wide separated slightly from the rest, outlining a trapdoor. "This door leads to a tunnel and to the main land. Don't even think about going through it unless Elder's Keep is compromised."

"But you said no one can come in," Connor said, skeptically eyeing the hatch, but Stone ignored him.

"The tunnel is one way." Stone stomped hard on the hatch, which disappeared back into the floor. "If you go through it, there is no way for you to get back to the island. Not without permission from the head of the Gray Clan. Now, I suggest you all get settled in. You'll hear from Ms. Gray as soon as it's safe."

"Hear from her?" Emilia said, walking behind Stone as he headed to the cabin door. "Where are you going?"

"To the Graylock Preserve. If they're going in there, I want to be with them," Stone said.

Of course Stone would want to be with Larkin if she was going back into the tunnels. The Dragons had captured and tortured her.

"Good luck," Jacob said as Stone shut the door.

"Dibs on the best room!" Claire shouted, dropping her bag and racing to the far side of the cabin where four doors sat along the far wall.

"Which one is the best room?" Connor asked, sitting on the couch, which puffed with dust.

"Haven't decided yet!"

DIED LIVING

*I*t took Claire twenty minutes to decide which room she wanted. Connor chose the one closest to the kitchen.

"You can pick first," Jacob said as Emilia got up from the floor, leaving the warmth of the woodstove behind.

"I don't care." Emilia ran her fingers through her hair. The wind from the boat had tangled it. She should brush her hair or eat, probably shower, too. But all she wanted was sleep.

She walked to the room next to Claire's. The only furniture was a tiny dresser with chipped paint, a chair by the vine-covered window, and a bed with a frame made of roughly hewn wood. The tiny branches had been sawed off, and the shellac that covered the bark reflected the light of the cracked ceramic lamp.

"How's the room?" Jacob peeked in.

"Not what I expected from Aunt Iz." Emilia sank down onto the bed.

"She probably didn't think many people would come here." Jacob sat next to her. "And she probably didn't want a bunch of workers coming in and out."

"She could have done it by magic." Emilia flopped back. At least the mattress was soft. "How long have we been back?"

"Five days." Jacob laced his fingers through hers.

"It seems like forever."

"We should do something for Connor and Claire for Christmas," Jacob said.

"They're missing it because of me." Emilia twisted to hide her face in the pillow.

They had to flee the Mansion House because she brought Rosalie there. The Pendragon was after them because he was Emilia's father. She had made them leave their home, and now they wouldn't even get Christmas.

Jacob lay down on the bed behind her and rolled Emilia over so her head rested on his shoulder. "You can't think like that. The Pendragon is responsible, not you. He's the one that hurts people, not you. You can't be blamed for what a madman does."

Emilia snuggled her head into the spot on Jacob's collarbone where she seemed to fit perfectly. She took Jacob's left hand in hers. The golden glow that came from the streaks on their palms seemed so warm, so perfect. Her eyes drifted shut.

"Sleep, Emi," Jacob murmured. "We're all safe here."

~

The sun peering through the vines woke Emilia the next morning. Jacob lay next to her, sleeping soundly with his mouth open. Emilia laughed silently and snuggled back onto his shoulder, trying to remember the last time she had slept through a whole night.

"Don't put that in there," Connor's voice came from the living room.

"It won't hurt anything," Claire said.

There was a *bang* and a *crash*.

Jacob shot up in bed. "What's wrong?" He grabbed his wand and was on his feet in an instant.

The living room went silent.

"Connor and Claire are fighting," Emilia whispered, pressing on Jacob's wrist to lower his wand.

"Should I climb out the window?" Jacob asked.

She hadn't thought about Connor and Claire being here.

"No. They aren't stupid." Emilia wished she had brought her pack into the room. Then she would at least have a hairbrush.

"Shall we?" Jacob gestured toward the door.

Emilia nodded.

As soon as they stepped into the living room, Connor and Claire froze, staring right at them.

Connor blushed bright red before spinning toward the stove.

"How did you sleep?" Claire asked.

Connor kicked back like a donkey and caught her in the shin.

"What?" Claire asked through gritted teeth. "I was being polite."

"What are you making?" Jacob asked, walking over to look into the pot on the stove, studiously ignoring Claire.

"It *was* oatmeal, but Claire kept tossing things—"

"Improvements," Claire interrupted.

"Breakfast is now oatmeal with croutons and chocolate chips. Bon appetite." Connor took the pan off the stove and set it onto the wobbling folding table that served as their dining room.

Glaring at them all, Claire began slopping portions into four bowls.

"Looks"—Jacob paused as a chocolate covered crouton fell from his spoon—"interesting."

"I just couldn't take normal oatmeal, okay?" Claire said, tears creeping into her voice as she shoved a spitefully big spoonful into her mouth.

Emilia had forgotten the professor always ate oatmeal for

breakfast. Molly made a bowl for him every morning and had it waiting at his seat. Or at least she used to.

"We all miss him, Claire," Jacob said.

"Do we though?" Claire asked.

"Claire—" Emilia started.

"I'm serious," Claire said. "We hadn't seen or heard from him in months. Everyone else from the Mansion House who isn't in this room is trying to free Samuel. We could all be dead tomorrow. The professor died in his sleep. Maybe it's better that way. If *we* die, it'll probably be really painful and bloody." Tears slid down Claire's cheeks.

Emilia moved to stand, but before she could, Connor already had his arms wrapped around Claire.

"He was old," Connor said so softly Emilia wondered if she was supposed to hear. "Maybe it was less painful for him to go quietly. And maybe we didn't see him for a while. But Professor Eames loved all of us. If he could have stayed to fight with us, you know he would have. He didn't die on purpose. He was just old."

"Now, even if we win," Claire said, her voice thick with tears, "we can never go back to how it was. Even if we stop the Dragons, fix the Council, and save Samuel, we can never have our home back because it won't be the same without him."

Emilia reached for Jacob's hand under the table. He squeezed her hand, and she took a deep breath, trying to keep herself from crying. Tears wouldn't do her any good.

"And we can't even have a funeral because we're hiding in a cabin, and Christmas was the professor's favorite." Claire sobbed into Connor's shoulder.

"We all miss him, Claire," Jacob said again. "We all want to be back home."

Emilia's heart caught in her chest. He was talking about the Mansion House. It was his home as much as any of theirs now. And he had only lived there for a few short months.

"But they'll make sure he has a proper funeral. And when all this is over, we can go pay our respects. And at least the four of us are together," Jacob said.

"He should have gone down fighting," Claire coughed. "He should have died doing something important."

"He died living, Claire," Emilia said. "That's as important as it gets."

⟿

*C*onnor and Claire spent the day working their way through every board game they could find on the faded wooden shelf. Emilia had pulled an old Agatha Christie novel down and was on the couch reading with Jacob's arm around her while he leafed through a tattered copy of *An Account of Magic* by Nathan Smith.

"How long do you think it will take?" Jacob whispered when Claire started to sing a loud victory song after trouncing Connor in backgammon for the third time.

"What do you mean?" Emilia asked, turning to Jacob.

His face was drawn and his brow furrowed.

"How long do you think it will take them to get Samuel out of Graylock?"

"Longer than today," Emilia said, taking Jacob's chin and guiding his face to look away from the windows. "Dexter has to make them a map of the caves. Then they have to make a plan once Stone reaches them. Then they have to…"

"Break into the base of the people who keep trying to kill us all," Jacob finished.

Emilia laced her fingers through Jacob's. She wanted to be there. She wanted to fight to find Samuel. But the thought of going back to those caves, back into the stone and the dark…

"I won't let him take you back there." Jacob kissed her forehead, tightening his arms around her. "I will never let him take you away from me."

Emilia leaned in, but before she could kiss him, Claire coughed loudly.

"Excuse me, but could you please get a room? Oh wait, you already moved in together. Wha!" Claire squealed as the pillow Emilia threw hit her squarely in the face.

PEACE WITHIN

*N*one of them even left the cabin to go out onto the island for two days. None of them had wanted to. Somehow, the tiny, human-looking cabin felt safe, as though the evil magic that hunted them couldn't exist within its walls.

The room had sunken into an afternoon stupor, all of them poking lazily at their lunches.

"I'm going outside." Jacob set his fork down on his plate of spaghetti.

Emilia had taken over the cooking after Claire had tried to make bacon and almost burned the cabin down with a grease fire.

"Why?" Emilia asked, looking at him sideways.

"Because I can see a few little pine trees out the window, and I'm going to cut one down. We missed the 25th by a few days, but we need something normal. We're having Christmas." He knew it was silly, knew it wouldn't fix anything. But it was something. And Stone had only said not to leave the shield, though even opening the front door seemed dangerous.

Emilia stared at him, frozen, book still in hand.

Jacob almost missed seeing Emilia smile as Claire launched

herself across the table, knocking the rest of the spaghetti into Connor's lap as she clung to Jacob's neck.

"Thank you, thank you, thank you!" Claire squealed.

"I was going to eat more of that," Connor said. *"Ablutere."* The pasta disappeared from his lap.

"I'll go with you," Emilia said.

"Us too," Connor said.

But Jacob was already shaking his head. "We need lookouts."

"And we'll be able to see better from outside." Claire stood up.

Five minutes later, they all stood at the front door bundled up in their coats, each of them staring at the doorknob. Seconds ticked past.

Jacob kept flexing his fingers, willing himself to reach for the knob.

"Oh, this is getting ridiculous." Claire pushed the little golden lock aside, turned the knob, and wrenched the door open.

Crisp, cold air swooped into the cabin. Jacob took a deep breath, feeling the chill whirl into his lungs. He hadn't realized how much he had missed the fresh air. He took a step out of the cabin, relishing the *crackle* of the frozen ground and the bright winter sun glistening on the lake.

"It's beautiful," Emilia said, taking Jacob's left arm. His right held his wand, ready for attack.

"We should get the tree and get back inside," Connor said, moving to the edge of the water. The sand crunched under his feet as he broke through the thin layer of frost with every step.

Claire followed, her eyes trained on the distant beach far across the water.

"Come on." Jacob walked quickly around to the left side of the cabin.

A pine tree stood close to the wall. It was barely five feet tall, and the vibrant green of its branches stood out sharply against the brown of the sandy dirt.

"I feel bad cutting it down." Jacob pointed his wand at the base of the trunk.

"We don't have to," Emilia said. *"Elevare."* She cupped her hands, as though scooping water from a stream. As she raised them, the earth around the tree shuddered. Slowly, the tree rose, its roots bringing a basin of soil with them.

"So what do we put the roots in?" Jacob asked, trying to hide his surprise. How many times had he seen Emilia do magic? How many times had *he* done magic? And still, it amazed him.

"We can deal with that inside."

Emilia guided the tree back toward the door, her hands still held out in front of her as though she were cupping the tree's roots.

The door swung open as she reached it, and gently she tipped her hands, lowering the top of the tree to drift under the door-frame and into the cabin.

"You next, Claire," Connor said, his gaze still sweeping back and forth over the glistening water.

"You next." Claire rolled her eyes. "I am perfectly capable of standing guard while you walk through a door."

Something flew toward them in the distance. A little black dot high in the sky. Jacob tensed, and Claire gasped. The dot flew lower, closer to the surface of the water. Jacob raised his wand ready to fight, squinting to see what the dot could be.

It looked too small to be a broom, almost the size of a bird. What if the Pendragon had used another horrible spell and given some of the Dragons wings? The wings spread, and a seagull showed his white belly. The lost seabird grazed his wings over the shield that protected them and took off, back up high into the sky.

"Both of you just get inside," Jacob said.

Connor and Claire scrambled through the door, and Jacob backed in after them, not breathing until the little golden bolt had been slid firmly into place.

"What was it?" Emilia asked, standing in the corner next to the still hovering tree.

"An evil killer bird." Claire flopped down onto the couch.

Jacob made himself laugh. "So, what do we do with the tree?"

"Claire, give me the blanket," Emilia said, nodding to the blanket Claire was lying on.

"But I like this one," Claire moaned.

Emilia raised her eyebrow.

"Fine." Claire stood and ran to her room.

Thuds like books falling to the ground and grunts of "stupid shelves for giants" came from Claire's room before she ran back out to Emilia, holding an old, greying blanket.

Jacob covered his nose, trying to block the smell of mothballs and mold.

"Thanks," Emilia said, eyeing the blanket. "Jacob, can you hold the tree?"

"Umm." Jacob rummaged through all the spells in his mind to try and find something that would let him make a tree hover without losing the dirt from its roots.

"I've got it." Connor stood opposite Emilia and placed one hand on top of the other as though he were holding someone's foot to help them climb a tree.

"Thanks." Emilia turned to the blanket. *"Bellusavis."* The stench of mothballs disappeared, and the room was flooded with the scent of lilacs. *"Seplicio."*

The greying blanket folded up its edges, making a perfect basin.

Slowly, Connor lowered his hands until the roots of the tree were perfectly nestled in the basin.

When the tree was down as far as it could go, Emilia muttered, *"Glacio,"* and with a *crack* the blanket became as hard as metal.

"Bravo!" Claire cheered, running to the sink and grabbing a

cup of water. "Deck the halls with boughs of holly. Fa-la-la-la-la-la-la-la-la! Give the tree a cup of water!"

"Claire," Connor groaned.

"You're supposed to give the tree water when you bring it inside," Claire said.

"But you didn't need to use the tap." Connor rolled his eyes.

"That's how my parents always do it." Claire furrowed her brow.

"They're human," Connor laughed. "You're a witch. You could have just used *parunda.*"

"Fine. *Parunda,*" Claire said, laughing as a jet of water leaped from her hand to douse Connor's face.

Connor coughed and spluttered, diving away from Claire's spell.

"Or, we could decorate the Christmas tree." Jacob stepped between them, getting splashed with the spell before Claire tucked her hands sheepishly behind her back with a grin.

"Who wants to make the tree topper?" Emilia clapped her hands together.

An hour later the tree glimmered with the glow of spoons and sparkles.

Connor had taken all the spoons from the kitchen drawer and bent them into circles to decorate the branches of the tree. Claire had insisted on conjuring glitter that drifted down from the ceiling, leaving the tree to sparkle.

Jacob watched in wonder at the unending stream of glitter, but the branches never became covered enough to mask the brilliant green of the tree.

"I know. I'm that good." Claire winked when she caught Jacob poking at the glitter on the tree.

Emilia had found old newspapers in the bottom of one of the cupboards and made paper chains that hung from the tree and ceiling. Jacob had sat at the coffee table, trying to make an angel out of tinfoil.

He remembered the Christmas trees at the Gray house when they had lived in Fairfield. They were tall and dripping with ornaments and candies. He had never had a tree in his own home. At least not since his mother had died.

Claire was cutting out paper stars and sticking them to the branches with magic.

"Don't hurt the tree," Emilia said, looking over Claire's shoulder.

"I'm being careful," Claire said before starting on another Christmas carol.

If Jacob thought hard, he could almost remember a Christmas tree in his house. His mother had decorated it with an angel on the top. Where was that angel now?

"It looks more like a fairy than an angel," Claire said, picking up Jacob's creation.

"How would you know?" Connor examined the molded foil.

"It's in the wing shape." Claire held the angel up by the tips of its wings. "Fairies have pointed wings."

"How would you know?" Connor asked again.

"I happen to be an expert on fairies," Claire said with an airy voice.

"I think it's wonderful," Emilia said, taking the angel in one hand and Jacob's hand in the other.

Jacob's heart hummed. She was happy. He could feel it. In this moment, decorating their tiny tree, Emilia was happy.

"You do it," Emilia said, passing the angel to Jacob.

Carefully, Jacob settled the angel into the top branches of the tree.

"*Perluxeo*," Emilia said, and the lights went out.

"*Lumenustris*," Connor said, and the paper stars on the tree began to shine, bathing them all in quiet brilliance.

17

CHRISTMAS WISH

*E*milia lay in bed, blinking to adjust her eyes to the darkness. Jacob's breathing was deep and even. She rolled over as slowly as she could, lifting his hand gently away from her shoulder.

She bit her lips to stifle her gasp as her feet touched the freezing floor.

Jacob had left his socks by the door. Emilia slipped them on before carefully opening the door to the living room.

The tree sparkled with tiny starlights that made even the dullest of the spoons glint. The tree was beautiful, even if there weren't fancy decorations. They had made it themselves. And it was something normal.

"*Inluesco.*" A ball of shining blue light appeared in her palm.

If she could make cookies or muffins or something, they would have a treat for Christmas morning. Then presents. She would have to find a way to make everyone presents.

Emilia had barely reached for the canister of flour when a doorknob rattled behind her. Emilia spun to look at the front door. Had they found Samuel in time for Christmas?

But it was Claire's door that began to open as Emilia dove to hide behind the couch. The cookies and presents were supposed to be a surprise. Why did Claire have to be up now?

Emilia peered around the edge of the couch and watched as Claire crept to Connor's door and knocked softly. Claire waited a moment. Emilia pressed herself to the floor as Claire glanced in her direction.

The knocking was louder this time and followed by Connor's door creaking open.

"What do you want?" Connor whispered in a hoarse voice.

"I want you to come here," Claire said.

Emilia chanced another glance around the side of the couch. Claire had taken Connor's hand and was dragging him in front of the Christmas tree.

"*Viscum alescere,*" Claire said. The branches at the top of the tree began to shudder, but Claire had turned her attention back to Connor. "We've been too afraid to go outside."

"We have to be careful."

"Because there are people trying to murder us. That's not the point. The point is they could get to us. They found us with Proteus. They could find us here."

"We'll fight—"

"I know we will," Claire said. "But if they kill us, there are a few things I need to do first."

"Like what?" Connor said, his ginger eyebrows rising.

"First off," Claire said in a business-like whisper, "I have never been kissed. And I refuse to die like that."

Claire pointed to the branches on the tree that had been shuddering just a moment before.

A sprig of mistletoe had grown right from the Christmas tree.

"And since we've already established we're getting married someday if we aren't all slaughtered in a horrific manner, I think you're the best choice for kissing," Claire said.

Emilia shrunk back down behind the couch. She shouldn't be

seeing this, shouldn't be hearing this. But there was no way out. And Claire *had* turned thirteen.

But she was still a baby.

"I'm also the only boy here who isn't tethered to Emilia." Connor's voice trembled as he spoke.

"Well, I was trying to be polite by not pointing that out."

"All right," Connor said.

The room was silent. Emilia wished she could hum loudly.

Why was it so quiet? But as first kisses went, silent was probably a good sign. No squelchy sounds. That was a good thing.

"Thank you," Claire said finally. "Goodnight."

Footsteps moved toward the bedroom doors.

"Claire," Connor said as a door squeaked open, "Merry Christmas."

Emilia held her breath in the silence. Claire got her first kiss. And Emilia was going to make sure she got a good Christmas, too. As quietly as she could, Emilia began pulling flour and mixing bowls from the cupboards. How hard could it be to make Christmas cookies anyway?

～

*H*ours later, Emilia stood in front of the oven, willing her eyes not to close. Soon, the cookies would be done. There was a present for everyone under the tree. As soon as the cookies were settled on the only non-chipped plate she could find, she could curl up next to Jacob and sleep.

Her eyes began to drift closed. How late was it? Three? Maybe four now?

Emilia's feet itched as though a thousand tiny insects were swarming across them where they touched the floor. She rubbed her feet together, but the feeling didn't go away.

"*Inluesco.*" The blue light didn't show anything, on her socks or on the floor.

"Emilia," Jacob's muffled call came from the bedroom.

She turned to go and shush Jacob, but there was a new noise, a low buzzing that tingled Emilia's feet.

"Emi." Jacob threw open the bedroom door and ran to her side as Claire burst out of her room.

"Emilia, are you okay?" Claire asked, rubbing her eyes.

Emilia opened her mouth to say she was fine, but before she could speak, the room around them began to hum, rattling the windows in their frames.

"What is that?" Connor ran out of his room, his wand pointing at the front door.

"I don't know." Jacob raised his wand, moving toward the window.

A light, brighter even than lightning, flashed outside.

Emilia covered her eyes a moment too late. Everything in the room looked too dark now and fuzzy around the edges. She wanted to squeeze her eyes shut to make the light stop dancing in front of Jacob's face, but the humming had gotten worse.

"Emilia LeFay," a horribly familiar voice pounded through the cabin walls.

Emilia ran to the window, knocking her shins hard on the coffee table that had disappeared into the bright white spots that still swam before her.

"Emilia, stay back!" Jacob shouted.

But Emilia had already reached the window and was staring horrorstruck at the lake. The surface should have been bright with stars. Instead, gazing out of the water, was the Pendragon.

It was as though he had skryed the entire lake, turning its shimmering surface into one terrifyingly large mirror.

"Emilia." The Pendragon's voice shook Emilia's bones. "I know you are hiding in the cabin. I know it is there, though I cannot see it. As I know you are in it, though I cannot see you."

Emilia scanned the edge of their island. Twenty feet from the shore, where the shield spell lay, the water was still dark. The

Pendragon was projecting his image into the lake, but he hadn't broken through the shield.

"Please don't be afraid, my sweet Emilia," the Pendragon said. "I haven't come to hurt you. You see, I thought I had lost my family. I thought I would never see your mother again. You have been bound to a traitor. But now I have new hope. I know how to break the tethering without causing you to feel the pain of the traitor's death."

Emilia gripped Jacob's hand.

"And now I have your mother." The Pendragon's face split into a smile that filled the lake.

"No!" Emilia screamed, but the Pendragon couldn't hear her.

"I want to have a family reunion. A nice big party. And you, my daughter, will be the guest of honor. You might not want to come and see me, but I know you, my daughter. I know you will come and save Rosalie. She has her magic back now. It's surprising how easy the unbinding spell is to find when you have the right resources. She may seem unhappy right now, but I think in time both of you will see I am only doing what I must to protect you."

The lake began to turn red under the dawning sun, giving the Pendragon a halo of fire.

"Come to the Immortal Crows Concert in Tarrytown," the Pendragon said. "The reunion will begin at ten o'clock this evening. And if you don't show up...well, there will be lots of humans crashing our party, and I am more than willing to kill them if it means teaching you a lesson in punctuality. I've missed so much of your life, but I want to make up for all that lost time now. See you tonight." A blaze of red and gold flooded the lake before the Pendragon disappeared, leaving the dawn chillingly pale.

18

THE PENDRAGON'S DEMANDS

*E*milia couldn't breathe. The Pendragon had Rosalie. How could he have found Rosalie?

"He's lying." Claire grabbed Emilia's face and turned it toward hers. "He's trying to lure you out. There's no way he could have found Rosalie."

Emilia shook her head. Jacob's arms wrapped around her.

"Claire's right," Connor said. "Someone would have had to tell the Pendragon where she was, and no one we know would have done that."

"Oh no," Claire breathed, horror in her voice.

Emilia turned to see Claire's pale face turn grey.

"What if he captured them in the caves? What if he hurt them? What if he's he torturing Aunt Iz?" Tears slid down Claire's face. "We have to go and rescue them." Claire ran to the door and pulled on her sneakers as though preparing to go on an instant rescue mission.

"They might be fine," Jacob said, gently taking the shoes from Claire's hand. "They might not have even made it to Graylock yet."

"Or they might be dying." Claire snatched her shoes back. "How else could the Pendragon find Rosalie?"

"He's probably lying," Connor said. "He might not have her, let alone know where she is."

"Then how did he find us?" Claire shouted.

"Someone told him," Emilia whispered. "They told him how to find Rosalie and how to find us."

"It wasn't Iz." Jacob paced the room. Emilia could feel the panic bubbling inside his chest even though his voice was calm. "If she had given him permission, he would have been able to get into Elder's Keep."

"So what are we supposed to do?" Claire sank down onto the couch. "Sit here and hope we're just being plain old betrayed by a lying rat and no one we know and love is being tortured for information? Hope the Pendragon doesn't kill us in our beds?"

"I have to go," Emilia said, turning to Jacob and staring into his bright blue eyes. "If I don't show up, he'll kill all the humans at the concert. That could be, what, hundreds of people? A thousand maybe?"

"He won't just kill people out in the open like that," Connor said. "That's crazy."

"Yes, it is!" Emilia screamed. "He tried to burn his own daughter to death. He's flooded cities and tried to bring down planes. This isn't about me or Rosalie. He doesn't care about actually having a family. He doesn't care about innocent people getting hurt."

"But he does care about Rosalie," Jacob said, taking Emilia's hands in his. "He said he wants her back, you back. He must know that if he kills people in front of her, she'll hate him even more."

"So you think he'll bring her flowers instead? He's a sociopath," Emilia said. They were wasting time. She needed to get to Rosalie. "You know I'm right. All he wants is to create his magical order. He likes the idea of a wife and daughter at his side.

But if Rosalie doesn't fit into his picture of the perfect magical First Family, do you really think he'll keep her around? She ran away from him. She hid me. She betrayed him."

"Emi—"

"And even if he doesn't have her. Even if he isn't going to kill her, do you really think he won't kill a bunch of innocent humans at a concert just because he wants to?" Emilia pressed her forehead to Jacob's chest, willing him to understand. "I can't sit here and let him murder innocent people."

"I know." Jacob held her tight. "We can go through the tunnel."

"Hold up," Claire said, shoving her arms between Jacob and Emilia, prying them apart. "No one is going into any tunnel."

Emilia started to argue, but Claire put a hand over her mouth. "Mr. Evil Killer out there is trying to get you to show up to a nice little kidnapping and murder shindig."

"I can't let him—"

"Hush," Claire said, sounding frighteningly like Aunt Iz. "I am not suggesting we sit here and eat cookies. I am saying we should try to contact Aunt Iz, Proteus, anyone we know who is still alive and might be able to help us before we go running toward the murderer. If we can't find help or come up with another plan, then we go through the dark, scary tunnel toward the murdering maniac. You said we couldn't go running to Graylock. Well, we can't go running after Rosalie, either. I'm all for adventure and no one else in the family getting killed, but I would also love to see my fourteenth birthday."

Emilia nodded silently, and they immediately scattered to their rooms to skry anyone who might help. Emilia tried everything she could think of to get a hold of Aunt Iz, Molly, or Larkin, skrying each in turn. Connor tried to contact his parents at the High Peaks Preserve. Claire tried to reach any of the centaurs. But there was nothing. No help to be found.

"Could he have gotten to all of them?" Jacob murmured to

Emilia as Claire threw her skrying mirror across the room, smashing it against the far wall.

"*Reparactus,*" Claire said, pulling the mirror back together before smashing it on the wall again.

"I don't know." Emilia shook her head. "Maybe he's found a way to block the skries." The how wasn't important. They were on their own. She needed to go.

Emilia stood and walked to the trapdoor. It was invisible now, hidden perfectly with the rest of the floor. But she could feel it, the darkness lurking right beneath them. "I have to go. I can't waste more time."

"*We*, Emilia." Jacob took her hand. "Remember, we fight together."

"So, into the tunnel it is then?" Claire stomped on the floor, sending a cloud of dust into the air. With a high pitched *squeak*, the trapdoor began to separate from the floor. "That looks promising."

"You two should stay here," Emilia said, taking Claire's hands in hers. "Please, stay here. Stay safe."

"The Pendragon knows where we are," Connor said. "Now that he knows we're here, he'll get inside."

"He shouldn't be able to get through the shield," Jacob said.

"If anyone can find a way, it'll be him," Connor said. "I'd rather not be here when he does."

"Aunt Iz might try to contact you soon. Tell her where we went," Emilia said, putting her foot on the trapdoor as Connor reached to open it.

"Nope," Connor said. "Last time you two disappeared, you were gone for weeks. If you're really going after the Pendragon, we're coming with you."

"It's too dangerous. This is a trap. We know it's a trap," Jacob said. "If anything happened to either of you—"

"You'd never forgive yourselves blah, blah, blah," Claire said, cutting across him. "You keep acting like this whole *mortal peril* thing is new. Well it's not. And the second you leave, we'll just follow you."

Connor nodded his agreement.

"And if we're going into the scary tunnel, I vote we all go together," Claire finished.

"Fine." Emilia dragged her fingers through her hair. "But when we get to the concert, you two are guards. Lookouts. You stay back, all right?" She pointed between Claire and Connor.

They looked at each other with raised eyebrows before turning back to Emilia with silent scowls.

"Promise you'll only be on lookout," Emilia said in a low growl that reminded Jacob of Samuel.

Connor shifted Emilia to the side. "I promise to be just as good at guard duty as Jacob," Connor grunted as he lifted the heavy wooden door.

The door slammed loudly to the ground, shaking the floor and leaving a black hole below them just wide enough for a person.

"Merry Christmas," Claire said, grimacing down at the hole.

INTO THE DARK

"I'll go first." Jacob knelt by the trapdoor. *"Inluesco."* A shining blue light appeared in his palm. He leaned down into the blackness, stretching to make the light reach as far as it could.

There was an old wooden ladder packed into the dirt wall.

"I can see a way down." Jacob wished he could see the floor as well.

Twisting around, he found a foothold with the toe of his sneaker. The wooden rung of the ladder creaked and sagged under his weight.

Emilia grabbed his arm, steadying him as he tipped back.

"I'm fine." Jacob took a shaky breath. He moved his foot to the next rung and heard Emilia scream as he tumbled backward.

The fall lasted only a moment before he hit the dirt floor with a *crunch* and a *thud*. Pain shot through his back.

"Jacob!" Emilia shouted, silhouetted by the light of the cabin creeping down through the trapdoor.

"I'm fine," Jacob coughed, forcing air back into his lungs. *"Inluesco."* The blue light flickered back into being on his palm.

"It's only about nine feet. Just hang and drop. I think it'll hurt less."

Jacob pushed himself to his feet, reaching around to feel something hot and sticky on his back. His fingers glistened darkly in the pale blue light.

"Watch out." Emilia lowered herself through the trapdoor and dropped to the ground. She stumbled as she landed, and Jacob caught her, wrapping his free arm tightly around her waist. His heart raced as she placed her hand on his chest.

"Thanks," Emilia said before looking down at the blood Jacob had smeared on her arm.

"You said you were fine," Emilia said, holding out his hand.

"My back got cut on something. I'm okay," Jacob tried to argue, but Emilia had already spun him around.

"*Pelluere.*"

Jacob gritted his teeth as the sting of the healing spell bit his flesh. "See, no big deal," he said, his voice tight and strained.

"What did you even fall on? *Inluesco.*" A light in Emilia's hand joined Jacob's.

The glowing sphere cast shadows on a small, white, crushed skull. He had fallen onto the bones of some poor dead rodent. Jacob rubbed the back of his hand over his mouth, willing himself not to be ill at the thought of the rodent's bones piercing his flesh.

"If you two lovebirds are done down there, would you mind scooting over?" Claire said.

Jacob and Emilia pressed themselves against the wall.

"I'll go first." Connor leaped down and staggered into the wall. "Don't worry, I can catch you," he said as he found his footing.

But Claire had already landed gracefully on her feet. "Thanks, but I think I can manage." Claire tucked her hair daintily behind her ears with a grin.

"Shall we?" Jacob turned to peer down the tunnel. Even with

the glowing spells in their hands and the shaft of light coming down from the cabin, he could see no twist or end to the tunnel.

With a *creak* and a *boom* that shook dirt down from the walls around them, the door above them slammed closed. They were trapped in the dark.

"On the bright side, I don't think the ladder would have held us on the way back up anyway." Claire's voice sounded hollow and dull as the dirt walls of the tunnel swallowed her words.

Jacob led the way into the darkness, holding his light up high. Emilia was at his shoulder, matching his every step. Every few feet, something would *crunch* underfoot. Jacob didn't look down. He didn't want to know what sort of animal would have been trapped here in the dark long enough to die.

"I suppose the tunnel would have to be long to cross all the way under the lake," Emilia said after a few minutes, sliding her hand into Jacob's.

Could she feel him getting claustrophobic already? He hated being underground, trapped beneath the earth with no way out. Jacob forced himself to breathe as the thought of all the water from the lake pouring down on them nearly froze him midstride. Could a wizard even survive that?

The tunnel began to change, narrowing and widening every few feet, twisting and turning under the lake.

Emilia pulled on Jacob's hand, slowing his step. "This doesn't feel right," Emilia whispered when Connor and Claire had skirted around them, moving a few feet ahead. "If we're under the lake, why does the tunnel keep twisting?"

"Bedrock?" Jacob shrugged.

But Emilia was right. The tunnels at Graylock had been dug deep into the stone. The walls had been roughly hewn, and the tunnels had curved, but not like this. This path seemed to be curving around invisible barriers leading somewhere that was not the other side of the lake.

Jacob trailed his free hand along the dirt wall. The earth was warm under his touch. His heart raced.

This wasn't right. The bones underfoot had vanished. His neck began to prickle. Someone—something—was here watching them. He spun around, but all he could see in the tunnel behind him was impenetrable darkness.

"Connor, Claire, slow down," Jacob called, quickening his pace and dragging Emilia to catch up. They were only fifteen feet behind, but in the dark it felt too far. He could barely see them. The walls were absorbing his light.

"Why don't you two speed up?" Claire shouted back. Her voice sounded distant and small.

"Claire, stop!" Emilia shouted.

With a *crack* and a scream, Claire and Connor were gone.

Jacob sprinted forward. "Connor! Claire!" He searched the ground, expecting to find the chasm that had swallowed them. Instead, a wall blocked the tunnel.

"Claire!" Emilia shrieked, pounding the wall with her fists. Dirt fell away, cascading onto them as Jacob joined her, trying to claw through the barrier.

But the wall regrew, filling itself back in as soon as they made a dent.

What if they were buried in the wall, suffocating under the weight of the lake?

"*Manuvis!*" Emilia shouted. A ball of brilliant, red light struck the wall. The spell shattered, leaving shards of sparkling red glittering on the ground.

"*Magneverto!*" Jacob plunged the tip of his wand into the wall. But nothing happened.

A rumbling, a crackling, and a laugh like wind chimes echoed down the hall behind them. "Oh you wizards with your funny little spells."

Jacob whipped around to see a woman dressed in pure white with scarlet painted lips sauntering toward him.

"Hello, beautiful boy." The Hag smiled. "I'm so glad you haven't managed to die yet."

20

THE FORGOTTEN GRAY

*S*he looked just as she had before. Perfect dark curls kissed her porcelain skin. Her white dress and heels were unmarked by the dirt that surrounded them.

"Where are Connor and Claire?" Jacob asked, pressing Emilia into the wall behind him, shielding her from the Hag's view.

"Don't worry," the Hag laughed, her red painted mouth curving into a grin, "if I'd wanted them dead, they wouldn't have made it past the trapdoor. If I had wanted you dead, I would have told you to jump off the wrong cliff. Or let you die on the dock in Newport. You're welcome for that, by the way."

"If you don't want to hurt us, why are you here?" Emilia asked, trying to push Jacob aside.

"I didn't say I didn't want to hurt you," the Hag said. "Pain is inevitable. Hurt can be the only way to move forward. And I so desperately want you to move forward. I may be the outcast of the Gray Clan, but that doesn't mean I'm not on your side."

"I thought you hated the Grays," Jacob said.

"I hate the ones who cast me out. But they've been dead for hundreds of years. I hate the Clan heads who sit on their pretty thrones of magic, making rules no one could hope to obey. But right now the Gray Clan is all that stands between the Pendragon and the humans. I know what humans are like when they're afraid. I've seen what they can do." The Hag twirled a perfect curl around her finger. "Besides, I've always helped the Grays. Who do you think cast the *fortaceria* around your quaint little home?"

"The shield spell for the Mansion House?" Emilia asked. "What does that have to do with you?"

"Everything."

"Edna had a shield spell. Did you make hers, too?" Jacob asked. "Do you just run around putting up spells for the Clans?"

"Our shield is different," Emilia said. "There are no chanters at the Mansion House. We don't have people hidden in a barn like Edna did."

Jacob shivered, thinking of the men he had seen bloody and dead on the ground.

"No one is making the spell. The *fortaceria* just exists," Emilia finished.

"Unlike any other shield." The Hag's eyes twinkled.

"I never really thought about it," Emilia said.

"How like a spoiled little Gray." The Hag took another step toward them. "Extraordinary magic protecting them, and they don't even notice or bother to say thank you."

"Why would Aunt Iz let you do the shield?" Emilia asked, ducking under Jacob's outstretched arm. "No member of the Gray Clan is supposed to speak to you."

"It wasn't Isadora," the Hag said. "Two elders before her, long before even your Daddy Dearest's time, there an elder desperate to hold onto his position. He was so afraid his people would see how very selfish he had become, he wanted a shield unlike any other to protect himself. He came to me.

"I made him two shields: one for the Mansion House and one for a little cabin in the center of a lake. A place to hide even from his own children if they came for his head. And you're welcome for the hospitality. Though the décor leaves something to be desired, I had nothing to do with that. I've never seen a reason for flannel to exist."

"Thank you for your incredible hospitality," Jacob said, his voice even and cold. "We appreciate your protecting us from the Pendragon, but we need to get out of here."

The Hag tilted her head back and laughed. The brightness and joy in the sound made Jacob tense as though they were being attacked. He wanted to take Emilia and run, but there was nowhere to go.

"Please," Emilia said, "just show us where Connor and Claire are, and let us out."

"So you can go running right into the Pendragon's waiting arms?" The Hag laughed again, but her smile didn't reach her eyes. "The last time you asked for my help, I gave it, free from obligation. You went to the Siren's Realm, and what have you done but make things worse? Worse for poor Rosalie. And infinitely worse for all Magickind."

"How?" Emilia said, her voice rising to a shout. "We brought Rosalie back to give her a chance to live. And what does it matter to Magickind if I brought my mother back from that horrible place? It only affects me and my family. You have nothing to do with this, so please don't pretend it could possibly matter to you."

"But it does, little Gray. You with your horrible dreams of a happy ending have made the Pendragon into something infinitely more dangerous than he has ever been before." The Hag's voice rang in the darkness as though she were speaking in a cathedral.

"We have never done anything to make him stronger," Emilia said. "All we've done is fight him."

"The Pendragon is strong." Jacob stepped around Emilia. He was close enough to the Hag he could have reached out and touched her, and that only made him more afraid. "He can do spells the rest of us can't because we don't even know what they are. He has a book—"

"A book?" The Hag said. "The Pendragon has magic beyond

what normal wizards can do not because he is stronger—though he is, incidentally, remarkably powerful—but because he doesn't care whom he hurts or who finds out he did it. Humans could wipe out their whole sorry race everyday. They could take their little pistols and shoot each other until there was no one left. But they won't do it because that isn't how the world survives. The humans have learned to live with violent uncertainty.

"But the Pendragon doesn't want the world to survive, not as it is now anyway, with all the rules and humans messing it up. He wants magic to reign over the world and doesn't care about the death left behind. He won't play by the rules that keep the grass from being painted with blood and ash. He does as he chooses and burns the earth in his wake. And now you've helped him to grow stronger than he has ever been before."

"How have we helped him?" Emilia growled. "We've done nothing to help him."

"You'll see. When it's too late, you'll know. The well runs deep, little Gray, and now it has no end," the Hag said, her voice soft and dangerous. "You had a way to stop all of this. The Siren would have ended it. But you, silly little mortal girl, had to keep *him*." The Hag pointed at Jacob. "She would have traded him for another hundred years of peace."

"I couldn't leave him there," Emilia said. "Is that what you wanted when you sent us to the Siren's Realm? For me to abandon Jacob in that hell?"

"A hell he could have survived," the Hag said. "But little Emilia couldn't stand the guilt of leaving her *coniunx*. So now the world will burn."

Jacob felt Emilia's guilt and fear flare in his gut.

"The Siren might not have even gotten rid of the Pendragon," Jacob said, stepping in closer to the Hag. "She might have stolen all magic from everyone. Wizards, centaurs, everybody could have lost their magic. You can't trust the Siren. It's better to fight the Pendragon on our own than to let the Siren have power in our world. Wizards made this fight, and wizards will end it."

"And what if your life is ended with his?" the Hag asked, staring at Jacob.

"Then so be it," Jacob said.

"You foolish boy." The Hag reached out, touching the burn on Jacob's cheek. "You would be an extraordinary loss."

"Don't touch him." Emilia leaped forward, knocking the Hag's hand away.

A shattering *crack* like a window slamming shut pounded through Jacob's ears. He reached for Emilia ready to run, but his hand met solid air and slid away.

"Emilia!" Jacob pounded on the invisible barrier, but Emilia didn't look back at him.

"Jacob!" Emilia screamed. "*Inluesco.*" A ball of blue light ignited in her hand. "Jacob!" Emilia looked wildly around.

"Emilia!" Jacob banged his fists on the wall.

"Bring him back!" Emilia shouted.

"Funny how she thinks I took you away," the Hag said.

"Let her out of there." Jacob rounded on the Hag.

"All in good time," the Hag said. "There's something you need to see first."

"I don't want to see anything you have to show me." Jacob raised his wand.

The Hag laughed. "Don't try to fight me. I'm here to help you. I'm here because I like you, Jacob Evans. I'm here because you are the one interesting thing left in this world, and I am giving you one last way out. There is nothing beyond here but pain and death."

"If we're all doomed, why are you here?" Jacob growled. "Why do you even care?"

"Because I was like you once." The Hag's smile faded. "I was a powerful witch. The most powerful my Clan had ever seen. I could have lived a *full* life. A life filled with marvelous things. But

I decided I wanted love instead. They murdered my love, and here I am."

"I'm sorry," Jacob said, imagining the Hag young, mortal, and in love.

"Don't be." The Hag paced across the dirt floor, her white pumps gaining no trace of filth. "At least I know he loved me."

"I love Emilia."

"I know. That's one of the things that makes you so interesting." The Hag stopped, her face inches from Jacob's. "The question is does she love you? Or is it just a bit of gold and magic that keeps her from abandoning you as everyone else has? You are extraordinary. Haven't you ever wondered how you destroyed your school? How you killed that foul Domina?"

"The professor…" He had never finished his last conversation with the professor.

"You have powers beyond the normal witch or wizard," the Hag said. "You are stronger, more magical than Isadora Gray could ever wish to be."

"No, I'm not."

"Yes, love, you are. Before wizards were wizards, they were humans, and now you, you are more than most wizards could ever begin to understand. Learning so quickly, did you really think you were just that smart?"

"Is that"—Jacob's mind raced back to the impossible spell—"is that how I survived in the woods?"

"No. But I could give you that answer, if you're willing to trade something to me."

"What?" Jacob's heart raced.

"Your magic," the Hag whispered.

Jacob watched her red lips form the words but somehow could not make sense of them.

"You are willing to give up an extraordinary life for that girl." The Hag slapped a hand against the barrier that trapped Emilia. "And you don't even know if she loves you. Magic, or love.

Magic, or love." The Hag said softly in a singsong voice. "What a silly question to decide the fate of the world."

Jacob swallowed. "It doesn't matter. I would do anything to protect Emilia."

"You would die?"

"Yes," Jacob said without pause.

"Sometimes I forget how foolish youth can be."

"Fine," Jacob said, throwing his arms out to his sides. "I'm a fool! I don't care. I don't care if—"

"If she loves you?" the Hag spat. "Now you're even lying to yourself."

"Jacob!" Emilia's shout rose through the barrier. Jacob could feel the panic and fear surging through her.

"The Pendragon took Emilia's choice away. He bound you together," the Hag whispered, leaning in close to Jacob's ear. "That was a horrible thing to do. He'll make you die for her. If you won't fight this awful fate for yourself, fine. Fight it for her. Find freedom for her."

"What do you mean?" Jacob tore his hands through his hair. "You can't break a tethering."

"Rosalie's chain was shattered." The Hag's warm breath tickled Jacob's neck.

"Rosalie's magic was bound," Jacob began softly before remembering how to breathe properly. "I need my magic. We have to go rescue Rosalie. And if we survive that, trying to stay alive with the Pendragon looking for us will definitely take magic."

"I would protect you." The Hag held her hand out to Jacob. "I would keep you safe, and Emilia would be free."

"No. I won't leave her."

"It doesn't have to be forever. I'm trying to make you a deal. I can bind your powers for an instant or a day. Let Emilia go. If she wants you back, you say the word and your magic returns. Your souls get strung back together."

Jacob watched Emilia, who was still circling her cage, digging her fingers into the earth, searching for a way out.

"There has to be a way to undo the tethering without binding my magic," Jacob said. "You've got to know a way."

"Magic, love. Not miracles. I can't just change a spell like that." The Hag snapped her fingers, and a tiny light appeared between them. "But I can take away your magic. It's what feeds the bond. Without it"—the Hag snapped again, and the light faded away —"nothing. Normally, I would only offer to *take* your magic, but under the circumstances, I'm willing to wait and see what happens."

"Why?"

"It's amazing how much can ride on the shoulders of two teenagers. Making muddy the path of Magickind. You know, I became a hag and didn't cause this much trouble." The Hag brushed an invisible speck from her chest.

"I can't just choose to be a human and leave her behind. I love her, and she needs me."

"Of course you love her." The Hag's smile faded. "But does she love you?"

"She needs me right now." Jacob pressed his hands to the barrier between him and Emilia. "Once this is over, then maybe you could bind my powers. Then we wouldn't be—" Jacob choked. He couldn't say the words. "I have to protect her."

"Do you? Or would she be safer without you? Would you have a better chance of survival without her? Imagine Emilia, safe. Emilia, free."

Jacob's head spun. "She said she chooses me."

"Choosing you and loving you are not the same thing," the Hag snapped, her voice sharp. "Before you die for her, don't you want to know what she really wants? Without spells? Without magic?"

Jacob looked down at the golden mark on his palm. He could feel Emilia. She was terrified. "We need to get out of here," Jacob said, raising his wand and trying to think of a spell that might free Emilia.

"There's something you need to see first. And Jacob, I'm sorry."

Jacob wanted to scream at her for apologizing for keeping them here, but Emilia gasped. Jacob spun around, sure the Hag had hurt her. But instead, the entire wall in front of Emilia had begun to glow like sun pouring through a window. And through the light, he could see Iz and Molly creeping down the tunnels of Graylock.

21

RETURNED TO GRAYLOCK

*E*milia gazed in horror as the wall of the tunnel became a window to a familiar scene. Caged light bulbs hung from the ceiling, leading to more wires and no way out.

Graylock.

The barely audible *crunch* of dirt made Emilia look as far left as she could.

"Aunt Iz." Emilia pounded on the wall. "Molly!"

Dexter led them down the tunnel, but they didn't seem to see her or even hear her pounding.

This was her punishment for being rude to the Hag, being transported back to Graylock.

"Jacob," Emilia breathed. "Jacob!"

She could feel his pull next to her heart. He was afraid, but alive. And close. Very close. "Please don't let the Pendragon find Jacob," Emilia said, gazing at the top of the cell, hoping the Hag would hear her and take pity.

"This way," a voice whispered in front of Emilia, and her eyes were drawn back to the window.

Dexter was making them go faster through the tunnel.

For a moment, Emilia was afraid they would travel past the

edge of her window and be gone, out of sight, and beyond her knowing what was happening to them. But as they moved, her window moved with them, showing Dexter pressing a finger to his lips before leading Iz and Molly around a corner.

Larkin was a few steps behind, her hands shaking and her face pale as her gaze swept back and forth across the tunnels behind them, making sure they hadn't been followed.

They were moving down into tunnels lower and deeper than the ones Emilia had run through as she escaped the Dragons. The ceiling was barely taller than Dexter's head, and the walls were too close for two people to pass.

Aunt Iz looked back at Molly, placing one hand on each of the walls and raising her eyebrow in a way that clearly said *this could be a trap.* Molly nodded, but still they continued to follow Dexter.

Dexter raised a hand, stopping Iz mid-step. He held up two fingers and pointed around the corner. "Next to the cell," Dexter mouthed.

Emilia pressed herself to the window, trying to see what Dexter was seeing.

Aunt Iz motioned for Dexter to let her pass. He plastered himself to the wall, and she squeezed by before peering around the corner.

Aunt Iz twirled her wand through the air like someone making a stick of cotton candy. The air around the tip of her wand thickened and darkened into a deep violet. With a smooth flick of the wrist, Iz guided the violet mist around the corner.

"What the—" came a voice from out of sight followed by two *thuds.*

Iz took a step around the corner, and Emilia could finally see what Iz had been seeing.

Two men with dragon tattoos wrapping from their cheeks to their necks now lay crumpled on the floor.

Iz nodded and began to move forward again, gingerly stepping over the downed Dragons.

Dexter tapped her on the arm and motioned to switch places again. But Iz shook her head. Dexter slipped as he trod on one of the Dragons. He took Iz's arm, trying again to move past her. Iz lifted her wand to Dexter's face and shook her head.

Dexter turned to Molly, but she too shook her head.

He stood frozen for a moment, one foot still on the chest of a Dragon before nodding and turning to follow Iz.

Emilia was so close to him, only a few inches away. Dexter's brow was furrowed, and his eyes darted back and forth across the hall. She should be there with them, rescuing Samuel.

The tunnel sloped down now, and the bends became more severe. Every few feet, Aunt Iz had to stop and peer around a corner before continuing on.

After a few minutes, Dexter tapped Aunt Iz on the arm. When she turned to look at him, he mouthed, "The next bend."

Aunt Iz slunk forward. "*Aurictus,*" she murmured, pointing her wand at something Emilia couldn't see.

There was a blast of golden light and a grunt. Iz stepped around the corner, her wand still raised.

They had reached a small room that had four roughly hewn doors surrounding it, flanking the tunnel that continued beyond.

"This is where I was," Larkin whispered, placing a hand on one of the doors. "This is where you found me?" she asked, turning to Dexter.

"Yes," Dexter said.

"How much farther?" Molly said.

"I don't think it's very far." Dexter moved to continue down the hall.

"Keep watch," Iz said, nodding to Larkin and Molly as she followed Dexter.

There were no lights hanging from the ceiling here. Dexter and Iz both held balls of blue light in their hands as they continued down the tunnel.

A voice called from deeper within the hall. "Ian? Emmet?"

Dexter paused, extinguishing the light in his hand. Emilia could see him straining to listen for a moment before the picture went black.

"Aunt Iz," Emilia whispered, pressing her ear to the darkened image, afraid the darkness would never lift, or worse, that the light would reveal something terrible.

Another voice came from down the hall. "Ian, don't be an arse."

"Don't call me an arse for delivering a message from the chamber." The voice was gravelly but came from where Dexter had been standing when everything went dark.

"Then tell us the message." It was the first voice again, this time pitched higher in poorly concealed excitement.

The picture moved again as Dexter's shadow crept forward. Dim torchlight seeped around a corner, showing Dexter plastered against the wall.

"They want you up for training," Dexter said in the same gravelly voice.

"Are we getting moved?" the second unseen person asked.

"Don't know, only I was told to come get you and watch the prisoner while you're gone," Dexter said, stopping so his shadow froze against the stone wall.

"Bet we're going to be moved to the uppers," the second voice said as footfalls began to pound the stone floor.

"*Crepacitus!*" Aunt Iz shouted.

Everything seemed to go still for a moment.

Emilia wondered if the spell had done something out of view.

Dexter staggered backward, as though hit in the stomach by an invisible wave.

The *boom* that followed made Emilia scream, sure something had gone wrong with Iz's spell.

"What happened?" Dexter called in his husky voice. When there was no answer he rounded the corner at a run.

Two men were pinned against the wall, their arms and legs

splayed at their sides. Their heads lolled forward, mouths dangling open.

Dexter paused to look at the men for only a moment before running to the single door that ended the hallway.

Dexter placed his palm on the door. *"Resero ab tessera Rex Draco,"* he chanted, head down and eyes closed.

The door began to *scrape* into the cell, rasping and shrieking as stone ground against stone.

A figure lay on the floor in the corner, huddled in a ball, covering its face against the light.

"Samuel." Dexter stepped forward.

"Not again," a voice mumbled from under the dirty rags. "Please don't do it again. It won't help anything. I won't talk."

"We don't want to hurt you." Dexter knelt next to Samuel.

"Then kill me!" Samuel screamed, sitting up, his eyes wide with fury and fear.

"We've come to take you home." Aunt Iz finally stepped into the cell.

"Iz?" Samuel tried to push himself to his feet, but collapsed back to his knees. "Emilia and Jacob?" Samuel breathed. "Larkin?"

"They're safe," Dexter said, reaching out to help Samuel.

Samuel swatted his hand away. "You did this."

"He rescued Larkin and brought her home," Aunt Iz said. "He led us back here to help get you out."

"It's a trap," Samuel said.

"Well, if it is, I would like to leave as quickly as possible." Aunt Iz bent down and wrapped Samuel's arm around her shoulder. With surprising strength for her age, Iz helped Samuel to his feet.

Samuel gasped and stumbled.

"Hold still," Dexter said, examining Samuel's ankle. It was twisted at an odd angle and crusted with dried blood. *"Pelluere."*

Samuel groaned as the spell began its work.

"Drink this." Iz handed Samuel a flask.

Samuel gulped down the liquid, sighing when he was done.

"Good." Iz started toward the door. "Now, let's get Larkin and Molly."

"And get the hell out of here," Dexter added as the stone door ground shut behind him.

They traveled back up the tunnel more slowly than they had come. Dexter took the lead, Aunt Iz walking sideways, her arm still around Samuel who limped behind her, his face paling with every step. He was ill and in pain. Emilia wasn't sure how much farther he could go.

It took twice as long to get back to where they had left Molly and Larkin. "Well, I do get a whole rescue party, don't I?" Samuel mumbled.

"Sam," Molly gasped, running to throw her arms around him.

He grunted but didn't move away from her. "Good to see you, too, Molly." Samuel kissed Molly's greying red hair.

Emilia wiped the tears from her eyes, wishing she could be there to hold Samuel, too. He'd been trapped for months. And now he was coming home.

"Let's get out of here." Larkin nodded toward the tunnel, taking the first steps toward the outside.

"Wait," Iz murmured. A soft rumbling came from the tunnel ahead, growing steadily louder.

"Ms. Gray, we have to go—"

"Quiet," Iz hissed at Dexter.

The rumbling had grown so loud Emilia covered her ears. She leaned closer to the window, searching the corners for whatever was making the horrible noise.

The air shifted, shimmering into a giant wave that engulfed the tunnel. Dexter choked, clawing at his throat. The others were gasping and looking around.

"They're here!" called a triumphant voice somewhere up the tunnel. "They're here! He said they would be!"

Four Dragons charged into view.

Iz aimed her wand at the nearest Dragon and coughed, "*Velloras!*"

With a grunt, the Dragon was jerked forward into Molly's waiting hands. Molly shot the Dragon back, tossing him into the other Dragons and knocking them to the ground.

"Watch out!" Emilia and Larkin screamed together as another of the Dragons charged forward, trampling his compatriots, his wand pointed at Dexter's heart.

"It's the Wayland bas—" the Dragon began before a streak of shining black shot out of Larkin's palm and into the Dragon's chest. The Dragon crumpled lifeless to the ground.

"More of them," Samuel croaked, pointing to the tunnel.

The Dragons who were struggling up from the ground had been joined by a half dozen more.

"We have to go back!" Dexter yelled. "There's another way!"

Just as they turned to run back the way they had come, an eerie hissing filled the air as the tunnel before them darkened.

"What's happening to the light?" Emilia asked, though she knew no one could hear.

"Turn back!" Iz yelled as a dozen *somnerri* appeared, tumbling from the ceiling, blocking their retreat.

"*Evomine saxum munio!*" Molly screamed. Rocks from the walls flew from their places, forming stone men that blocked the tunnel.

"*Immospatha!*" shouted one of the Dragons from behind them.

"No!" Dexter shouted, throwing himself in front of Samuel. The red light whipped across his face, cutting down through his chest.

Blood blossomed from the wound, and Dexter swayed, sagging to the floor.

"Help him!" Emilia screamed.

"*Primionis,*" Iz shouted. A shimmering barrier blocked the next spell the Dragon shot.

"*Recora!*" the Dragons' shouts echoed. "*Crevexo!*"

The shield shook and bubbled as spells exploded on its surface.

Larkin chanted, running her hand over the oozing slash in Dexter's chest.

"No time," Dexter gasped, pushing Larkin's hands away. "Take Samuel and go," Dexter choked. More blood pooled on the stone floor, surrounding him in a sea of red.

"Oh, to Hell with that." Larkin kept chanting, pressing her hands to the sides of Dexter's wounds as though trying to match two sides of fabric.

"Please fix him, Larkin," Emilia whispered.

"The stones won't hold much longer," Molly said, adjusting herself to stand in front of Samuel who sank against the wall.

"Almost there," Larkin said, wiping the blood from Dexter's stomach with her hand. "Get up." She wrapped her arm around Dexter and yanked him to his feet.

"*Expulsio!*" Iz bellowed just in time as the stone men were torn apart by the claws of the *somnerri*. Her shield shot behind her, sending the Dragons staggering back.

A whip of bright red light flew from the tip of Molly's wand, wrapping around the waists of three Dragons and tossing them up to the ceiling.

"Go!" Aunt Iz shouted.

Molly took the lead, Samuel leaning heavily on her. Larkin had Dexter propped up next to her, and Aunt Iz was behind them all, shooting spell after spell at the Dragons, who fell from the ceiling one by one.

"We have to get out!" Larkin shouted.

"Move back," Dexter grunted, shoving Larkin away from him. "Move back!" he shouted again as Iz and Molly reached toward him.

"*Primurgo,*" Dexter said, his voice cold and calm.

Emilia watched the shield shimmer around him.

"No!" Emilia screamed, knowing what he would do a moment

before it was done. But Iz didn't know. She hadn't seen the tunnels collapse. "Dexter, don't!"

"*Magneverto!*" Dexter shouted, his hands raised to the ceiling above him.

There was a *crack* and a *shatter*, and they were gone. Swallowed by a darkness so complete, Emilia couldn't see her hands as she pounded on the glass, screaming, sobbing, and begging Dexter to answer her.

22

RIPPED APART

*J*acob knelt, watching Emilia, feeling her fear and pain rip him apart.

"Let me go to her," Jacob whispered. "Please let me go to her."

He needed to hold her, to feel she was safe. Tell her the Dragons were far away.

"Are you sure that's what you want?" the Hag asked, her voice soft.

"Yes, I need to be with her."

"Why?"

"Because she needs me."

"Does she?" The Hag raised one perfect eyebrow, the genuineness of her question making Jacob want to scream.

"Was what you showed her real?"

"Yes." The Hag nodded. "I would never lie to you. Not about that."

"Are they alive?" Jacob pressed his forehead against the barrier. The rocks falling from above—he and Emilia had survived it. But Dexter hadn't warned Aunt Iz and the others what he was going to do. They didn't have shield spells to protect them.

"It's too soon to say," the Hag said.

"Then Emilia could have just lost most of her family. I need to be with her."

"Are you sure it's you she wants to be with?" The Hag knelt, her shoulder brushing Jacob's. Her face was the most human he had ever seen it. "She's in there, sobbing for Dexter Wayland. Do you really want to risk your life for a girl who is begging the boy who betrayed her to not be dead?" The Hag looked through the barrier at Emilia. "She doesn't love you."

"You don't know that!" Jacob stood up, walking away from the Hag.

"And you'll never know if she does!" the Hag shouted.

"She chose me! She *chooses* me! Not Dexter. Her family could be dead. He was her friend. That's why she's crying."

"Are you willing to risk everything you are, everything you could become, on a girl whose heart is clouded by a spell?"

"Yes!" Jacob shouted. "Always!"

"Well I'm not. You are worth far more than you know." She studied Jacob, looking from the mark on his palm to the scar on his cheek. "I'll make you a deal," the Hag continued, her voice calm, almost peaceful.

"I'm not going to make any deal with you." Jacob pointed his wand at the barrier. "Let her out, or I will."

"The Dragons had a trap set for Isadora," the Hag said, ignoring Jacob's wand as she planted herself in front of him.

"Someone must have seen them coming in."

"And they waited until after they had reached Samuel to attack? Does that really seem reasonable to you? I thought you were smarter than that."

"Then it was Dexter," Jacob spat, reveling in a reason to hate him, feeling the fury rise in his chest.

"Perhaps," the Hag said. "But he did just risk his life to save your gardener."

"Don't call Samuel that." Jacob raised his wand, aiming the tip at the Hag's face.

The Hag narrowed her eyes as though appraising Jacob. "My apologies." The Hag smiled. "Someone told the Dragons that you and *Samuel* were in the woods at Graylock. Someone who knew when Larkin joined him. Someone told the Pendragon those two children were with the Elis. That you were with Edna. Where Rosalie was hiding. Every step of the way, the Pendragon has known where you were. Do you really think Dexter could have managed that?"

"Who was it?" Jacob asked, his head spinning as he tried to sort through every time the Dragons had found them.

"I'll tell you, if you do something for me." The Hag took a step toward Jacob, brushing his wand out of the way.

"What do you want?"

"I want you to find out if the Gray girl really does love you," the Hag whispered. "It's more than your fate that lies with the girl."

"There's no way to know. That's the point. Tethering is forever."

"No, little boy," the Hag cooed. "I really thought you were smarter than this."

"You want to bind my powers?" Jacob gripped his wand tighter.

"It's a simple proposition. You get your powers nicely bound, the tethering is broken. We'll finally know if Emilia really loves you. If she does, you get your magic back. If she doesn't, you're mine."

"What do you mean, *yours*?"

"So, you *are* afraid she doesn't want you." The Hag grinned.

"Why does it matter to you? Why do you even care?"

"No, no, Jacob. The questions are for me to ask, not you. I

know who the traitor is. I am the one who can keep you here till the end of your time. Lives will end, Jacob Evans. Lives of the ones you love. There is no way to stop it. But I can help you save a few." The Hag paused. "If you know who the traitor is. You risk your magic and your heart. I save the lives of those you love."

"Is there a way to do it without taking my magic?" Jacob's mouth was as dry as parchment as he formed the words. If he could save Iz, Molly, or Samuel, he had to do it.

But Emilia. He looked through the barrier. Emilia was still crying on the ground. What if he lost her?

The Hag traced her finger across her chest, leaving a glistening golden line.

She took his hand in hers. "All powers must be bound. But if you all pass my little test, all powers will be returned."

"We have to save Rosalie—"

"Time in my tunnels is for me to decide. A week takes an hour, an hour takes a century. I have the lifespan of the world to wait. But don't worry. You'll make it to Rosalie in time."

Jacob thought for a moment. He wanted to ask Emilia what to do. He was going to rip both of their souls in half. He couldn't do that to her. But if someone was killed because of him…

"Why?" Jacob asked, his mind racing. He needed to get to Emilia, to be sure she was safe. "Why does it matter to you?"

"I've seen more death and torment in my existence than you could ever hope to match, Jacob Evans. Never ask me to explain myself. The answer would make your heart bleed, and how could you force Emilia to feel such pain? This is important, Jacob. You see only Emilia, but I see a burning world, and a thousand years of darkness to endure."

The Hag stepped forward, laying her hand on Jacob's chest. "The only things you're risking are your heart and your magic. If she doesn't love you, then Emilia will be free, her family will be safer. If you don't have magic, well, I think you'd be used to that anyway. The only one who can possibly lose is you. So say yes, and hope Emilia forgives you for ripping her heart in two. I promise I'll be gentle."

Jacob looked back at Emilia. If he could only hold her for one more moment. "Fine."

~

*E*milia lay on the floor, trying to make sense of everything. Maybe what she had seen wasn't even real. Maybe it was only a horrible trick of the Hag's.

Fear began to pull at her chest, not the terror of watching her family fight for their lives, something deeper.

"Jacob!" Emilia leaped to her feet. He was close by. She could feel it. Had the Dragons found him, too?

"Jacob! Where are you? *Profindo! Manuvis!*" Emilia shouted, sending spell after spell into the walls around her. "Jacob," she tried to scream again, but there was no air left in her lungs.

Emilia gasped, clawing at her throat. The pain started at her heart. A horrible ripping that would surely kill her. She clutched her chest, desperate to hold together whatever was being torn apart inside her, but her arms were too weak. She stumbled, falling back onto the cold stone floor. The pain engulfed her, searing every nerve she had. Her arms glowed gold, the light radiating from her.

"Jacob," she mouthed his name. She had no air even to scream in pain.

And Jacob. He was being tortured, his agony more than hers. His pain separated from her own, drifting away so she couldn't feel it anymore.

Jacob was gone.

And then her own pain ebbed away, and she was left alone in the dark.

Emilia screamed, clutching her heart. Surely there must be a hole in her chest. A terrible void where her heart had been. Surely if Jacob was gone, she would die soon, too.

"Jacob," Emilia murmured, struggling to breathe. There were no tears for her to cry. Half of her had vanished. Tears were impossible now. All that was left was to wait in the dark. The Dragons would find her, and that would be the end. The pain would stop.

A *whoosh* of fresh air entered her tomb. This was it. They were coming to end it. Staggering footsteps came nearer. They had sent a wounded Dragon to kill her. How very fitting.

"Emilia," a voice whispered. A warm hand brushed the hair away from her face. Strong arms cradled her to a chest that smelled of freshly mowed grass.

"Emi," the voice whispered, "you're all right. Everything is going to be all right."

"Jacob?" Emilia pushed herself up so she could look at his face.

It was Jacob. The tousled hair, the bright blue eyes, the scar on his cheek. Even the look of concern he only ever had for her.

Perhaps they were both dead. It seemed wrong for dying to hurt so very badly. But if this was death, if they were going to be trapped in the dark, at least they would be together.

"I'm so sorry," Jacob said, helping Emilia to sit up. "I had to let the Hag bind my powers. Someone's been betraying all of us. The Hag knows who it is. She promised to tell us if I let her bind my magic, but—"

"She did what?" Emilia asked, taking Jacob's hand in her own. His shaking hand was covered in sweat and dirt. But the golden streak had disappeared from his palm, and from hers. "You're not dead?"

"No."

"Where is she?" Emilia stood, trembling at the pain that shot through her. "Where are you?"

"Right here, little Gray." The Hag stepped out of the shadows.

"Give him back his magic," Emilia growled.

"Perhaps I will." The Hag smiled. "We made a bargain. Jacob can tell you all about it if he wishes."

Emilia turned to Jacob.

"I can get my powers back when we get out of the tunnels," he said.

"Oh, little Gray, I would have thought you would be more concerned about me taking all of your magic too." The Hag took a step forward as though daring Emilia to strike.

"That wasn't part of the bargain," Jacob said.

"*Inluesco,*" Emilia said. But there was no tingle of magic. Emilia closed her eyes, searching for the energy that had always lived in her chest, but it was gone.

"I'm surprised you didn't notice. But then I suppose breaking the tethering was probably more shocking."

"The deal was for my magic, not Emilia's." Jacob planted himself in front of Emilia, blocking her path as she stepped forward to punch the Hag.

"*All powers must be bound. But if you all pass my little test, all powers will be returned,*" the Hag said in a singsong voice. "It's not my fault you didn't listen."

"You evil—" Emilia began.

"Don't worry. The only risk is the one Jacob agreed to. If you can make it through the tunnels, you'll make it to Rosalie. You and those children will get your magic back. The only one who might live forever in the dark is Jacob. And it was a risk he was willing to take." The Hag backed away into the shadows. "Best be going now. I have quite the little adventure planned for you all, and I wouldn't want the timing to be off. Then where would poor Rosalie be?" With a swish and a laugh, she was gone.

"Emilia," Jacob said after a silent moment.

"Why would you agree to this?" Emilia asked, staring out into the dark tunnel, wondering how they were supposed to start finding Connor and Claire.

"What you saw in the Graylock tunnels. It really happened. If the Hag can tell us who the traitor is, we'll all be safer. The Pendragon has Rosalie because someone told him where she was." Jacob reached for Emilia, hesitating before wrapping his arms around her.

"Do you really think you can trust her?" Emilia asked, painfully forcing a deep breath into her lungs. "She could keep us down here forever. We need to get to Rosalie."

"The Hag said we could still make it."

"And you trust her?"

"She doesn't want to hurt us," Jacob said.

His voice sounded sure, but Emilia couldn't feel what he was feeling.

"Then why is she doing this?"

"She wants to know what will happen," Jacob said. "What we'll do without magic. She said it was important, but…"

"I suppose a real answer would be too much to ask for." Emilia ran her fingers through her tangled hair.

"Once she knows, we'll all get out in time to get to Rosalie," Jacob said, resolution and fatigue filling his voice.

Emilia stepped forward, burying her face on his chest. It felt so familiar, but the buzz, the tingle that flowed through her veins screaming *this is right, this is home* was silent. Now it was just her and Jacob in the dark.

"We need to find Connor and Claire," Emilia said.

The light that had filled the room while the Hag was there had begun to slowly fade away.

"Let's go." Jacob nodded and led Emilia into the dark.

STUMBLING THROUGH THE DARK

  For the first few steps, the dim light of the room followed them, but before they had traveled twenty feet, the path in front of them went pitch black. Emilia glanced back to where the Hag had left them. Only darkness remained.

Emilia reached out, tracing her fingers along the dirt wall, feeling pieces of it crumble away beneath her touch.

"Claire." Jacob's voice echoed, carrying through some unseen expanse.

"Touch the right wall," Emilia whispered, not wanting to hear her voice bouncing in the dark. "I'll touch the left."

Jacob stretched away from her. The darkness seemed worse when she could only feel his hand.

"Connor! Claire!" Jacob called as they began to move forward again.

There was a rustling behind them.

"Connor?" Emilia whispered.

But the rustling grew louder and closer.

"What's—" Jacob began, but the sound of hundreds of rubbery wings flapping was too close to mistake now.

Emilia screamed as something brushed across her cheek.

Shrill squeaking filled her ears, and Jacob pushed her to her knees.

She could feel him in the dark, covering her head with his body.

"Stay down," Jacob shouted in Emilia's ear, his voice nearly swallowed by the bats flying past.

It felt like an eternity before the wings finally began to slow, their sound fading away in the distance.

"Did they hurt you?" Emilia asked, feeling Jacob's head in the dark. She ran her fingers through his hair, searching for a sign of blood.

"I'm fine," Jacob answered, sounding out of breath. "Are you —" Jacob began before cursing loudly.

"What's wrong?"

"Do you remember which way we were going?"

Emilia put her hand on one wall and turned to face down the corridor. "Claire," she called. Her voice sounded muffled, as though she were standing in a closet. "I think it's this way." Emilia began to lead Jacob in the opposite direction.

"Connor," Jacob shouted as they crept forward. But again, the sound was muffled.

"Claire," Emilia called one way. "Connor," she called the other. But neither direction sounded different. The echo was gone.

Emilia took a breath, willing herself not to panic. "How are we supposed to find them? We can't see, we don't have magic, we don't know where we are."

"The Hag wants us to survive like humans." Jacob led Emilia down the corridor. "So we search as best we can in the dark."

They kept their hands on the walls, feeling for another corridor. But there was nothing. Just a seemingly endless journey of blackness.

"We need to get out of here," Emilia finally said. "We need to find Rosalie." Saying the words somehow made her feel worse.

"We'll find a way," Jacob pressed on, keeping a slow and steady pace.

Minutes ticked by, or hours. There was no way to tell which.

A ball of anger grew in Emilia's chest. She gritted her teeth, wanting to scream in frustration. But finally, another noise began in the distance. Something muffled, like a voice through a pillow.

"Connor! Claire!"

Emilia stood in silence for a moment, waiting for the muffled voice to try and call to them. But the muttering continued.

Inch by inch, Jacob and Emilia moved forward, Emilia sweeping the ground in front of her with her toe, afraid of stumbling over whatever was in front of them.

Emilia's toe met something fleshy, and she gasped.

"Claire," Emilia said. "Connor, is that you?" But whatever was lying at her feet continued to wriggle as though she had never spoken.

"Emilia, don't," Jacob began, but Emilia had already knelt down, reaching one hand out toward the thing.

It was warm and covered in cloth. As she touched it, the wriggling thing started to scream through whatever was covering it. Emilia pulled something furry back. The screaming became louder as the thing began to writhe on the ground. A head banged hard into her shin.

"It has two heads," Jacob said. "Emilia, back up."

Emilia reached back out to the thing, and something silky brushed her fingers. She yanked her hand away. She took a deep breath and reached forward again. There was a head of hair, a face, and a nose. A strip of fabric was tied tightly in the mouth of the thing.

"Let me help you," Emilia said, finding the knot on the back of the head and trying to pull it free. "Hold still." Emilia dug her fingers into the knot. Her skin tore as she ripped the fabric free. Emilia screamed as teeth sank into her arm.

"Don't touch me!" Claire's voice screamed in the dark. "I'll bite you again!"

"Claire, it's us," Jacob said.

"Don't—what?" Claire stopped mid-scream. "Jacob? Emilia? Is that you?"

"Of course it's us," Emilia answered. "Didn't you hear us calling?"

"I didn't hear anything," Claire said. "I just felt someone tugging at my face."

Emilia reached for the other head, which was still thrashing and screaming through its bonds.

"Is this Connor?" Emilia asked, feeling her blood leak onto the knot of the other gag as she tried to untie it.

"I should hope so," Claire said. "I would hate to have been tied butt to butt with a total stranger."

"Claire," Connor shouted as soon as Emilia untied his gag. "Are you okay?"

"I'm fine," Claire said, "and it was very nice of you to ask. By the way, Jacob and Emilia are here."

"Make a light," Connor said. "I can't get my magic to work."

"Neither can we," Jacob said. "The Hag bound all of our powers."

Emilia dug her fingers into the ropes that tied Claire and Conner together.

"The Hag," Claire said. "*The* Hag? The Hag none of us are even supposed to know about bound our powers? Did she tie us up, too? Is she trying to kill us?"

"Not kill us, no," Jacob grunted as Claire sat up, knocking him backward.

"How do you even know about the Hag, Claire?" Emilia asked, finding Jacob's hand in the dark and helping him to his feet.

"A powerful witch who causes chaos and was banned from discussion by the Council of Elders. You really think I wouldn't know about her? I'm a little hurt by your underestimation of my curiosity," Claire said.

"So this Hag lady decided to tie us up underground and bind our powers?" Connor asked, his words muffled in the sounds of him squirming on the ground. "Did she bother to mention why?"

"To make us find our way out of here in the dark. She's testing us," Jacob said.

"Why?" Connor asked.

Emilia hesitated. "She wants to see what we'll do. Getting out of here like humans."

"So is the whole darkness thing some sort of metaphor?" Claire asked, her voice rising as she stood. "We have to stumble through the dark without magic, just as humans stumble through life blind to the world around them?"

Light flashed in the tunnel. Emilia fell backward into the dirt, covering her eyes.

Blinking, she could see Connor, Claire, and Jacob all staring at the same place where three torches sat in golden brackets mounted on the dirt wall.

"So," Connor said, clearing his throat. "This woman—"

"The Hag," Claire inserted.

"Yeah, her," Connor said. "She said she would let us get to the other side?"

"Yes." Emilia reached up, pulling a torch from its bracket and handing it to Claire.

"All four of us?" Connor asked as Emilia handed him a torch.

"Yes." Emilia hesitated, her fingers on the last torch.

"So, which one of us doesn't get a light?" Connor asked, looking from Emilia to Jacob to Claire.

"I don't," Jacob said, stepping next to Emilia. "I don't need one. I already know what it's like to be human. A torch doesn't make much difference."

Emilia laced her fingers through his. She stared for a moment, waiting for their palms to begin to glow. Waiting for the thrum that beat through her body every time they touched. But there was no light, no hum that shook her nerves. Only a desire for him to hold her close. To feel his heart beating and know that whatever was waiting for them in the darkness they would face it together.

Jacob would follow her, protect her however he could. He always had. But the magic was gone. He was no longer tied to her. He was just a boy who was her best friend.

He twisted their joined hands this way and that, as though searching for the golden light. Emilia watched his face as he studied their hands, but she didn't know what he was thinking. Was he afraid that they were trapped in the dark, or relieved that, for the first time in months, Emilia didn't know what his heart was saying?

"Let's go." Emilia held the torch in front of her as she led the way into the dark.

A TEST IN BLOOD

*S*hadows bounced off the uneven dirt of the tunnel. Emilia gasped and stumbled into Jacob as a face emerged from the wall, a long, hooked nose pressing out through the dirt.

Claire shrieked as the head turned to watch them all back away.

"Who are you?" Jacob asked, taking a step in front of Emilia. But the face remained frozen, its mouth stretched in grotesque silent laughter.

Jacob pulled the torch from Claire's hand, waving it back and forth in front of him, as though trying to scare away an animal, as he approached the face.

"Leave us alone," Jacob shouted, but the figure didn't move. "We have been granted safe passage by the Hag." He was only a foot from the shadowy face, but still it did not speak.

His torch was close enough to the face now that any person would have shied away from the heat of the flame. Jacob reached a trembling hand toward the face, ready to fight whatever creature waited in the wall.

As he touched the nose an ear splitting wail rent the air,

sending Jacob stumbling back. The scream stopped, and the face crumbled away, falling into a pile of dirt at his feet as the echo of terror carried down the tunnel.

"What was that?" Emilia said.

Even though she was standing so close to Jacob he could feel her chest rise and fall with each frightened breath, he could barely hear her over the ringing in his ears.

"A hello from the Hag would be my guess." Jacob poked the mound of dirt with his toe, half-expecting it to turn into some horrible creature.

"I think you two need to be more careful about who you make friends with." Claire stomped on the pile of dirt, grinding it with her foot.

The tunnel seemed as though it would never end. Was this part of the Hag's plan? Drive them to insanity by making them walk forever?

The path in front of them curved, but whenever Jacob looked behind, all he could see was a straight corridor.

Jacob took Emilia's hand and pulled her a step behind the others. "She's making it up as she goes," Jacob whispered.

"What?" Emilia blinked for a moment, before looking down the corridor where Jacob was pointing. "Have we moved forward at all?"

"We'll make it out of here," Jacob said, forcing his voice to sound steady.

"I know." Emilia ran a hand over her face, leaving smudges of dirt on her cheeks. "But Iz and the others could already be dead. We need to tell Claire and Connor."

Jacob wanted to pull Emilia into his arms. To hold her and comfort her. To tell her Aunt Iz, Molly, Larkin, and Samuel would all be all right. But what if her tears were for Dexter? What if she didn't want Jacob to hold her?

"Umm, guys," Claire called.

The lights of her and Connor's torches were down the tunnel, far ahead of them.

"We're coming," Emilia called as she and Jacob ran toward the lights.

"I think we might have a problem." Connor's voice reached back to them.

"Don't move," Jacob shouted, pictures of crumbling floors and hungry beasts flying unbidden through his mind.

"Not really a choice," Claire shouted.

"What's wrong?" Jacob asked, but he didn't need them to answer. A thick wall of brambles and branches blocked the tunnel.

Jacob stared at the thicket in front of them. If they could use magic, just one little spell, they could get through in a minute.

"Maybe we took a wrong turn?" Connor shrugged.

"There were no turns." Jacob reached into the thicket. "Well, that's great." He pulled his hand, now covered in scratches, back from the brambles.

"Can we climb over it?" Claire asked hopefully.

Emilia held her torch high. The branches and thorns reached up to the top of the corridor.

"I say we go back and look for another way," Connor said, turning and starting back down the hall.

With a *crack* that shook the tunnel, a solid wall of dirt and rock fell to the ground inches in front of Connor.

Jacob grabbed Emilia and Claire, pulling them both to the ground and shielding them with his body. The tunnel groaned, protesting the added weight. Jacob held his breath, waiting for more earth to fall. But after a few seconds, everything was silent.

"Thanks for including me in that heroism," Connor said, pulling Jacob to his feet.

The ceiling hadn't collapsed in a heap. Instead, the stone had formed a solid and impenetrable wall.

"Through the briar patch it is," Emilia sighed.

She held her torch to the brambles in front of her. A minute passed as the flames licked the thorns. Finally, she pulled her torch away, but the wood showed no sign of having been singed. "Well, it was worth a try."

Emilia sighed again and began pushing her way into the brambles. Jacob followed close behind, afraid of letting her get too far ahead where he couldn't reach her.

The brambles were tangled just loose enough that if Jacob used all his weight to force them apart, he could push himself between the branches.

Emilia moved faster than Jacob, ducking through gaps that were too narrow for him. Branches creaked and snapped behind her. Emilia ducked under a thick branch, its bark grabbing at her hair. She ducked lower, pulling her hair free from the thorns.

"Ouch," Jacob gasped as the branch swung backward and caught him hard across the cheek.

Emilia grimaced. "Sorry."

"It's fine." Jacob pushed another step forward.

The thorns tore at Jacob's arms. Soon, he was covered in little red drops of his own blood. They sank into silence. The only noises were their clothes being torn and the cracking and whipping of branches.

"Why does the crazy psycho lady want us to look like we've been mauled by house cats?" Claire asked a few minutes later. "Does she think mild to moderate scratches are going to stop us?"

"Be nice, Claire," Jacob warned, his voice low.

"Why?" Claire asked. "Am I supposed to be worried she's listening?"

With a *groan* and a *crack*, a branch hit Claire hard in the stomach, knocking her sideways into a patch of brambles.

"She *is* listening," Emilia said, pushing herself over to Claire and stretching her arms between the branches to grab Claire's fingertips.

"Fine," Claire grunted as Emilia dragged her back to her feet.

"She's listening. Then would she mind"—Claire shoved herself a foot forward—"telling"—she pushed another step—"me why"—she dove headfirst between two branches—"this is necessary?"

"Million dollar question, Claire," Jacob said, stepping past Claire and pulling her through the branches.

There was a *crack* and a yelp from behind Emilia.

"Don't worry," Connor said, "it's fine. I'm only bleeding a little. From my eyelid."

"We'll get through," Jacob panted, his breath coming in short gasps. "This won't last forever." He pushed a branch aside, swallowing his gasp as a thorn tore deep into his hand. Blood trickled from his palm where the golden mark should have been.

How much longer would the Hag keep them here? How much blood was enough?

He pushed a cluster of brambles and thorns aside, gritting his teeth against the sting he knew would come from the new cuts. But stepping forward, he stumbled, landing face down in the clear, cold dirt. Jacob rolled onto his back, gasping. There were no branches overhead.

"We're through," Jacob panted. Emilia's hand emerged, and Jacob grabbed it, pulling her forward. "We made it."

Emilia looked at Jacob but didn't return his tired smile. Instead, her gaze drifted over Jacob's shoulder.

"What?" Jacob spun around and found himself looking at a sheer dirt wall, twenty feet high.

CLIMB

*a*s Connor and Claire burst free from the brambles, Jacob silently pointed to the wall, not trusting himself to do anything but curse if he tried to speak.

There were no rungs, no rocks, no rope.

"Any bright ideas?" Emilia asked, turning to Jacob.

"I would say we could use a simple *adsurgo* spell and float up there," Connor said, his voice rising to a shout. "But somebody had to take our magic!"

Jacob ran his hand over the wall. The dirt was hard and packed together. He searched for a button or lever, something they were supposed to find to make a door or, even better, a staircase to the pitch black opening at the top of the wall. But he already knew what needed to be done, even if he didn't want to admit it.

"We have to climb." Jacob kicked his toe into the dirt wall and found a place where he could dig in his fingers. He hung like that for a moment, waiting to see if the dirt would give way. Chunks of earth fell under his weight, but not enough that he couldn't hold on.

"Great," Emilia said, nodding and twisting her hair into a tight bun before putting her torch between her teeth.

Jacob went slowly, testing every hold before transferring his weight. He glanced down at Emilia. She was a few feet below him with Connor and Claire just starting up the wall. Jacob turned to look back at the top. Just a few more feet.

The dirt around him seemed to change. The hardened, moist dirt was shifting into something dryer and more powdery.

Jacob's heart leaped into his throat as the earth beneath his right hand crumbled away. He dug his left fingers in as hard as he could while his balance wobbled away from the wall. Jacob shut his eyes tight, not wanting to see the wall drift away if he fell. His arms burned as he pulled his chest to the wall, panting.

"Be careful," he choked out, his right hand looking for another purchase. "The dirt isn't as sturdy up here."

"Great," Claire said, her words muddied by the torch clenched in her teeth. She was closer to him than she had been before, climbing fast up the wall.

Jacob's hands found the top, and he pulled with all his might, trying to swing one leg over the wall and hoping to find a solid surface. The sandy dirt scraped against his face as he dragged himself onto the flat top, gasping for breath. He rolled onto his back, watching the shadows of the torches dance on the ceiling.

Dancing like puppets, that was what they were all doing. Entertaining the Hag.

A hand appeared over the top of the wall, and Jacob reached out, recognizing the feel of her hand in his without even needing to look at her face. He pulled Emilia up and over the edge of the wall. She landed on his chest, her face so close to his. They had been here before. But he had felt her heart pound with his own. His stomach purred for him to kiss her, for something to feel right and wonderful. But that wasn't what the Hag wanted, and it wasn't what he wanted either. Emilia needed to choose.

A horrible scream came from below. Then a *crack* and a *thud*.

"Connor!" Claire screamed.

Jacob twisted to see over the edge. Claire was already climbing back down the wall. Her torchlight cast shadows on the ground below, but the light from Connor's torch was gone. In the shadows lay Connor, clutching his leg.

"Connor, are you all right?" Emilia said.

Claire had jumped the last five feet down from the wall and knelt at Connor's side. Connor turned his face up to them. It looked pale and strained even in the flickering torchlight.

"I think it's broken." Connor spoke through gritted teeth.

Claire screamed, turning toward the straight expanse of tunnel they had already traveled. "The stupid, evil, plotting—"

"Claire, don't!" Emilia shouted.

"Why not?" Claire screamed. "He's hurt. The game's over. She has to let us out of here."

"That's not the point," Jacob called down. "She won't let us out because it's hard or we're hurt. That's what she wants. She wants us to know what it's like to struggle. She won't let us out till she's done with us."

"So we're being held captive by a creepy masochist? Well, that's just great," Connor said, pain echoing in his voice.

"I've met worse," Jacob muttered, digging the heel of his hand into his forehead. "I'm coming back down." Jacob twisted to lower his leg over the wall.

"Me, too," Emilia said.

"No." Jacob shook his head.

"You think I'll be safer up here alone?" Emilia gave a dry laugh.

"I think I might need you to help Connor over the edge when I figure out how to get him this far." Jacob planted both feet in the wall.

"Jacob." Emilia bent over and kissed the top of his head. "Be careful."

It took Jacob longer to climb down the wall than it had to climb up. Each time he reached toward a place where there was already a gouge in the dirt from one of them using it as a hold, the earth would crumble, leaving nothing but shifting sand in its place.

Jacob let himself drop the last few feet to the ground.

Connor lay on the dirt, clutching his leg. Claire knelt next to him, brushing his bright red hair away from his face.

"Let me look at it," Jacob said, reaching for Connor's leg.

Connor tried to shy away like a wounded animal, but Claire held him in place. "Don't be a baby."

Jacob carefully pulled up the ankle of Connor's pants. His foot twisted at a strange angle.

"You should keep going," Connor said.

"We are not leaving you," Claire said. "No man left behind, right?" She turned to Jacob.

"She's right." Jacob nodded.

"And how do you expect me to climb that?" Connor stared up at the wall.

"With help." Jacob picked up Connor's torch, touching it to Claire's, but when he pulled it away, Connor's still had no flame.

"Let me do it." Claire held the two torches together again, but Connor's still wouldn't light.

Jacob touched the blackened tip, but there was no heat, no warmth to show it had touched fire at all.

"Well, that makes this easier." Jacob stood and brought the torch down hard across his knee, snapping it in two. "This is going to hurt," he said apologetically to Connor as he gently placed one piece of wood on each side of Connor's hurt ankle. Jacob took off his sweatshirt and began tearing it into strips. When he had enough cloth, he gently lifted Connor's leg and began binding the sticks to his ankle.

Connor groaned, his face scrunching up against the pain.

"That should help," Jacob said as he finished tying on the makeshift splint.

"I forgot what weird things humans do when they're hurt." Claire eyed the splint suspiciously.

"Come on." Jacob helped Connor to his feet.

Connor gasped, his face turning grey with pain as he tested his ankle. "It's great. Thanks." He looked up at the wall. "This should be easy."

"Claire, you go first," Jacob said. "Keep the torch low so we can see where we're going. Then you go, Connor."

"And what do you do?" Connor asked as he limped toward the wall.

"I push you up," Jacob said, hoping his voice sounded more confident than he felt.

Claire started climbing, awkwardly switching her torch from hand to hand, trying to give Connor light to climb by.

"Go without me," Connor whispered when Claire was a few feet above them. "I didn't make it up with two good legs. Take the girls and keep going. The Hag told you she would let us all out. Well, I'll wait here."

"Not a chance," Jacob said, trying to turn Connor toward the wall, but Connor clung to the front of Jacob's shirt.

"There are people aboveground who need saving. You won't get to them if I'm slowing you down." Connor's eyes were earnest. He meant it. He wanted to be left behind.

A low *rumble* shook the ceiling above them. The *roar* grew closer and fiercer. Water began to trickle down from the ceiling in the center of the chamber.

"Climb. Now," Jacob said, planting Connor's hands on the wall and half-lifting him as he started to climb.

Jacob looked back as he steadied Connor. A heavy stream of water poured from above.

Connor spat curses as he put his weight on his broken ankle.

Jacob grabbed the back of Connor's thigh and pushed up until Connor had his other foot back on the wall.

The water sloshed above Jacob's ankles, its smell of must and filth making him gag as he started up the wall. They stopped every few seconds, Jacob steadying Connor as he moved his good leg up the wall.

"I feel so close to you right now," Connor grunted as Jacob began to use his shoulder as a seat, pushing Connor to move more quickly. The water was rising fast, faster than they were climbing.

"Watch out!" Claire screamed as her torch fell past Jacob's face. He didn't turn to see what had happened to the torch. The sizzling as it hit the water meant it was useless.

"Sorry," Claire said.

Emilia reached down, dragging her to the top.

"Go," Jacob shouted up. "Both of you go, now!" The water was up to his waist.

"Climb ahead," Connor gasped, pulling himself up another painful step. "I'll catch up."

"Just keep moving." Jacob pushed Connor up higher. They were almost to the top. If they could make it just a few feet...

Jacob shook. The water was freezing and up to his chest now.

The wall crumbled under Connor's fingers, sending a stream of dirt onto Jacob's face. "Sorry," Connor grunted. "Almost there."

Emilia leaned as far over the wall as she could. If Jacob could lift Connor a foot more, she would be able to pull him up.

"Reach for my hands," Emilia said, her fingers dancing in the air as they searched for Connor's, making shadows creep across the wall in the light of the only torch they had left.

Jacob gave one final heave, lifting Connor as high as he dared.

"I got him," Emilia said.

Jacob felt Connor's weight leave him as the wall gave way. He heard Emilia's scream before the water closed over his head.

Jacob opened his eyes, but the dim torchlight was only a glimmer through the muddy water.

He kicked, fighting against the current he was sure would try to pull him down to the bottom where there would be no light, no air. He kicked as hard as he could, but there was no way to push himself up. He waited for his lungs to burn, but the pain didn't come. Instead a voice echoed in his head.

"How long until you drown? When will the darkness close around you forever? I give you a chance for light."

The water rushed past him, faster than wind. He felt the cold air whip his face for a moment before he hit the wall of the tunnel and dropped to the floor.

"Jacob!" Emilia knelt next to him, brushing the wet hair from his face. "Are you okay?"

"Fine," Jacob said, expecting to sound out of breath, but he just sounded tired.

"You went under, and I couldn't even see where." Emilia shook her head, holding Jacob's face in her hands.

"I'm so sorry," Connor said as Claire helped him lower himself to the ground.

"You didn't do anything." Jacob stood, shaking his hair out like a wet dog.

The roar of the water tumbling from the ceiling had stopped. The water rested perfectly level with their safe haven, still as glass, and blacker than water should ever be.

"She blocked the way back." Jacob ran his hands over his face. "Why do you have to block us in?" Jacob punched the dirt wall.

"We have to keep going forward," Claire said.

"I just need a minute," Connor said, his voice close to a whimper.

Jacob took a few steps down the darkened corridor. It was the only way out. Into the darkness. He was shivering. His clothes were soaked through. If only the Hag had decided to torment them with a nice warm bed.

"Here," Emilia said from behind him.

Jacob hadn't felt her standing there.

She planted the end of her torch in the ground and lifted his hands toward the warmth of the flame.

She shrugged out of her sweater and held it out to Jacob.

"I'm fine." Jacob pushed the sweater back to her. "I don't want you to get cold."

"You're the one who's shaking. I'll be fine." Emilia smiled, but her eyes were afraid.

"I won't let anything happen to you," Jacob said, dragging the sweater over his head. It was warm and smelled like lilacs.

"It's not me I'm worried about. I could have lost all three of you. And there was nothing I could do. I thought I knew what being a human felt like. Before, when the Pendragon had those awful cuffs on me to bind my power, I felt like I was covered in rubber. All of my magic was trapped inside with no way out." Emilia shuddered. "But now it feels like my magic is dead. I feel so hollow. It's hard to breathe. I couldn't help you. I can't fight. We have to find Rosalie, save Iz, Molly, Samuel, Larkin."

"And Dexter," Jacob said.

"I don't think he's—" Emilia began, her voice catching in her throat. "The Hag showed you what happened."

"She showed me you watching it all happen."

Emilia stiffened.

"I thought she was making you watch Aunt Iz, but it was him," Jacob said. "She wanted you to see him. You were terrified. You screamed for him."

Jacob's hands were shaking now, from more than just cold.

"Jacob," Emilia murmured.

"You care about him."

Emilia took his face in her hands and forced him to look at her.

"I want to hate him," Emilia said, "but he freed Larkin. You've seen what the Pendragon can do. Is it so hard to believe he manipulated Dexter?"

Jacob ran his hands over his face, digging his palms hard into his eyes. "You dated for a long time." It felt like someone had stabbed a knife into his throat. "You care about him."

"He saved Larkin," Emilia whispered. "I know you don't really know her, but she's like my big sister."

"And now you're free from me and want to be with Larkin's savior."

Emilia flinched as though he had slapped her. Jacob turned and paced into the darkness, grateful his magic was gone. He felt like he would explode, and his magic might have let him.

"I never said that," Emilia said softly. "I don't want to be with Dexter."

"You were crying for him." Jacob turned back to her, ripping his hands through his hair.

"I don't want him to die," Emilia said, her face furious as she strode over to Jacob. "He messed up. He betrayed us all. I could never trust Dexter Wayland. I would never ever want to date Dexter Wayland again. But I don't want him to die to protect us. Jacob"— Emilia laid her hands on his chest—"the way he was fighting, he wanted to die. He was sacrificing himself, even when he didn't need to. If those rocks killed him, it would be my fault. And if the Dragons captured him, it would be even worse."

She was right. They had tortured him and Larkin just for trying to rescue Emilia. What would the Dragons do to Dexter?

"I know Dexter," Emilia said, her voice barely above a whisper. "Even if he did some awful things, he was still a part of my life." Emilia swallowed, staring desperately into Jacob's eyes. "And I can't keep losing people."

Jacob drew Emilia into his arms. She buried her face on his shoulder.

"I'm sorry," Emilia murmured.

"Don't be," Jacob said, his lips brushing the top of her head.

"No one deserves to be a prisoner of the Dragons. But they could have made it out. Even if he was hurt, Iz wouldn't leave him."

"If I'm going to hobble through this hell maze, I think I'd like to start now," Connor said, his breath hissing through his teeth as Claire hoisted him to his feet.

"Let me help." Jacob ran over and wrapped Connor's arm around his shoulder. They did need to keep moving. Only the Hag knew how much farther they had to go.

SAFELY HOME

*E*milia led the way, holding her torch high. Claire was under one of Connor's arms and Jacob the other. Connor gasped and winced with every step.

"We should rest," Claire whispered after a while.

Connor's face had turned an eerie shade of green.

"Not yet," Connor said through clenched teeth. "I can do a bit more."

The tunnel twisted lazily around, sloping up and down as though it had no purpose other than to make them keep moving.

"I see something. I think it's a—" Emilia stopped, kneeling down and reaching her hand forward.

"It's a what?" Claire asked.

"We're going to have to crawl through" Emilia lowered her torch for them all to see.

The tunnel had narrowed and turned to rock. There was a hole at the base of the wall that would barely be big enough for Jacob to squeeze through.

"Well, at least it's something different." Connor slid down the rock wall.

"I'll go first," Jacob said, running his hand along the stone opening, half-expecting it to grow teeth and bite his arm off.

"I should go," Emilia said. "I have the light."

"Which means you should stay with the others." Jacob flattened himself to the ground. "She spit me out of the water. I doubt she'll crush me."

Jacob stuck his head through the opening, wishing for a light on the other side. But there was nothing, no sign of how long the tunnel might be. He twisted his shoulders sideways and pushed himself into the wall. Digging his fingers into the rock, he inched his way forward, pushing as hard as he could with his feet.

But soon there wasn't enough room for his knees to bend. He was trapped, caught between rocks. Alone in the dark. Jacob twisted his neck. Beyond his feet, he could see the light glinting. He had to keep moving. They had to go forward, and he had to get out of the others' way.

His fingers ripped on the rocks. His knees bruised from banging into the stone wall. How long would he have to do this? He reached as high above his head as he could, but there was no rock wall, only air. Jacob gripped the edge of the tunnel and pulled, his shoulders screaming and the skin on his sides tearing as he pulled himself into the open air and scrambled to his feet.

"It's only about fifteen feet," he shouted at the opening.

No one responded.

"Emi."

He knelt down, feeling in the darkness for the opening he had just crawled through, but it was gone. A solid, smooth stone had taken its place.

"Emilia!" Jacob felt behind, but there was no wall, only open air. He took a step forward, sure he hadn't moved that far from the opening in the wall. He took a step back, grateful to find the stone wall still there. Kneeling, he crawled to the right and left, searching for the opening, but it was gone. The Hag had sealed him in.

"Bring Emilia back," Jacob said, his voice cold and calm. "Open the tunnel, and bring Emilia here now."

A hand wrapped around Jacob's ankle in the darkness. Jacob pulled his foot free, leaping away.

"I found the end," Claire shouted.

Jacob took a step forward.

"Jacob is that you?" The hand patted Jacob's foot.

"It's me." Jacob knelt.

"He's here," Claire called as she wriggled out of the crack. "We called for you. Why didn't you answer?"

"I was trying to, but I couldn't hear you or find the opening."

"Come on, Connor. It's not that bad, I—" Claire stopped. "I can't find the opening," Claire said, the slapping of her hands on the rocks echoing in the dark. "I can't find the way out."

"That's because it isn't the way out," Jacob sighed. "It's only the way in."

~

"Jacob? Claire, did you find him?" Emilia held her breath, waiting for a noise, a *thump*, anything that meant they were still alive and moving.

"Claire," Connor called into the darkness.

Still, there was nothing.

"You take the torch," Emilia said, pressing it into Connor's hand. "I'll go see if I can find them."

"In the dark?" Connor handed the torch back. "While I sit here and defend us from the rear? I'll go and see if I can find them."

Connor lowered himself to the ground. His slim shoulders let him crawl on his stomach like Claire had.

"Keep talking," Emilia said as Connor started to move forward. "Keep talking to me."

"Well," Connor said as he dragged himself forward, "a few

days ago, I was studying with the centaurs and living on the preserve. I had moved up to broadsword training. Then we were attacked, and the centaurs started cutting people's heads off, which really turned me off of the whole sword concept. I think I'm going to be sticking to my wand for a while." There was a muffled grunt.

"What happened?" Emilia pushed the torch into the crack and leaned in as far as she could, trying to see Connor.

"Nothing. Banged my ankle, more pain and suffering. Where was I? Oh right, then we lost the best mentor I've ever had. Then we ran to another safe place that really wasn't safe at all, only to be surrounded by a nice watery death threat to pretty much the whole magical world. Now, I'm crawling through a stone crack with a broken leg and no magic, so I would say my December has been a real pile of—"

"Connor," Emilia said softly. "Connor!"

He was gone, swallowed by the darkness.

Emilia curled up, her head in her hands. She had to go forward. There was no way back. Jacob was forward. But if something was wrong and she got herself stuck, how could she help them? But then how could she help them stuck out here?

Emilia looked to the ceiling. "If you hurt them, I will find a way to hurt you. I don't care how long you keep us trapped. I don't care how strong your magic is. I will find you, and I will hurt you."

Emilia waited, expecting the Hag to smite her or at least crush her with rocks, but there was nothing. Only silence and the tunnel in front of her.

Emilia cursed at the ceiling before placing her torch in the crack and beginning to crawl.

The light made the tunnel seem to shrink in front of her. She was like Alice, too big to fit through the door.

"Jacob," Emilia called, her heart pounding in her chest. "Jacob!"

The rocks scraped her arms and legs. She could feel bruises forming on her shoulders and knees. Twice, she nearly dropped the torch trying to pull herself forward.

Was this where the others were? Crawling through an endless tunnel? Alone? Tears dripped from Emilia's eyes to the filthy stone floor. If she could find them, just find them alive, it would be all right.

Emilia forced herself to look to the end of the tunnel, choking on her tears. The end was close. A wall of black her light could not pass through. "Are you there?"

Her torch pierced the black, sending her into darkness. Is that what happened to them all? Were the others swallowed by a sea of inky blackness?

Emilia moved forward, brushing her fingers against the dark. It felt like air, like nothing. She took a deep breath and reached farther into the void. A hand closed around hers, pulling her forward. Before Emilia could gasp, strong arms had wrapped around her.

Jacob held her tight, his cheek pressed to her hair.

"I'm okay," Emilia said, looking up into his bright, blue eyes. Her heart skipped a beat. Jacob brushed the tears from her cheeks before pulling her back into his arms.

His heart beat loud and strong in his chest, but she couldn't feel it echoing with her own. A moment ago he could have been dead, and she wouldn't have known it.

"Where are we now?" Emilia turned away from Jacob, holding her torch up high.

They were trapped in a room the same size as their cabin had been. There were no breaks in the solid stone walls. Emilia looked up at the ceiling, hoping they weren't going to have to climb again. But there was no break in the stone above them, either.

Plink, plop.

The sound echoed through the room.

Plop, smack.

Drops of water fell from the ceiling, forming puddles on the stone floor.

"Again?" Claire screamed. "Gonna trap us in here and fill it with water? Well that's just great since I really felt like treading water today!"

But the water wasn't spreading across the floor. It was forming five pools.

"Look," Emilia gasped, running to the pool in the far corner. The most beautiful and warm golden light radiated from its center. "It's gorgeous."

"Look at that one." Claire stared open-mouthed at another pool. "It's so bright."

But Emilia couldn't see anything.

"No, this one is." Connor had lowered himself next to a pool and was gazing into it, rapture filling his face.

"My light is in that one." Jacob pointed to the pool to the left of Emilia's, but he didn't leave her side.

Emilia took his hand in hers before leaning over the pool and gazing into its brilliant glow.

"It's them." Emilia squinted through the light, trying to see every detail.

It was Iz, Larkin, Molly, Samuel, and Dexter all fighting their way through the woods at Graylock.

"It's them. They're safe." Tears streamed down Emilia's cheeks. She knelt next to the pool, wanting to see every detail. "Dexter didn't get hurt." Jacob's hand flinched in hers. "He's helping Samuel. Molly's fighting one of the guards, but I think Iz has a way for them to get out."

"Molly's not fighting," Connor said from his pool. "She's back home at the High Peaks Preserve. She's with my dad. But..." Connor paused. "It's not happening now. It can't be."

"Why?" Jacob asked.

"Because I'm there, too," Connor said.

"I can see myself in my pool, too," Claire said, longing filling her voice.

Jacob let go of Emilia's hand, but she followed him the few steps to his pool. All she could see was less than an inch of water and the rock beneath.

"It's us," Jacob said, his voice soft, a sad smile filling his face. "We're home. We're at the table at the Mansion House."

"Can we go there through the water?" Claire asked, reaching her arm down deep into her pool.

"Claire, don't," Emilia shouted, running over and lifting Claire away from the water.

"But *there* is better than *here*." Claire turned back to her pool.

"There is no *there*," Emilia said, reaching in and touching the rock beneath the water.

"Yes, there is." Claire knelt down and reached her arm into the water up to her elbow.

Emilia walked back over to her pool and reached her hand down into the water. The water was warm and deep. The fighting was over now. They were driving away, Iz behind the wheel.

"Give me your hand," Emilia said, reaching for Jacob. He knelt next to her. They had jumped into another world together. They should be able to go to Aunt Iz now.

She laced her fingers through Jacob's, his palm resting on the back of her hand. Emilia dipped her hand into the water, but Jacob's stopped just below the surface.

"Try again," Emilia said, switching so her hand was on top of Jacob's, but his fingers could barely touch the water.

"What now?" Claire walked to the pool in the center of the room.

The surface had begun to shimmer red, casting its horrible light on the walls, making the shadows seem to drip blood.

"Can you see the light, too?" Emilia asked, walking to the center pool and staring down into its depths. But she didn't need

Claire's answer to know she could see. The horrified look on her face was enough.

This pool glowed crimson, and its scene was not one of triumph or joy.

The hillside was covered in blood, shining red in the light of the spells flying above it. Bodies lay on the ground, twisted and broken by swords and spells. A dark figure leaped over a body lying face down in the dirt, a boy with dark blond hair who didn't move. Emilia searched the faces of the fighters. Could this be Graylock? But her own shining, black hair appeared in the pool. Her face contorted with rage as she cursed an unknown foe.

Emilia turned away. If this was her future, she didn't want to know the ending.

"This is the only one we can all see?" Connor asked, his voice already quavering with the answer.

"So." Claire shuddered. "We either jump into the happy pools alone or the death pool together. I really think the whole treading water thing would have been better."

"I'm going to the fight," Jacob said.

"Why?" Emilia asked, forcing herself to keep breathing as she wondered if dead boy with the blond hair in the pool had been Jacob.

"Because we have to get through the fight before we can go home anyway. And if I go into that Mansion House"—Jacob pointed at his pool—"it won't be real."

"I'm going with you." Emilia gripped Jacob's hand.

"Because happiness has to be earned with fighting?" Connor sank to the ground.

"Because it's where Jacob is going," Emilia whispered. Her throat was tight. The scene of Graylock was a lie. They would have to fight to know if the rescue party was alive and hope they could survive to find out.

"Well, let's all jump in and hope we don't die." Claire yanked

Connor back to his feet. "Maybe this is what's waiting for us. But at least we'd be free."

"On three?" Emilia asked.

"Forget three." Connor stepped into the water. The light flashed red as he disappeared.

"See you." Claire balled her hands into tight fists before stepping into the water.

"Our turn," Jacob said as the light that had swallowed Claire began to fade.

"One, two, three." Together, they stepped into the water and fell.

A PERFECT PARADISE

*J*acob felt Emilia twist away from him as they sped through the dark. He wouldn't let her be dragged away. He tightened his grip on her hand, and her arms wrapped around him. White light flashed in Jacob's eyes before he saw the ground racing toward them. Twisting, he lifted Emilia to fall on top of him. He hit the ground with a grunt, shielding Emilia from the hard earth.

"Thanks," Emilia murmured, rolling off of Jacob and tumbling to the ground.

Pain seized Jacob's back as he turned over. His hand met something soft and warm on the ground. They were lying in grass. Jacob ran his fingers over the bright green blades. The ground was warm as though the sun had just been shining on it.

Something tiny and white drifted through the torchlight.

Jacob reached out to catch it, assuming he would find some sort of insect in his hand.

He opened his fingers slowly, but lying in his palm was a tiny speck of white.

"Emi." Jacob held his hand out for her to see. But Emilia's eyes were tracking more tiny bits of white floating toward them.

"Snow," Connor said. "We must be getting toward the surface."

Claire ran ahead. "It means it's snowing on Christmas!"

"Christmas was days ago," Connor called after her.

"Don't ruin my childlike dreams!" Clare shouted back.

"Claire, slow down." Emilia quickened her pace.

"There's something different up here." Claire froze.

"What is it?" Jacob asked, helping Connor limp after the girls, but in the few feet he had to cross, Claire had already gasped, staring at the scene in front of her.

Jacob opened his mouth to ask if she was hurt but lost the words as he stared into the vast cavern before them.

He couldn't see how large the cavern was, only that it was too large for Emilia's torchlight to reach the other side. White birch trees grew in the cavern. Some straight and tall, as though reaching for a sun he could not see, and some curved and bent by a wind he couldn't feel. But each of them reflected the flame of the torch, sending sparkling light dancing from tree to tree.

"It's beautiful." Emilia stepped into the cavern. As her torchlight entered the room, its fire reached the ceiling, sending flickering waves of light across its dazzling surface.

"What is this place?" Connor asked.

"Probably some kind of trap." Claire reached out to touch a tree.

As her fingers grazed the papery bark, a wind stirred, sending flakes of white swirling through the air, floating around them like a shower of petals in a spring wind.

"I mean, if we have to walk into a death trap, this isn't so bad." Claire sat on the grass that blanketed the ground.

"We can't stop here," Emilia said, taking Claire's hand and trying to pull her to her feet.

"Actually, we can," Connor said, lowering himself shakily down next to Claire and lying back in the grass. "The Hag said we would get out of here in time to find Rosalie, right? We've been walking for what feels like a week, not to mention I don't know how much more my ankle can take. Let's sit and rest for a minute."

"Or sleep for a few hours." Claire lay down. "If we get out of here exhausted, we won't be in as good a shape to fight the Pendragon. Think of this as a no penalty nap. We don't lose time, and we get to sleep."

Jacob looked at Emilia. Her face was pale, and her eyes looked tired. "She's right. You need to rest. We all do."

"But—" Emilia began.

"If the Hag wants to trap us, she'll do it whether we sleep or not." Jacob lay down in the grass.

Emilia chewed her bottom lip. "Fine, but the first one to wake up gets the others up, all right?" Emilia knelt down on the grass. She stuck her torch into the earth, its flames still dancing, before curling up on Jacob's shoulder. Her breath was even and steady before he could whisper, "Sleep well," into her ear.

~

he girl in the mirror barely looked like her. The eyes were the same grey, but everything else seemed different. Emilia touched her cheek, watching the girl in the mirror do the same. Her long, black hair was curled and elegant, sweeping gently along her neck. Her face looked calm, happy, and healthy. She turned slightly, and the beads on the front of her white dress shimmered in the light.

"You look beautiful," Aunt Iz said, lifting a veil to place it onto Emilia's head.

Iz beamed as she adjusted the delicate lace to frame Emilia's face.

"Aunt Iz," Emilia said, shaking her head. "I don't understand."

"Some people deserve happy endings." Claire handed Emilia a bouquet of delicate white roses.

"Where did you come from?" Emilia asked. Claire hadn't been in the room a moment before.

"Everyone's here for your wedding." Claire laughed, spinning in her pale pink bridesmaid's dress. The chiffon of her skirt floated in the air.

"It's time." Samuel appeared next to Emilia, holding his arm out to her.

"Samuel," Emilia gasped, throwing her arms around his neck. He was here. Whole and happy. Emilia took his face in her hands, studying each of the creases near his eyes when he smiled at her.

"I thought I would never see you again." Tears streamed down Emilia's cheeks.

"I would never miss this," Samuel said.

"You look perfect, baby," Rosalie's soft voice came from behind Emilia.

"Rosalie," Emilia whispered.

"Shh," Rosalie hushed, kissing Emilia on the forehead.

"I was so afraid," Emilia said, wiping tears away with the back of her hand.

"No crying. You'll ruin your makeup, and you haven't even seen the groom yet," Claire said.

"It's time." Molly waved a hand through the air, and the room dissolved.

They were in the garden at the Mansion House. Candles hovered everywhere, casting a glowing light onto everyone. Larkin stood next to Proteus. Sabbe twisted her head to look at Emilia with her good eye, her face alight with joy, her white coat shining next to Raven's shimmering black.

And at the end of the aisle stood Jacob, beaming at her in his suit, gazing at her as though she were not just the most beautiful thing in the world, but the only thing that could ever matter.

"You can thank me later for getting him into the suit," Claire whispered as she half-skipped down the aisle in front of Emilia.

"Ready?" Samuel said, wrapping Emilia's arm through his elbow.

"Is this real?" Emilia whispered only loudly enough for Samuel to hear.

"If this is what you want," Samuel said.

Emilia took her first step down the aisle, toward Jacob, toward happiness and life. Connor stepped forward, standing next to Jacob, his red hair clashing so horribly with the pale pink of his vest Emilia laughed.

Jacob's laugh joined hers, his joy radiating toward her as she took each slow step.

Professor Eames smiled, standing next to Jacob, his arms outstretched, welcoming Emilia to her future.

With a gut-wrenching crack, *Larkin fell into the dark ground.*

"No!" Emilia screamed. "No!"

Samuel and Iz disappeared from her side.

"Please stop!"

The centaurs disappeared with a shattering crack.

"Help!" Rosalie was gone. There was no one left but Jacob and the professor, standing impossibly far from her.

"Jacob!" Emilia called for him, but he had already been swallowed by the darkness.

DECIDED

"*J*acob." Emilia's muffled sob wrenched Jacob from sleep.

"Emilia!" Jacob sat up, his gaze sweeping over the trees, expecting blood or danger. But Emilia was curled up next to him on the grass, sobbing and reaching for some unseen thing. Her eyes were shut tight as the nightmare kept her in its grip.

"Emi," Jacob whispered, pulling her into his arms. "Emi, you're okay."

Emilia woke with a gasp, pushing herself away from Jacob and staring wildly around the cavern.

"Emilia," Jacob said gently, holding out a hand to her. "It's all right. You were having a nightmare."

Emilia looked at him, her eyes focusing on his face in the dim light before she launched herself at him, sobbing again.

"You're safe," Jacob whispered, rocking Emilia gently in his arms.

Claire stirred in the grass, mumbling something Jacob couldn't understand and rolling closer to Connor, who lay still on his back, his mouth wide open.

"I won't let anyone hurt you." Jacob held Emilia even tighter.

"Oh, God," Emilia sobbed before standing and running into the trees.

"Emilia," Jacob called after her, chasing her pale figure into the dark.

She was deep into the trees before Jacob caught up to her, curled up and sobbing into the grass.

"Emilia," he said softly, wanting to reach out and hold her, but afraid she would run again. "It was just a dream." He knelt down beside her. "What happened?"

"It was my wedding," Emilia whispered, her breath ragged. "Our wedding."

Jacob's heart stopped. It was him. She was crying and running away from him.

"I had a dress, and Claire, and Samuel, and Iz, and Rosalie. Everyone was there." Emilia pressed a hand over her mouth. "But it can't happen, it'll never happen." Emilia shook her head, sending tears flying from her face.

"It could," Jacob said, his voice shaking. "I could stay human."

"What?"

"I lived without magic most of my life," Jacob said, hoping he had the strength to get the words out. "I'll stay human. No more tethering. You could marry whoever you want. White dress, flowers, all of it. You could be happy."

Emilia stayed silent for a moment. He wished he knew what she was feeling, but that was part of the bond he had to leave behind.

"Eames was the one performing the ceremony," Emilia said, her voice low and hollow. "Then everyone started to disappear, just falling away. My whole family, gone. And then you." Emilia took Jacob's hand, pressing it to her tearstained face. "It doesn't matter if we beat the Pendragon tonight. My family is still broken."

"Emilia—"

"I won't lose you, too."

"You wouldn't lose me," Jacob said. "I would still be here. I would still be your—" He couldn't bring himself to say the world *friend*. "I will always be here when you need me."

"I need you all the time. You're the one I want. You always were, I just didn't know it. We should have had years to figure that out. I would have dumped Dexter. And you would have been there. We would have dated and grown up. Then someday you would have gotten down on one knee and asked me to marry you. We would have had the perfect wedding in the garden. But I won't lose our future because someone pushed us into it too soon. I won't lose you." Emilia leaned forward, her lips brushing against Jacob's. "I love you, Jacob Evans."

Jacob breathed in Emilia's scent. Lilacs. It was really her, and she really loved him. He took her face in his hands, brushing away her tears.

"Emilia," he breathed.

Clap, clap, clap. The noise echoed from the tress behind them.

"Well done," the Hag said, still clapping slowly and sarcastically. "You know, I really thought it would take her much longer to figure out what she wanted. I mean, the girl's been waffling about it for how long now?"

"It was you." Emilia stood, pointing a quivering finger at the Hag. "You made me have that nightmare."

"I don't play in people's heads." The Hag smirked. "If I'm going to play with someone, I want to be able to see what happens. I may be a Hag, but I can't float into people's minds and watch like television. Your nightmares are your own."

"You just trap people in your crazy tunnels and take away their powers," Emilia spat.

"Oh, you're done here," the Hag said, taking a step closer to Emilia. "We had a deal." The Hag turned to Jacob. "She really does want you." She shrugged.

"I love him," Emilia said.

"Enough to keep risking his life?" the Hag asked. "I think it's clear he would die to protect you, but would you want him to?"

"Of course not," Emilia said, taking Jacob's hand tightly in her own.

"You want to stay a witch to go save your mommy. He wants to go with you to protect you. But *I* could protect *him*," the Hag whispered, her eyes for the first time seeming afraid. "I could keep him human. Keep him safe with me. The magical world may crumble, but I will endure. I always endure. Let him live, safe, with me."

Emilia turned to Jacob, her eyes filled with confusion. "If he comes with me, will he be hurt? Will the Pendragon—" Emilia stopped, her hand trembling in Jacob's. "Will he kill him?"

"There is no way to know," the Hag said. "The Gray Clan is crumbling, and the losses are only beginning."

"I could come back for you," Emilia whispered, leaning in close to Jacob, "as soon as the Pendragon is gone."

"Emi—"

"You would be safe here," Emilia cut across. "You've done so much to protect me. I'll save Rosalie and come back for you."

"Oh, silly child, no amount of magic will let you have everything. You have to make a choice," the Hag said. "Rosalie will never be free if you don't fight with Jacob by your side. You can't win a war alone, little Gray. If you want to kill your father, you need your boyfriend's help. The tethering makes you stronger. Makes your magic more than you could ever hope to be on your own. Makes you able to ignite the forest without getting burned."

The trees around them began to flicker. Jacob gasped, pushing Emilia behind him as flames devoured the trees and screams echoed in the distance.

"The well runs deep, Jacob," the Hag whispered, her faint voice cutting through the pained cries, "and with your *coniunx* at your side, it has no end."

His heart raced at the screams grew louder. "It wasn't just my magic."

The flames on the trees disappeared, and the voices vanished.

"It was both of us, together," Emilia whispered.

"The Pendragon is the strongest wizard I've seen in many years. Only one other comes close to his power. And you, little girl Gray, brought the Pendragon back the other half of his soul. You've made him more dangerous than ever before and have no hope of defeating him alone."

"But we could fight him together. We're stronger together, Emi. I'm coming with you. That is my choice to make," Jacob said, looking into Emilia's fear-filled eyes. "I've already lost my whole family once. I won't be left behind again. I don't care about safe. I couldn't survive hiding while you, while anyone in our family, was in danger. I love you, Emilia. If we fight, we fight together."

"Together." Emilia wrapped her arms around him, pulling herself close.

He would do anything to protect her. And if she loved him, that meant always being by her side.

She kissed him, their lips touching gently, before letting the kiss become more urgent. He felt Emilia sigh as heat began to glow in the center of his chest. A light that felt like the soul of magic itself coursed through his veins. Jacob gasped as his lungs filled for what seemed like the first time in years.

Emilia pulled herself closer to him, and everywhere their bodies met, heat flooded through him. Jacob's heart began to race, and in one brilliant moment, he could feel Emilia's heart beating joyfully with his own.

Magic burst from within him. Golden light surrounded them, and they were frozen, Jacob gazing into Emilia's eyes. Calm and happy grey eyes.

This was where they belonged. Whatever was to come, they would meet it together.

Emilia took Jacob's hand, lifting it up to see the golden streak shining across his palm. She pressed the mark to her lips, kissing the glow that showed their bond.

Jacob brushed the hair back from her face, and she smiled at him before turning to the Hag.

"We have our magic back," Emilia said. "Now tell us who the traitor is, and let us out of here."

THE IMMORTAL CROWS

"You know, I think I may have been immortal for too long," the Hag laughed. "I forget what it's like to be in such a desperate hurry all the time. It must be exhausting."

"You promised you would tell us when we got our magic back." Emilia's voice dripped with anger she could no longer conceal. "We went through your tunnels. We performed like ponies so you could have a good laugh. We survived. Now tell us—"

"You survived, but survival wasn't the point. This wasn't for my entertainment. Haven't you realized by now that everything I have done has been with a purpose? Can't you see it?" The Hag's eyes gleamed in the dim light, making her terrifying in her fervor.

"No," Jacob said, before Emilia could speak. "No more questions, please." His voice trembled. "No more lies. No more tests. No more darkness and tunnels. I love Emilia. She loves me. We are going to heal Connor and get out there. We'll save Emilia's mother and keep fighting the Pendragon. And maybe you're right. Maybe we'll all die trying. But it's our choice to fight, and it's our choice to do it together."

"It is your choice to fight and die, Jacob Evans. I've done all I can. You were left for years to wander alone. I have been alone for centuries. When magic crumbles, I will be left alone for a thousand years because a boy loved a girl more than he wanted eternity. You have condemned us both to darkness," the Hag said, her voice low and quiet, not with anger but with sadness. "You will fight. You have to. The Pendragon will kill countless humans. And then the humans will kill all of you.

"The humans stumble through life in the dark, without power, without hope. They will swarm over us like ants until there is nothing left of our world. But you feel sorry for the little ants. So you will fight for them. For the little creatures with enough hate in their hearts to destroy all of Magickind. If you don't stop the Pendragon, our world will burn, and the humans will start the fire. You could be saved. You're strong enough." The Hag reached out to Jacob. "You could be like me. Beautiful and powerful until the end of magic itself. Together, we would endure the flames."

"No," Jacob said, taking the Hag's hand. "I'll fight with Emilia."

"You'll give up an eternity to wallow in blood and violence? As you wish." The Hag flicked Jacob's hand away, all trace of sadness gone from her voice, and turned to study Emilia. "You really do love him, don't you?" The Hag tilted her head as though trying to catch Emilia in the light. "How pleasant to be surprised after all this time. Perhaps watching the world end won't be so dull after all. It doesn't matter if he'll die by the Pendragon's hand or not. He won't leave you. And besides, if you fail, all of you will die soon enough."

The Hag's words hung in the air. Emilia felt as though her chest would explode. If Jacob died because of her…

"Tell us who the traitor is," Jacob said.

"I would have thought you'd have guessed by now. No matter." The Hag shrugged. "MAGI Jeremy Stone."

Emilia forgot to breathe as her mind raced.

"He let the Dragons into the MAGI headquarters so they could destroy everything. He told the Pendragon which plane you would be on and how to find you in New York. That you had gone to Graylock to rescue Emilia. That Larkin was there, too."

"He knew where Connor and Claire were," Emilia said, forcing the words past her rage and panic. "He knew we were at Elder's Keep. And Rosalie. He knew where she was hidden."

"Imagine how proud he must have felt when he told your darling daddy he could bring your mother to him. And how he will be rewarded for helping to lure you out tonight," the Hag said, examining Emilia's face.

Sparks flew from Emilia's hands as her blood boiled, seething with an anger that didn't feel like it could possibly be her own. Never before had she wanted to kill.

Emilia clenched her fists, feeling the sparks burn her palms. "We'll find him. We'll find them both."

"And what will happen when you do?" The Hag asked. "Will you fight?"

"Yes," Emilia spat.

"You're walking into a trap set by one of the most powerful wizards alive," the Hag said, all traces of her smile gone. "He is dangerous and evil beyond your measly little comprehension. But please, go and fight."

"You could help us," Jacob said. "You could fight with us. With you on our side, we could stop the Pendragon tonight."

"I cannot live. I cannot die. Why would you think I have the ability to take a life? The only way for me to murder is to influence others and then watch time do its work. I cannot fight the Pendragon for you because the only way to defeat the Pendragon is to kill him. Why would I fight if I can't win?" The Hag turned and walked away through the trees. "Leave when you like, though truth be told, you would be better off staying down here." Her voice hung in Emilia's ear as though she were standing next to her. "And good luck, Jacob Evans. Try not to die."

Emilia wanted to scream, to toss spells at the Hag's head. "Connor," she said instead. "We need to heal him." Emilia turned to walk back through the trees.

"Emi, wait." Jacob caught her around the waist.

"She traps us down here to tell us we need to kill the Pendragon," Emilia said. "To try and convince you to become like her so she can have a toy to play with if the world ends. And now if something happens to you—"

"I would rather die fighting by your side than live a thousand years without you." Jacob held Emilia tight. Her heart lightened at his touch, his warmth flooding through her. "Nothing the Hag could do would ever change that."

"And if we walk into his trap and the Pendragon kills you?" Emilia choked out the words. "I won't lose you. I can't survive that."

"Then we'll have to make sure we win." Jacob kissed Emilia's forehead.

Emilia's soul shivered at the words that hung so heavy in the air.

We'll have to make sure we kill your father.

~

"*C*onnor," Jacob said, softly shaking Connor's shoulder. "Wake up."

"Don't touch him!" Claire shouted, bolting upright, her eyes wide.

"It's us, Claire," Emilia said, brushing away the blond hair that stuck to Claire's sleep-creased face.

"Oh." Claire blinked as she looked from Jacob to Emilia. "Sorry. Bad dream."

"Connor." Jacob shook Connor harder.

"Wake up." Claire flicked Connor's ear.

"What? What do you want?" Connor said, rubbing his ear.

"We have our magic back," Jacob said. He could feel Emilia's fear and anger, but he smiled. Connor and Claire didn't need to know why or how. Not now.

"*Pelluere.*" Jacob touched the tip of his wand to Connor's leg. The magic flowed from him. His fingers tingled, and his breath caught in his chest.

Connor gasped and dug his fingers into the dirt. There was a horrible *crack* that turned Jacob's stomach before Connor lay back in the grass, his face sweaty and his eyes clenched shut. "Thanks," he grunted after a minute.

Claire dug her fingers into the ground and, after chewing on her lips for a moment, pulled out a tiny, filthy pebble. Cupping her hands around it she muttered, "*Sarubesco.*" A bright, rose-colored light shown from her hands before she opened them, revealing a pink sapphire. "What?" she asked, wrinkling her nose at Connor's bemused expression. "I made it through this hell hole. I think I deserve a present."

"So what do we do now?" Connor asked, shaking his head and standing up, gently shifting his weight on and off his healed leg.

"We get out of here," Jacob said, looking around.

An echoing *crack* shook the ceiling of the cavern. Jacob covered his head as a stream of earth crumbled onto them. He coughed the dirt from his throat and brushed a cloud of brown from his hair.

A distant and rhythmic thumping pounded high above.

A rectangle of light had appeared over their heads. As Jacob watched, a fine silver ladder fell from the light, landing at Jacob's feet. Jacob reached out and touched the polished metal. It vibrated with each *thump* from above. Delicate scrolls were carved into each rung. Flowers and spirals covered every inch. A note was attached to the front.

Jacob read the two words written in a hand he had only seen once before.

I tried.

The paper burst into flames that did not burn him as he crumpled the ashes in his hands.

"What did it say?" Emilia asked.

"Good luck." Jacob pulled himself up the first rung of the ladder.

The ceiling of the dome was more than a hundred feet up. Jacob was first to climb. The ladder swayed when any of them moved. Every time the ladder twitched, he warred with himself. He wanted to look down to make sure everyone was all right, but if he looked down and saw how high he had climbed, would he be able to grab the next rung up?

Every second, the pounding from above them grew louder. It sounded like a giant having a temper tantrum, beating his fists on the ground. Jacob had never thought to ask if giants existed. What if the Pendragon had found one and brought it with him? Were there spells to fight a giant?

"I'm getting really tired of climbing things," Connor called from below. "Next time we rescue someone, no climbing, all right?"

"Sure. We'll just negotiate that into the bargain with the psycho killer. *Excuse me,*" Claire said in a very formal tone, " *but we really must insist that next time you're threatening someone's life as a trap to lure us out of hiding, you do it in a nice, easy to reach place. Preferably with cake and central heating.* I think he'd go for it."

The pounding from above was joined by a new noise. A low, rolling melody.

"Guitar," Jacob said. "It's a guitar. We're hearing the concert."

"The Hag did say she'd let us out there," Emilia said. "Somehow, I didn't think she meant it so literally."

"When we get up there," Jacob said, climbing faster now that their goal was in sight, "Claire and Connor, you stay back. Try again to get ahold of Iz and Proteus. Warn them about Stone, he's the one feeding the Pendragon information on all of us."

"That slimy, dirty, son of a," Claire shouted up the ladder.

"Claire," Emilia cut in.

"We trusted him. I was nice to him!" Claire growled.

"And Aunt Iz will take care of him," Emilia said, anger resonating in her voice. "She needs to know as soon as possible. Jacob and I will go look for Rosalie."

Silence carried up the ladder.

"Got it?" Jacob asked.

"Claire, Connor, do you understand?" Emilia said, sounding frighteningly like Aunt Iz.

"Got it. Stay in the rear, be lookouts, give warnings, find help," Connor said.

"And be ready to run in and save both your butts when you realize that while you were out cliff jumping, Connor and I were being trained to fight, so maybe, just maybe, if you're going to have a battle with the evil wizard who has your mother, you might want our help," Claire added.

"It isn't about not wanting help," Jacob called down. The roar of the crowd from the concert above was loud enough to make him shout. "It's about keeping you safe." He reached the last rung of the ladder. The cold winter air lifted the hair on his head. The crowd above cheered. The band had just finished a song.

"Ready?" Emilia asked.

He could feel how close she was, and how afraid, even though her voice was calm.

"Yep." Jacob grabbed the earth and pushed himself up to the surface.

He pulled himself out of the ground and scrambled to his knees, turning to take Emilia's hand, but before he could look back at the hole in the ground, he was knocked over and trod on. Jacob coughed and pushed himself back up. He was surrounded by a packed sea of legs, their owners all seemingly oblivious to the hole in the ground.

Jacob leaped to his feet as Emilia pushed herself up. He took her hands and lifted her to her feet before she could get stepped on.

"Sorry," a teenage girl with dyed black hair and piercings covering her face said as she bumped into Emilia while dancing with her hands over her head, "didn't see you."

"They can't see the hole," Jacob screamed into Emilia's ear over the music.

They took up positions on either side of the hole as first Claire emerged and then Connor.

"So, we're waiting outside the concert?" Connor screamed.

Jacob looked to Emilia. They were in the center of a mass of bodies. Who knew how many men the Pendragon had brought with him? Stone would have told him Claire and Connor would be staying with them. He would know to look for them here. If the Dragons found Connor and Claire, they could kill them before Jacob and Emilia knew what was happening.

Emilia chewed her bottom lip, her brow furrowed. "We stay together."

"Now we're getting somewhere," Claire said as Connor pulled his wand from his pocket and held it casually at his side.

Linked together like a train, they waded into the surging mass of bodies, Jacob holding onto Emilia, who held onto Claire, who held onto Connor.

The vibrations of the speakers shook Jacob's chest, making his heart pound even harder as though it were trying to drown out the noise of the drums. There were thousands of people on this lawn. If the Pendragon really was here, how many of them could he kill before anyone even knew what was happening?

Jacob shuddered, his blood turning to ice. He tightened his grip on Emilia's hand and pulled her farther into the crowd. She had been snatched from him on a packed street once. He wouldn't let that happen again.

The band ended the number, their guitars screeching one final riff. The crowd screamed and cheered.

"We'll be right back!" The singer's voice echoed through the speaker over the crowd. He took a beer and shook it before spraying the audience. The girls at the front of the stage laughed and squealed. One took off her soaked shirt and threw it at the singer. He caught it and ran off the stage, following the rest of the band. The sweat from the people rose above them as steam, leaving a mist of human heat hanging over the crowd in the frigid night air.

The cheers died down as people started talking to their friends.

Jacob took a breath, willing his ears to stop pounding.

"Do a search spell while we can think," Claire muttered to Emilia.

"*Venescopo,*" Emilia said.

Jacob listened for the faint ringing that would lead them to magic. His body hummed, but he couldn't hear anything over the noise of the crowd.

After a few seconds Connor said, "I don't think we're going to find him like that. It's too noisy. Maybe we should—"

But Connor never said what his new idea was. The crowd had started cheering again. A man had walked onto the stage—a tall man with dark, curly hair, wearing a black uniform with a golden dragon emblazoned across the front. The Pendragon waved, smiling at the crowd.

30

ON THREE

*N*o one heard Jacob curse as the Pendragon jerked a chain in his left hand, dragging Rosalie onto the stage by a metal collar around her neck.

"No!" Emilia screamed.

Before Jacob could quiet her, Claire already had a hand over Emilia's mouth and had shoved her down to duck below the crowd.

"Friends," the Pendragon spoke over the masses, but there was no echo as there had been with the singer. His voice didn't come through the speakers. It reverberated through the air itself.

"I hope you will forgive my interrupting the festivities. I assure you the band will not mind." The Pendragon spoke calmly, but Jacob had a gut numbing feeling he knew why the singer didn't mind his concert being interrupted. The band was probably dead.

"I have come to make this a night to remember!" the Pendragon shouted. His voice sounded exultant, and the audience cheered.

Rosalie's shouts of, "No! Please!" barely carried over the roar of the crowd.

Laughter rose from the front of the mob, mocking Rosalie's tears.

"But first, I need a volunteer from the audience!" the Pendragon said.

People began to jump up and down, waving their hands in the air to be chosen.

"I thank you for your enthusiasm," the Pendragon said, "but I am looking for someone very special for this part of the show. Emilia Gray, please come to the stage."

Emilia looked at Jacob with terror in her eyes.

"Emilia Gray, I know you are here," the Pendragon said.

Someone in the crowd shouted, "Pick someone else!"

Peeking through the shoulders of the people shielding him, Jacob watched the Pendragon's face twist into a bright smile.

"You're right. The show must go on!" the Pendragon said, his voice jubilant. "We cannot stop the show because Emilia doesn't want to be onstage."

The crowd cheered again.

"I choose the front two rows. *Terraminis.*"

A horrible *crack* rent the air as the ground beneath Jacob gave a horrible lurch.

Screams of terror began in a wave at the front of the crowd as a vast hole in the earth swallowed the spectators nearest the stage.

The crowd surged back, away from the gaping chasm.

Jacob spun, grabbing Claire and Emilia, trying to herd them away with the rest of the crowd. But Emilia wouldn't move.

She stood still, staring at the Pendragon, her eyes wide with fear. They were all being pushed and hit by the people trying to flee. A girl with mascara streaming down her face ran into Claire, knocking her feet out from under her.

Jacob and Connor both yanked on Claire's arms, making her scream with pain, but getting her back on her feet before she was trampled by the fleeing mass.

Suddenly, the hoard stopped. The people around them began stumbling backward as the earth around the crowd rose, forming a wall sixteen feet high.

Jacob turned, watching in horror as the barrier surrounded them. They had been trapped, penned in like animals for the slaughter.

"Please do not leave, my friends," the Pendragon said. "You see, my part of the show has just begun. And what would a show be without a captive audience? Now, where is my Emilia?"

Jacob wrapped an arm around Emilia, pushing her head back down just in time to stop her from standing up.

"Run, Emilia!" Rosalie screamed into the crowd.

"Quiet," the Pendragon ordered.

Rosalie's screaming stopped. She collapsed on the stage, a bright scarlet gag tied across her mouth. A wave of panic swept through the crowd. Every person stared at the Pendragon, afraid that what he had done to her, he would do to all of them.

"Jacob, I have to go," Emilia said, shaking as she tried to pull away from him, but Connor and Claire added their grips to Jacob's, holding Emilia firmly in place and hidden from view of the stage.

"I will give you until three, Emilia," the Pendragon said. "One, two—"

There was another horrible *crack*, and screams surged through the crowd as another group of people disappeared into the earth.

"Three."

"I have to go," Emilia shouted, struggling to break free. But Connor clamped a hand over her mouth.

"If he sees you, everyone dies," Connor shouted in her ear.

"They've seen magic, Emi. They've seen his face," Jacob said, feeling her guilt and terror rip through his heart. "If he gets what he wants, he'll kill them all."

A girl behind them started to sob.

"We have to do something," Emilia said, her eyes wide with panic. "We can't just stand here."

"Emilia." The Pendragon's voice was horribly calm. Jacob shivered down to his bones. "I know you're here. I can feel my blood surging through you. I know you have your friends with you, and your *coniunx*. I can feel the magic flowing between you."

Jacob looked down at his hand. The golden streak shimmered on his palm. Emilia's terror radiated through his chest. But how could the Pendragon feel Jacob's connection to Emilia?

"I know you don't want anything to happen to them." The Pendragon paced the front of the stage. "So I give you a choice. Come to me now, and I'll let your friends live. I'll have to bind that boy's powers to set you free, but he is a human. Let him live as one. I will take you and your mother from this place. And we will leave all of this horrible unpleasantness behind us."

Jacob felt Emilia move to stand and yanked her back down.

"Do you really think he'll let us walk away?" Claire whispered.

"Fine," the Pendragon said. "I had hoped to spare you watching the humans die, but if it is what you wish. *Fulgur mortella.*"

A bright flash came before the shrieks of pain. White, hot lightning streaked out of the Pendragon's hands, rushing through the crowd, darting between terrified people before choosing its marks. Jacob didn't know how many people had been hit, but he could smell their burning flesh.

A bolt struck a boy beside them. He writhed on the ground, shaking and screaming, and then suddenly went silent and still. The girl with the black hair who had knocked into Emilia knelt beside the boy.

"Bobby!" she screamed, trying to make the boy look at her. She rolled Bobby onto his back. The center of his chest was covered in charred, black, flaking skin. The girl turned away just in time to avoid vomiting onto Bobby's corpse.

"You see, Emilia," the Pendragon said, his voice still chillingly calm, "I can keep picking them off slowly, painfully. Or I can make it end now. I didn't think you would want to watch the humans suffer. Maybe you are more like me than I realized."

Emilia trembled in Jacob's arms, staring at the stage. "Jacob, if I distract him, you might be able to get some of these people out."

Jacob had to force himself to swallow the knot of fear in his throat before he could speak. "*We* distract him, Connor and Claire get people out."

Emilia gripped his hand. She didn't try to argue, didn't try to tell Jacob they would probably both be dead in the next ten minutes if they tried to fight the Pendragon. They had to do something. And losing her, feeling his soul permanently ripped in half with no hope of ever mending, was worse than dying. He couldn't survive it.

"Connor," Emilia said, "break a hole in the wall." She kept talking as he tried to interrupt. "I don't know how. Just find a way. Claire, get as many people out as you can and then run. Find a way to get Iz or Proteus. It doesn't matter who. They've seen magic. A centaur can't make it worse. Find someone and tell them what's happened here."

Claire threw herself at Jacob and Emilia, wrapping her arms tightly around their necks. "Be safe."

"Enough!" the Pendragon shouted. "I've grown weary of waiting. *Terramotus.*"

The ground around them began to shake and crack. Chunks of earth fell away into great chasms of nothing.

"Connor!" Claire screamed. The earth by his heels had fallen away. He whirled his arms as he tried to regain his balance.

Claire grabbed Connor's arm, but he was bigger than she was. They were both going to fall.

"*Evocio!*" Jacob cried. As though an invisible hand had grabbed him by the collar, Connor was wrenched forward, tumbling on top of Claire.

In an instant, the cracking stopped, and the screams went

silent. All around them people sobbed and screamed, but the sound had vanished. All of the humans were trapped in shimmering blue spheres, each person floating in the air as though riding in a bubble. Only the four wizards were left exposed with their feet on the ground.

"How noble. Trying to save your friends." The Pendragon smiled, staring right at Jacob. "I had hoped you wouldn't be willing to let them die simply to stay hidden."

Jacob shifted his weight to the side, hoping his body could block the others from view.

"Do you know, Emilia," the Pendragon said, laughing and raising his wand, "if this boy hadn't been a traitor who kidnapped my only child, I might have been glad to have you bound to him? He is wonderfully loyal and has exceptional magical ability."

"Thank you," Jacob shouted loudly, trying to cover the scuffling of Connor and Claire scrambling to their feet behind him.

"It does disappoint me to destroy you, but my Emilia must be saved."

"Saved?" Emilia screeched. "You tried to kill me. Or don't you remember trying to burn me alive? Or the assassin you sent after me?"

"Those were"—the Pendragon paused—"unfortunate mistakes. I had thought your betrayal meant you were lost to me forever. As Rosalie had been lost. She betrayed me, ran from me. I even thought she was dead. But you, my child, you brought her back to me from another Realm. Then they bound her powers, and our tethering was broken. Did you know tethering makes your magic stronger? You can use each other's magic without even trying. The well of magic becomes infinite when another's joins your own.

"I didn't know. Not until our tie was cut. So I had to find my sweet Rose. I unbound her magic, and now—" The Pendragon flicked his wrist. There was a sharp *zap*, and all of the humans around them screamed as though shocked by some horrible current. "I am stronger than ever. You betrayed me to bring your mother back to me. You were bound to a traitor to make you strong enough to serve your father. And now it is time for you to come home. The world awaits us, Emilia."

"I don't want to be a part of any kind of world you create," Emilia said.

"Jacob," Claire whispered in his ear, "on three, blast a *furvapos* spell. It should make enough smoke to cover us."

"My world shall be the only world, Emilia," the Pendragon said. "There is no other way but death."

"Run for the wall," Claire whispered.

Jacob slipped his hand into Emilia's, ready to drag her away. But Rosalie was left lying on the stage, bound and trapped.

"One," Claire whispered.

"Let the humans go!" Emilia shouted at the Pendragon. "They have nothing to do with this."

"Two."

"The humans are nothing," the Pendragon laughed. "*Terminulla.*"

With a *snap* that shook Jacob's bones, all of the shining bubbles disappeared. Emilia shrieked as ash tumbled from the air. They were dead. Hundreds, thousands of people, just dead.

"Three."

31

THE FALLEN LEFAY

"*Furvapos!*" Emilia heard three voices shout before a cloud of smoke erupted around them, throwing them into darkness.

"Run!" Jacob screamed, pulling on her hand.

She followed. There were cracks in the ground. She felt herself leaping over them, but the ground, even her feet, seemed strangely far away. Like she was watching a movie of someone else's life. Another girl with black hair had seen all those people turn to dust.

A burst of silver light flew past her left shoulder.

"Watch out!" Jacob shouted. He glanced back to make sure she hadn't been hurt. His eyes were filled with terror.

This must be real. She, Emilia, must really be running from her father. The murderer. The mass murderer. Jacob would never look at anyone else like that.

"*Ignisphera!*" A fiery, sparking ball taller than Emilia rolled toward them.

Emilia pulled Jacob out of the way as Claire leaped aside, dragging Connor with her. The smoke from their spells had started to clear. They were near the wall of earth. If they could only get a bit farther.

"*Recora!*"

Emilia screamed as the Pendragon's spell struck the ground only a foot from Jacob.

"*Somnectus!*" A flash of blue light streaked toward them. Jacob hunched over Emilia, protecting her.

"Connor!"

"Claire!" Connor bellowed.

Emilia spun around to see Claire's blonde hair blooming around her as she fell.

"No!"

"*Leferio!*" the Pendragon cried.

"*Primionis!*" A shield shimmered into being in front of them the instant before the Pendragon's spell struck. Jacob staggered under the weight of the attack.

Emilia ran to Claire. Her head was already in Connor's lap.

"She's still breathing." Connor brushed the blond hair and blood away from Claire's face. "*Pelluere.*" The cut on Claire's head shimmered with the spell but didn't knit itself back together.

"You have to get her out of here." Jacob backed toward them, only glancing down at Claire for a moment. "I can hold the shield spell for another minute. Get her over the wall."

"We can't leave you," Connor said.

"You have to go," Emilia said. "*Scalaxum.*" Stones from the earth wall pulled themselves free, making a staircase for Connor to climb. "Save Claire."

Connor nodded and lifted Claire easily. He was so much taller than Emilia remembered. Claire looked like a doll cradled in his arms. He didn't look like a little boy anymore. Why hadn't she noticed how much he'd grown while she and Jacob were gone?

Connor glanced back once before disappearing over the wall.

Please let them live. Please at least let them live.

"Emilia," Jacob said. The shield hummed and buzzed with each spell the Pendragon threw at them.

Emilia stepped forward to stand next to Jacob. He didn't tell her to leave, and she wouldn't have told him. Their place was together.

"Ready?" Emilia murmured.

"Ready." Jacob nodded.

Emilia felt the surge of magic in her chest as Jacob let go of his shield spell.

"*Manuvis!*" Emilia cried as Jacob shouted, "*Captio!*"

A ball of gleaming red appeared in Emilia's hands as a bolt of pure green light shot from the tip of Jacob's wand toward Rosalie.

The Pendragon laughed as he batted Jacob's spell away.

"Jacob, what are you doing?" Emilia flung her sphere of red at the Pendragon.

"We have to get Rosalie off that stage. *Procellita!*" A roar of fierce wind blasted toward the stage, bits of earth flying in its wake.

The Pendragon covered his face for a moment before swatting the filth away with a wave of his hand.

"We can't risk hurting her." Jacob seized Emilia's arm, pulling her behind him as an explosion shook the ground to their left.

"*Fulguratus!*" Emilia shouted, sending the lightning shard at the Pendragon's head.

The Pendragon shifted his head lazily to the side, laughing as he avoided the spell completely. "I really thought the Gray woman would have taught one of you to fight."

"Emilia, we have to get Rosalie before—"

The ground beneath Emilia's feet began to shift, tumbling away into the void in front of her. Emilia tilted forward toward the dark chasm. She screamed, and Jacob jerked her back onto solid ground.

"Emilia, are—"

"Get Rosalie. Go. Now!" Emilia shouted to Jacob.

Jacob looked at her a moment longer, then sprinted off to the left.

"Emilia," the Pendragon spoke in a conversational voice, "surely you must know you cannot beat me. *Terramotus.*"

The ground began to rumble again. Emilia widened her stance, trying to balance as more earth fell away. She glanced around for Jacob but couldn't see him anywhere. Had the Pendragon crumbled more of the earth? Had Jacob fallen into the darkness?

"Sometimes it's not about winning," Emilia spat, desperate the keep the Pendragon's attention on her. "What would I be if I didn't try to stop a demon like you? You're a monster. How many people did you just kill? And you don't even care."

The Pendragon smiled coldly. "They weren't people, they were humans."

"You're insane," Emilia said. Her voice was soft, but still the Pendragon heard.

"Someday, you will see. And it wasn't me who killed them. It was you. Everywhere you walk, destruction follows. Everywhere you go, flames and death trail behind."

"Because you bring them!"

"You chose to hide in Elder's Keep. You chose to come here tonight."

"To save Rosalie!" Emilia shrieked. "To save my mother."

"To save her, you came to a place with thousands, knowing what would happen. Did you think I would give her up? Did you think you could take her from me without anyone getting hurt?"

"We were actually hoping to hurt you," Emilia growled.

"Then you are guilty of insanity. I have spent decades learning to fight, learning to control. You are only children."

The Pendragon roared, and a terrible rumbling rent the air, shaking Emilia to the bone.

She threw herself to the ground as a jet of fire exploded out of the chasm in front of her. She covered her face, feeling the flames burn her hands. Another jet of bright orange leaped high into the air to her right, then another to her left. Soon flames were leaping at random from every hole in the earth, bringing with them debris from below.

Emilia swallowed the bile that soared to her throat as a scorched body flew into the air.

"Primurgo!" The heat of the flames still touched her skin, but the bits of fire-blackened debris that Emilia forced herself not to look at glanced harmlessly away from her shield.

Her heart raced, quickening with every second that passed. A flash of fear that was not her own coursed through her. She squinted past the fire, trying to find Jacob.

For a split second the flames in front of her parted, and she saw him. Out of the corner of her eye. Jacob was near the stage and closing in on Rosalie. Soon he would be within view of the Pendragon.

Sticking a hand through the shield, Emilia shouted, *"Magneverto!"*

The top of the scaffolding above the stage shattered, sending lights crashing down onto the Pendragon. The flames disappeared as the Pendragon fell face first onto the stage.

"Now, Jacob," Emilia whispered. As though he had heard her, Jacob ran at the stage. He was ten feet from Rosalie now. He was going to reach her.

The Pendragon soared back onto his feet. "There is nothing you can do to harm me. You are flies I can pick from the air."

Jacob froze midstride and floated into the air, away from the stage, caught inside the same giant bubble the Pendragon had used on the humans.

"Jacob!" Emilia shrieked, but he was already soaring far above her. *"Crusura!"*

The Pendragon batted her spell aside.

Emilia searched for a spell, any spell that could save them, and the Pendragon just stood and laughed.

"Primurgo," Jacob gasped. A thin shield shimmered around him, twisting and distorting in the bubble.

"Let him go!" Emilia shouted. She glanced up at Jacob.

Blood dripped from his nose and ears. He pushed against the walls of the bubble. The sheen of his shield faltered under the weight of the Pendragon's spell. He wouldn't be able to survive much longer.

"Let him go, and I'll come with you."

Jacob's faint shout of "No!" traveled to her as though from underwater.

"You will come with me after I kill him." The Pendragon raised his wand. "I will find you a new *coniunx*. A better, more loyal *coniunx*, and you will never leave me again."

"Leave her, Emile." It was Rosalie who spoke. She stood on the edge of the stage, her face red and raw from biting through her gag. Her wrists bled from the rope that had bound her. "Let her go."

"She is our child. I will keep her safe," the Pendragon said.

"Let Emilia go, and I will do whatever you ask," Rosalie said. "I will go where you go. I will fight where you fight."

"I will have you both!" the Pendragon shouted. "You are weak. You are both weak. But I will make you strong. I will make all of Magickind strong! *Alevitum!*"

Emilia felt the force of the spell lift her from her feet. She tumbled through the air, tossed like a doll by the Pendragon.

She stuck out her arms to try to brace herself as the ground flew toward her. Her throat burned with her own scream as her left arm shattered.

"Emile, no!" Rosalie shouted from the stage. There was something in her hands. Something shiny and sharp. Rosalie ran toward the Pendragon, raising her weapon. She was going to stab him.

But she was raising it the wrong way.

The metal flashed in her hands as Rosalie plunged the jagged end of the silver shaft into her chest.

a desperate roar of fear and pain echoed from the stage, but Emilia could barely hear it over the cry that ripped from her throat.

"Rose!" the Pendragon screamed as he ran toward her, clutching at his heart.

Rosalie sank to the ground as red blossomed from her chest.

"*Primurgo,*" Rosalie muttered. The Pendragon was knocked back as the shield shimmered around her.

Emilia ran toward the stage, leaping the cracks in the earth. If she could reach her in time, she could stop the bleeding. She could save Rosalie.

"*Pelluere!*" the Pendragon shouted, but the healing spell couldn't break through the barrier.

The Pendragon collapsed, gasping.

Emilia was close now. She could see her mother's blue eyes gazing at her.

"Goodbye, Emilia." Rosalie's mouth formed the words, but the sound was lost in the Pendragon's scream. It was a cry of agony beyond anything Emilia could have imagined.

Rosalie was dead.

The Pendragon knelt on the ground next to her body, shaking.

"*Calvinis!*" Jacob shouted from behind Emilia. He was covered in blood and cuts, but his spell struck the stage, engulfing the Pendragon in flames.

"No!" Emilia shouted as the flames crept toward Rosalie. Jacob caught her arm and pulled her back as she tried to run toward the stage.

But the Pendragon had already created a storm of rain as red as blood, which doused the flames.

"*Gelunda!*" Jacob shouted, and the rain became hard and sharp, its scarlet spikes skewering the stage.

"*Nebulafero!*" the Pendragon bellowed.

As though blown by an unseen wind, the hoard of spikes shifted slowly toward Jacob and Emilia.

"*Primionis!*" Jacob's shield spread over Emilia just in time. Red pelted down on them as the Pendragon hurled lights and speakers that crackled and glowed bright blue with his magic.

"Emilia, we can't keep this up." Blood trailed down Jacob's face.

Emilia reached up and touched his cheek. Was all that blood his own?

"We have to attack together."

Even though Jacob was shouting, Emilia could barely hear him over the roar of the blood made solid pounding down on his shield.

"We'll use the *calvinis* spell, together!"

She nodded, turning to gaze at where her mother lay.

"Emi!" Jacob took Emilia's shoulders, forcing her to look into his eyes. "Emilia, we can do this."

"On three." Emilia turned to face the Pendragon.

Together, she and Jacob pressed their hands to the surface of their shield. "One, two, three!"

"*Calvinis!*" they cried together, thrusting their hands through the barrier.

Instantly, the stage was engulfed in flames that leaped high into the sky, blocking out the darkness.

For a moment, the only noise was the roar of the fire. And then the roar began to grow. The flames pulled away from the sides of the stage, gathering around where the Pendragon had been standing.

The roar of the fire changed into a guttural howl as a monstrous head appeared with flaming fangs, burning bright.

Before Emilia could scream, a red-scaled body had formed, and a black blazing tongue tasted the night. Four massive, muscular legs grew up out of the embers on the stage. The entire beast was formed of the flames, and on its back rode the Pendragon.

The monster's golden teeth snapped as a tail of blue flames swished back and forth, bathing the stage in sparks. It was a dragon. A dragon of the brightest flames, gnashing its teeth as it reared up onto its hind legs, breathing a stream of fire.

Emilia ducked, hiding her face. The heat blistered the backs of her hands.

The fire dragon gave an anguished roar before leaping into the air.

"Perectus!" Jacob shouted. *"Fulguratus!"* But the heat was disappearing.

The dragon shone in the darkness, flying high above them, carrying the Pendragon out of reach.

Emilia pulled away from Jacob, stumbling toward the stage. Toward her mother. She climbed onto the platform, keeping her legs from collapsing by pure strength of will.

"Rosalie. Mother, please!" Emilia called like a child waiting for her mother to sit up and tell her it had all been pretend. A trick to make the boogie man go away. But Rosalie didn't sit up. She lay on the ground, unmoving.

"Mom!" Emilia screamed.

Rosalie would never have wanted to be called mom. She would never have answered.

She looked perfect. No fire or rain of blood had harmed her. If the silver pole were gone from her chest and her blood cleaned away, she could be sleeping. Her face looked peaceful. Happier and younger than Emilia had ever seen her.

She was kneeling and holding Rosalie's hand before she knew how she had gotten there. Rosalie's hands were still warm.

"She did it to save us," Emilia said as she felt Jacob draw near. "He was going to kill you. It was the only way she could stop him." Tears streamed down her face.

"I know," Jacob said, wrapping his arms around Emilia's waist. "She loved you."

"No, she didn't." Emilia clutched her mother's hand even tighter. "I was a mistake. I dragged her back to this world. And now she's dead. I didn't deserve her love."

"It's not about deserving. She loved you. She protected you, Emi."

But somehow that made it worse. If Rosalie had cared enough about Emilia to die for her, she had lost something more than a stranger who shared her face.

Emilia laid Rosalie's hand back on her chest. "We have to find Connor and Claire." Emilia started to shake. She couldn't lose Claire. Not after the professor. Not after Rosalie.

"Should we leave her?" Jacob asked, wrapping an arm around Emilia's waist as her legs wobbled. She grabbed for Jacob's hand as she swayed. Pain shot up her broken arm.

"*Pelluere*," Jacob said as he lifted her from the stage.

Pain seared her arm as the bones knit together. Emilia relished the pain. She deserved it.

"The police will come soon," Emilia said without looking back. "They'll take care of her until Aunt Iz—"

Emilia couldn't finish the sentence. Aunt Iz could be lying in a pool of blood, too.

She tripped over the cracks in the ground. How many people had fallen, and how many had turned to dust? Sirens blared in the distance. What would the police think had happened? Not even *terrorist attack* could explain this. What would they tell all the families of the people who had simply disappeared?

The steps Emilia had created for Connor still hung in the air, awaiting her command. She reached out to hold Jacob's hand behind her as they climbed. Blood and magic pumped through his veins. She could feel his heart beating with hers. He was alive. The Pendragon hadn't managed to steal him from her.

They reached the top of the dirt wall. Emilia stared down at the sixteen-foot drop on the other side.

"Let me go first," Jacob said. "I can catch you."

Emilia smiled weakly and ran a hand over her face. He wanted to make sure she didn't fall. After all this.

"It's fine. *Tardego.*" Emilia leaped from the wall and floated gently to the ground like a leaf on the wind.

"*Tardego?*" Jacob asked.

Emilia nodded.

"*Tardego,*" Jacob said before stepping out into the air. He fell as though through water, slow enough not to hurt, fast enough to be ungraceful.

"Connor," Emilia called. "Connor, where are you?" The sirens were getting closer. If they didn't leave now, the police would find them.

"Connor!" Jacob shouted.

"Here." Connor's faint voice carried out of the darkness.

Jacob took off running, and Emilia kept close behind. The pounding of her feet matched the rhythm of the siren, making a song that mocked her. *All gone, all gone, all dead, all gone.*

"Connor!" Jacob shouted again.

"There." Emilia pointed and began to run toward a shimmering pool of blond hair.

Connor knelt in the grass behind a tree with Claire's head in his lap. Tears streamed down his cheeks as he clasped Claire's hand in his.

"No," Jacob breathed.

"She's alive," Connor choked out the words. "I did all the healing I know how to do. She's still breathing, but she won't wake up. Where's Rosalie?"

"She didn't make it." The words sounded hollow as they left Emilia's mouth.

"Is the Pendragon gone?" Connor looked up at the sky. "I saw a big burning thing."

"He's gone," Jacob said, bending down to pick up Claire.

"I've got her." Connor shifted his weight and lifted Claire. "Where should we go?"

"Back to Elder's Keep," Emilia said.

"We can't get back in," Jacob said.

He was right. They had chosen a one-way ticket out of safety, and for what?

"We could go back to the Elis Tribe," Connor said. "They might be able to help her."

"We can't put them in danger like that," Jacob said. "If the Pendragon rode that fire thing against them—"

"It would be another massacre," Emilia finished for him, trying not to think of how many humans had just died.

"We have to do something," Connor growled. "Claire needs help."

"The Academy," Emilia said, her stomach churning at the sound of the words. "I don't think the Dragons have taken over there, and they have a nurse on staff."

"If he finds us there," Jacob said. "If anyone tells him—"

Jacob's words were lost in a fury of sirens. Police cars rushed in, surrounding the park, fire trucks and ambulances close behind.

Police officers jumped out of their cars, guns raised, staring at the wall of earth that blocked their view of the concert grounds.

Only the broken scaffolding that had been the top of the stage could be seen.

Jacob pulled Emilia into the shadows behind the tree, cursing under his breath.

"Do we let them find us?" he whispered.

"No." Connor held Claire to his chest. "They would ask too many questions, and we don't have time for that. Claire needs help."

He was right. Claire's normally pale skin had gone completely white. Blue veins pulsed slowly in her neck.

"There are ambulances here," Jacob said, pointing to the gurney that had been taken out of one of the buses waiting behind the lines of police.

None of the humans seemed to know what to do. It didn't matter. There was no one left to save anyway.

"Human doctors can't help her," Connor said.

"We're going to the Academy," Emilia said, her mind clearing with the force of her decision. "Give Claire to Jacob."

"How are we going to get out of here?" Connor asked, clutching Claire even tighter. The police were starting to move closer, a wall of uniforms with no break. "Are we fighting our way out?"

"No, we're traveling by magic," Emilia said. "Give Claire to Jacob. He'll take her. I'll take you."

Connor looked afraid, but how could he not be? Gently, he handed Claire to Jacob. Emilia took Connor's hand, holding it tightly.

"Are you sure?" Jacob asked.

"See you at the Academy," Emilia said.

Jacob nodded.

"*Retivanesco*," Jacob and Emilia said together.

A flash of bright light filled Emilia's eyes. Startled shouts from the police reached her ears as everything went black.

Emilia could feel Connor's warm hand in hers as he clung

desperately to her.

Something hard hit the bottoms of her feet, and she stumbled, falling to the ground, pulling Connor down with her.

Emilia blinked at the shadows of the trees that surrounded them.

"Sorry," Emilia coughed, pushing herself up onto her knees.

"Emi, are you all right?" Jacob stood over her, still holding Claire.

The trees swayed as Emilia helped Connor to his feet. "Fine."

"What the hell was that?" Connor asked, his voice and legs shaking.

"A gift from the Hag," Emilia said.

They had arrived in a stand of trees, old and weathered, closer to death than life. Dull lights broke through the branches in front of them.

Emilia walked slowly toward the lights, her hand raised, ready to fight. The frozen ground crunched as Jacob and Connor followed her.

A grey building appeared through the trees, square and dull surrounded by a high iron fence.

"The Academy," Jacob said.

"What do we do now?" Connor lifted Claire from Jacob's arms and held her close to his chest.

"We knock on the gate." Jacob stepped out of the shelter of the trees.

Emilia could feel the dread and exhaustion that filled him. She reached forward, taking his hand in hers, grateful for the hum that echoed in her heart.

"And if the people inside try to kill us?" Connor asked.

"Then we keep fighting till there are none of them left," Emilia said as a shadow appeared at the front door of the Academy.

Jacob and Emilia's story concludes in The Blood Heir.

JACOB AND EMILIA'S JOURNEY
CONCLUDES IN THE BLOOD HEIR

Read on for a sneak peek of *The Blood Heir*.

WALLS

"*Volavertus* Aunt Iz." Emilia's voice trembled. "*Volavertus* Isadora Gray."

The mirror in her hands shimmered for a moment before fading in the dim light.

"*Volavertus* Molly Wright." The mirror shook in Emilia's hand. "*Volavertus* Larkin Gardner."

Emilia brushed the tears from her cheeks with her sleeve. The fabric was rough with soot and scented with smoke.

Fire. Thousands of people turned to ash. The Pendragon flying away, leaving Rosalie—

"*Volavertus* Dexter Wayland!"

But the mirror didn't care how desperate Emilia sounded. No face appeared in the glass. Emilia pressed her forehead to the cold concrete wall. The florescent lights made the grey walls look sickly and filthy. Like the whole Academy was rotting from within.

Emilia lowered herself to the hall floor. She wanted to run away, to find Jacob and Connor. The Academy nurse wouldn't let Emilia go into the infirmary with her to try and heal Claire. The headmistress had taken Jacob and Connor to the boys' wing.

Emilia had been left alone and helpless in the shadowy corridor.

The pull in Emilia's chest told her Jacob was still nearby. He was angry, frightened, and tired. But so was she.

"He's fine," Emilia whispered to herself. "Jacob is fine."

Footsteps carried down the hall. Emilia leaped back to her feet. Her legs screamed in protest at being asked to move again.

"I want to see—" Emilia began, but it wasn't the headmistress who ran down the hall toward her. It was only a girl, the same age as Emilia, wearing the grey and black uniform of an Academy student.

The girl slowed as she reached Emilia, eyeing her up and down before shrugging and opening the door to the infirmary that Emilia had been forbidden from entering.

"Wait! Let me see"—the girl slammed the door—"Claire."

Emilia shut her eyes tight, forcing herself not to scream or pound on the door. They needed help. They needed the nurse to heal Claire.

Images flew unbidden through Emilia's mind. The Pendragon shooting spells at them. The spell missing Connor and hitting Claire.

Panic rose in Emilia's chest. The Pendragon was still out there. Emilia was pacing in front of the infirmary door before she even realized her feet were moving.

She needed to do something. She had to help.

"*Volavertus* Isadora Gray," Emilia said to the mirror again.

Aunt Iz wasn't answering. She had been rescuing Samuel with Larkin, Dexter, and Molly. Dexter had collapsed the tunnel. The Pendragon had known they were coming.

Stone. It all went back to the traitor MAGI Jeremy Stone.

"*Volavertus* Proteus." Emilia's voice echoed down the long hall.

The mirror shimmered again, but this time the light didn't fade into nothing. Instead, a face appeared. The man had long hair that was greyer than the last time Emilia had seen him only a week before. The creases on his face seemed deeper, and they shifted to lines of worry as he looked out of the mirror at Emilia.

"Emilia Gray," Proteus said, his deep voice resonating from the depths of the mirror, "I had not expected to hear from you. Isadora said you had been taken to safety."

"We had," Emilia said, trying to hide her fear, "but the Pendragon found us. He found Rosalie. He took her. Proteus, she's dead." Tears burned in the corners of Emilia's eyes, but now wasn't the time to cry, not when so many people were still in danger.

"It was Stone." Emilia's voice grew fierce. "He betrayed all of us to the Pendragon. Stone told him where we were hiding. He told them Aunt Iz and the others were going after Samuel."

Proteus's shoulders tightened, and his eyes flashed with anger. Even if Emilia hadn't known Proteus was a centaur with the enormous body of a powerful horse, his look would have been terrifying. "The MAGI scum betrayed the Gray Clan."

"Yes, and if he can, he'll send people to attack the Green Mountain Preserve. He'll send them after all of you." Emilia took a deep breath. "You need to move. You need to find a safer place for the Tribe."

"We will be prepared for the Dragons, and if Stone shows his face, I will kill him myself," Proteus growled.

"Good." For a moment, the fact that she had said *good* to a person promising to kill someone seemed absurd. But Rosalie was dead. Claire was unconscious. Aunt Iz and the others were missing. "Kill him."

Proteus nodded.

"Contact the Wrights at the High Peaks Preserve," Emilia said. "I don't know how much Stone knows about their settlement."

"I will contact the Wrights and make sure they are safe."

"Thank you, Proteus."

"Do you want me to send the fighters of the Tribe to Graylock to search for Isadora?"

Emilia's heart leaped to her throat just before a terrible sickness settled into her stomach. "No." Her voice cracked as she said the simple word. "We have no idea where they are. And we can't send anyone else to Graylock."

We can't lose anyone else.

Proteus bowed, and the mirror shimmered again before leaving Emilia staring at her own reflection.

Tears cut pale tracks through the dirt, ash, and blood that covered her face. Her grey eyes were bloodshot and looked much older than seventeen.

"This is what war does," Emilia murmured.

It had been coming for a long time, since before Emilia had really known it. Attacks on humans, disappearances, murder.

But Aunt Iz had been trapped at the Graylock Preserve. Rosalie was dead. Thousands of humans had been murdered. There was no mistaking it now.

The Gray Clan was at war.

Order The Blood Heir *to continue the story.*

ESCAPE INTO ADVENTURE

Thank you for reading *The Dragon Unbound*. If you enjoyed the book, please consider leaving a review to help other readers find Jacob and Emilia's story.

As always, thanks for reading,

Megan O'Russell

Never miss a moment of the magic and romance.

Join the Megan O'Russell mailing list to stay up to date on all the action by visiting https://www.meganorussell.com/book-signup.

ABOUT THE AUTHOR

 Megan O'Russell is the author of several Young Adult series that invite readers to escape into worlds of adventure. From *Girl of Glass*, which blends dystopian darkness with the heart-pounding danger of vampires, to *Ena of Ilbrea*, which draws readers into an epic world of magic and assassins.

With the *Girl of Glass* series, *The Tethering* series, *The Chronicles of Maggie Trent*, *The Tale of Bryant Adams,* the *Ena of Ilbrea* series, and several more projects planned for 2020, there are always exciting new books on the horizon. To be the first to hear about new releases, free short stories, and giveaways, sign up for Megan's newsletter by visiting the following:

https://www.meganorussell.com/book-signup.

Originally from Upstate New York, Megan is a professional musical theatre performer whose work has taken her across North America. Her chronic wanderlust has led her from Alaska to Thailand and many places in between. Wanting to travel has fostered Megan's love of books that allow her to visit countless new worlds from her favorite reading nook. Megan is also a lyricist and playwright. Information on her theatrical works can be found at RussellCompositions.com.

She would be thrilled to chat with you on Facebook or

Twitter @MeganORussell, elated if you'd visit her website MeganORussell.com, and over the moon if you'd like the pictures of her adventures on Instagram @ORussellMegan.

Feather and Flame

<u>Guilds of Ilbrea</u>

Inker and Crown

Made in the USA
Middletown, DE
24 December 2020

30104378R00151